P9-DOA-175

HUNGARIAN LIBRARY

GYULA KRÚDY

THE
CRIMSON COACH

CORVINA PRESS

Title of the Hungarian original:
A VÖRÖS POSTAKOCSI

Translated from the Hungarian by
PAUL TABORI

© Corvina 1967

Printed in Hungary
Zrínyi Printing House, Budapest

CONTENTS

INTRODUCTION

One fine spring morning, about sixty years ago, two young men met in the middle of Calvin Square, Budapest. One was smooth-shaven, with elegant sidewhiskers—he was coming from work, having finished his nightly stint as sub-editor of the leading morning paper. The other had a trim, black moustache and had just emerged from a dive, a notorious all-night drinking shop which had only one thing in its favour: it served the best red wine in the Hungarian capital. He wasn't drunk—few people ever saw him even half-seas-over—but he was decidedly in an expansive and adventurous mood.

The two greeted each other like long-lost brothers though they had met at the *Otthon* (Home), the journalists' and writers' club, only a couple of days before. Then the man with the moustache said:

'I need a little fresh air. I'm going to take a drive. Coming?'

His friend only hesitated for a moment, then he nodded.

The other man hailed a cab drawn by two glossy chestnuts. They climbed up and settled in the dove-grey, elegant interior. The coachman touched the rim of his bowler and asked: 'Where to, Your Lordship?'

'To Lake Balaton, Marcus. And don't hurry.'

Lake Balaton was about sixty miles from Budapest, in Transdanubia. The cabbie did not hesitate for a moment but flicked his whip and off they went. It took them almost three weeks before they turned homewards, making the circuit of the lovely lake, pausing to sample its great wines and inspect the food at the inns and hotels, picking up a change of linen on the way and sending postcards to their friends. It was a wonderful, an epic, a totally irresponsible journey—one that few people would make on the spur of the moment even in those halcyon days.

The smooth-shaven travelling companion was my father, Cornelius Tabori; the instigator of the journey was Gyula Krúdy, the author of this book. The story of this madcap, delightful trip was told and retold in our family as a sort of legend, growing in colour and excitement with every telling; still, it was essentially true and more characteristic of Krúdy than of my father who was more of an observer and chronicler of Bohemia than a participant in its defiantly irresponsible activities. Yet he remained a friend of Krúdy to the end of their lives—the author of *The Crimson Coach* died eleven years before my father's murder by the nazis—and though they never took such a journey again, it inspired them both in their individual ways. Krúdy wrote several stories set in Transdanubia, invoking the bibulous, amorous and balneary atmosphere of the great lake; and, for over twenty years, my father was the most enthusiastic propagandist of the Balaton and especially of its oldest watering-place, the venerable Füred. Thus I can claim a modest personal relationship with the man whom many consider one of Hungary's greatest and certainly most misunderstood writers; and this is one of the reasons why I found a particular pleasure and a special challenge in the almost impossible task of translating *The Crimson Coach*.

*

'I ran away from the parental home to become a journalist, I fell madly in love with a provincial actress, I was happy,

8

I was an artist, I drank, I caroused, I made love, I don't really know what happened to me,' wrote Krúdy in one of his numerous autobiographies.

There were few outside, actual events in Krúdy's life—and his real life is summed up perfectly in the above lines. He was born in 1878 in a small Hungarian town, centre of the Nyírség, a district named, poetically, after birch trees. His father was a well-to-do attorney, scion of an ancient noble family; his mother was a chambermaid, daughter of poor peasants. This twin heritage was decisive for his life and his work; he was always conscious of his landed gentry origins yet he preferred the company of the poor, the simple, the dispossessed. He had his roots in the Hungarian countryside and no one could invoke with greater mastery, with subtler colours the *puszta*, the Great Plains, the wooded hills, the snow-covered winter roads, the small, medieval or baroque towns than he. Yet he spent most of his life in the capital, Budapest, where he settled at the age of eighteen, in 1896— and he made certain districts, a few selected quarters his very own. Old Buda, the Inner Town, Margaret Island, Joseph Town (an old, lower middle-class ward or *arrondissement*) were his favourite haunts. He knew every street, every inn, almost every house. For him Budapest was Paris and London, Rome and New York; I don't think he spent more than a few months of his entire life away from Hungary.

His first short story was published when he was fifteen, at seventeen he was chief contributor to a provincial daily and his stories and articles were regularly appearing in national newspapers and magazines. He was not yet twenty when he published his first volume of short stories—and, except for some years after 1919, there was no year until his death in 1933 that one or two volumes bearing his name did not appear. He was prodigiously productive and versatile; yet, in a way, he was working all the time on an immense autobiography. As Aurélien Sauvageot, a French critic and editor (who had spent many years in Hungary) put it: 'He stands in different guises in front of us; he called himself Sindbad the Sailor, Casimir Rezeda, the poor amorous poet who is constantly on the move and full of desires, always frequenting the company of women and has a passion for food; a man who proclaims the vanity of life...' How far Rezeda was autobiographical, would be difficult to say—but that in many respects he represented the image Krúdy formed of himself, is undeniable.

He married twice—because the Bohemian in him always longed for the family hearth, for security and peace, much as the clown longs to play Hamlet or perhaps the great tragedian yearns to play the clown. His first wife was older than himself, a charming and wise woman named Bella who, under the pseudonym of Satanella, had published some striking short stories. This marriage cost Krúdy his paternal inheritance. Not that he was an ideal husband—in spite of his dreams of middle-class regularity. In one of his letters, written from a café at four a.m., he confessed to his first wife: '...Sneer at me if you like! I need every day two or three hours of *solitude* when I'm thinking. Laugh at me if you please—to gain these two or three hours' pause I could even kill my father. This is what I'm living for, this is why I exist, this is why I haven't died yet... because every day I was able to be alone for a while...'

Satanella bore him four children (one died in infancy) of whom two were girls and the third surviving one was a boy.

His second marriage started even more stormily. Early in the First World War Krúdy became the close friend of the manager of a great Budapest hotel and was introduced into his home. Unavoidably, he was attracted to his new friend's wife, a mature but beautiful woman to whom he wrote some of his most intimate love letters. 'My life that I had believed a year or so ago to be aimless and finished,' he wrote in one of them, 'now glows through your heart. I am filled with

10

pride and confidence that after all I may not be the least of men if am loved so much...'

But it was not the mature, understanding woman he married—it was her daughter. A very young, very beautiful girl who fell desperately in love with the famous writer. There was, of course, violent resistance. They eloped; the girl was retrieved by her family and kept in strict confinement—then, after years, there was a complete breach and Krúdy married a girl twenty years his junior. She bore him a daughter, his last child.

Krúdy was an affectionate husband, a loving and amusing father but he still needed his hours of solitude and these became longer and longer. He was an alcoholic whom drink never degraded. The favourite and characteristic image was a tall, solitary figure sitting over a bottle of wine in some smoky, low-ceilinged inn or wine-shop, silently watching the world both around and inside him—and then producing his stories and novels.

He was not a demonic, possessed drinker—for he retained his creative urge, his clear-minded conception of beauty and passion to the very end. He was an insomniac—but then, there were few Hungarian writers who escaped this curse. After the 1918–1919 revolutions during which he was editor of a newspaper destined for peasant readers, he suffered an eclipse. The reactionary, strongly conservative Hungary between the two wars considered him a traitor to his own class; his sympathies with the lower depths were considered to be doubly offensive because he did not come from them. For years he was unable to publish any books and he did not achieve financial security or even modest stability until the end of his life. He published almost a hundred books, wrote thousands of sketches, short stories and newspaper articles, contributed to innumerable magazines and newspapers—and when he died he left a sadly depleted wardrobe, a few scores of books—and no money at all.

11

Krúdy claimed kinship and named as his ancestors Dickens and Turgenev in the first place. There are elements of Byron's and Barbey d'Aurevilly's dandyism in him. These may have inspired him but he was utterly different from if not necessarily inferior to them. This is, of course, a large and daring claim to make for a writer who is virtually unknown outside his own country. Yet Krúdy has some unique qualities. He is a *petit maître* in the choice of his world and period—yet one of the truly great in the presentation of characters, in the evocation of all that five senses can experience. He is beyond doubt a great erotic writer though his love-scenes are always oblique; when he presents a brothel or a *maison d'assignation*, it is done with the objectivity and the total lack of moralizing of a Maupassant. He never glamorizes nor denounces his villains and his frail beauties; in *The Crimson Coach* the character of Estella is a good example of this approach. Above all, he seems to sheer away from consummation, from even the temporary happy ending. When his lovers get together, he drops them, forgets about them. While Mr Rezeda might be a passionate and highly expert Don Juan in his dreams, he barely dares to touch his true love of whom he claims and obtains little more than a fleeting kiss. There are other, more satisfactory love affairs in his books—but though his sensuality is as burning and tangible as Baudelaire's or Flaubert's, his men and women are mostly ships that pass in the night, ghostly lovers crying in the mist. Balzac, of course, spent so much time on exposition and the introduction of his characters that he seldom had time and space for a properly developed plot. Krúdy is again and again sidetracked by a secondary character; his books are a series of portraits, three-dimensional and extremely touching—but he is not really interested in telling a story that has a beginning, middle and end. His books end on a quivering note, on a point of indecision and uncertainty; and thus they are far more realistic than so many others

12

that neatly tie up the ends and give us, as Priestley puts it, 'all that is needed for those who insist upon the latest news.'

Though the titles of his books can mean little to the English-speaking reader, they are significant for his development. He began with volumes of short stories—*The Nest is Empty* was published in 1897, when he was nineteen; *Youth* in 1899 and *The Sad Tales of the Gay Man* a year later. In 1901 he published his novel *The Gold Mine* which was an almost savage denunciation of his own class, a bitterly detailed indictment of a corrupt and destructively passive landed gentry. Then came three more volumes of short stories, *On the Beard-Drier*, *The Naughty Gaáls* and *The Heroes of Dreams*. (The beard-drier is the Hungarian equivalent of the ingle-nook, the bench where the old men sit, drying their beards and telling tales.) He also published another novel, *The Heir of Andráscsik*. Around 1908–1910, as his Hungarian critics point out, a slow but definite change began in his writing, in his choice of subjects and his general approach—as if some yeast had been at work. He turned to medieval settings and published several short stories with the background of the Szepesség, a picturesque district of northern Hungary; a short novel or long short story, *Among Old Weathercocks*, was an invocation of Pest around the turn of the century. His first full-fledged historical novel was *The Hungarian Jacobins* about the ill-starred conspiracy of Hungarian nobles in the late eighteenth century, led by the romantic prelate Martinovics.

He created his most characteristic *alter ego,* his most striking incarnation, whom he named Sindbad the Sailor, in the years just before the First World War. *The French Château* was published in 1912, *Sindbad's Youth* in 1911 and *The Travels of Sindbad* a year later. The travels were as imaginary and as fantastic as those of the sailor of the *Arabian Nights;* but their settings were as real and actual as the world before the great flood of iron and blood overwhelmed it. *The Crimson Coach* itself was published in 1914, first as a serial and then as a book—and it brought Krúdy's first, decisive popular success. This was only enhanced by its sequel, *Autumn Voyages on the Crimson Coach* (1917). During the years of the war which were increasingly disastrous for Hungary he sought escape in the evocations of his youth and of a Bohemia that was far more eccentric than Murger's—and far less sentimental.

Krúdy's liberalism led him to embrace the revolutionary ideas of 1918–19; but he was unable to forsake the traditions and beliefs of his origins. He wrote a short book about the distribution of land among the landless peasantry and contributed a number of articles to the newspapers; but he was an apolitical being whose social criticism had to be refracted and distilled through his own special vision of the world. He never really looked forward; at the most he was concerned with the present but the past attracted him far more. His novel *Dreams of Palota* and the short story collection with the characteristic title *Fine Days in the Street of the Golden Hand* were totally detached from his age. Not that he was uncritical of the past or that his nostalgia was blinded by sentimentalism. His novels *Seven Owls* (1922), *The Prince of Wales* (1925), *The Fine Life of Casimir Rezeda* (posthumously, 1933) expressed a disillusionment, a reserve that was absent from the earlier books. His fine historical novel, *Three Kings* (1926–1930), his long short story, *The Devil Carries Off Someone* (1929), are far more realistic—and so are the final books, *In My Happy Youth* (1930), and *Life is a Dream*, a collection of short stories (1931). The tally of his *oeuvre* is really remarkable: he had written more than sixty novels, almost three thousand short stories, several hundred tales for young people, over a thousand articles and sketches and four plays. Certainly his huge output was partly explained by sheer financial necessity; for one of the finest Hungarian writers was outrageously underpaid and exploited by publishers and editors alike. And he was a wildly generous man who would share his last penny and his final half-litre of wine with a friend or a needy acquaintance.

Post-1945 Hungary rediscovered Krúdy in a remarkable fashion. Practically all of his works have been reissued and are selling in large editions. Many of his scattered, half-lost pieces have been collected into volumes. One of his one-act plays, *Gold and the Woman*, was set to music and included in the repertory of the State Opera House. It seems that to a generation that knows nothing about the times and characters that were Krúdy's main inspiration his writing represents a magic world, a plunging into a refreshingly different atmosphere. He has proved timeless because he was so firmly anchored in his own time; so firmly that he could defy its conventions.

*

The Crimson Coach was commissioned by József Kiss, Hungary's greatest Jewish poet who was the editor of the most popular literary weekly around the turn of the century. To be published in his magazine *A Hét* (The Week) was a much-coveted accolade. He had been watching Krúdy's work and in 1912 asked him to write a novel for his review. The first instalment was published in January 1913 and was immediately acclaimed as a work of special significance and power.

I have spoken of Krúdy and his treatment of time. Anachronism was a deliberate device with him. In *The Crimson Coach* telephones and stage-coaches, the mid-Victorian *ambiance* and the Edwardian lust for life coexist comfortably. His characters are taken from life yet are larger than life. His hero is the unheroic Casimir Rezeda, a partial self-portrait. But our imagination is rather caught by Edward Alvinczi, the Hungarian nabob, a man whose descent is far more ancient than that of the Habsburgs; a man who can

15

despise rank and title because the blood in his veins is the heritage of ninth-century chieftains and almost mythological leaders of pre-historic Hungarian tribes. Alvinczi was modelled after Miklós Szemere, a fantastic magnate, a gambler who lost and won immense fortunes in a single night, whose horses ran at the most famous racecourses of Europe, who could have walked over a living carpet of women's bodies if he had chosen to do so—but whose love affairs were as exotic and as tender as any prince's from the *Arabian Nights*. He was kin to Lermontov's *Hero of Our Age*, to Byron's *Don Juan*— he was utterly Magyar yet cosmopolitan. Krúdy was an anglomaniac who invoked fox-hunts, Tudor mansions, London fogs, the ideals of the English gentleman with an intuition that held research and fact in contempt yet was true to the essential England which he never saw.

His women are never idealized; they are very much flesh and blood and their virginity hides strong sex impulses. The full-blooded widow who keeps a series of gigolos is never ridiculous nor repulsive because she frankly admits her appetites—and insists on getting her money's worth in every bargain. Clara, the provincial actress who is fatally in love with the wrong man and cannot quite yield to the right one, has something of Ibsen's Nora and certain traits of Shaw's heroines. The poets and pimps, the actors and womanizers, the wise madame of the most exclusive brothel in town, the provincial matron who longs for metropolitan lovers and literary fame—the whole cavalcade of briefly-glimpsed yet fully realized characters passes in front of us, now gaily now tragically but always true to life.

*

To translate Krúdy is like working on a vast jigsaw-puzzle or design a huge tapestry. Every piece must fit, every colour must find its equivalent. His style is often more important than his subject-matter—and this supple, often evasive and allusive style can only be partially transposed to another language. I found it a challenge unlike any other book I had translated; and of course, it is for the reader to decide what measure of success I have achieved.

Street names are immensely important to Krúdy who uses them to create a special atmosphere. The Hungarian *Pattantyús* would mean nothing to a non-Hungarian—but *Bombardier Street*, I flatter myself, creates an echo, establishes a mood. So I have translated most of the street names into their English equivalents. Even so, there are certain names, dates, details in the book that cannot be translated. To have footnotes in a novel I consider a barbarian compromise; so I have grouped them at the end of the book and kept them as short as possible. For those who want to be informed about every person mentioned by Krúdy, every newspaper or book title quoted, those notes will provide the necessary help —the others might as well ignore them.

I have a reasonable though perhaps over-optimistic hope that with this book Krúdy, dead for more than thirty years, would have broken through the barrier of language, bridged the abyss between a strange, savoury and exquisite civilization and the modern West. If the publisher and myself have succeeded in this rash undertaking, other translations might follow and Krúdy might take his rightful place in the commonwealth of world literature.

New York, March 1967

Paul Tabori

I

SPRING SUNDAY IN BUDA

Shortly before Palm Sunday two new tenants made their appearance in Bombardier Street, two women, provincial actresses settling in Pest, because they hadn't been able to get an engagement away from the capital.

Bombardier Street was a survivor of the past in the very heart of Pest—as if the Slovak demolition workers had lost their way and had forgotten to raze the street which consisted of only four houses. Crowded together, these old burgher homes had narrow, deep courtyards which, at nightfall, became awesome, stretching into the distance. The worn-out stones were rinsed by invisible waters and the waterspout, topped by a lion's head, had ceased to function half a century ago. Under the gateway the hunched pavement echoed mysteriously as if there were a host of subterranean denizens dwelling beneath; the staircase spiralled daringly upwards though it was as wobbly as if about to collapse any moment. In short, these were ancient, ramshackle houses; beyond doubt, there were old people living behind the narrow windows, with musical clocks playing, and women whom the mouldy walls had turned phthisical. Not every apartment boasted of running water and one had to shout for the janitor to light the gas on the stairs in the evening. Whenever the wind rose outside, the doors and windows were inclined to cry. It may well have been true that someone was once murdered in the house and his corpse walled up. Such things had happened frequently in old Pest. One wondered in which of the flats the strangled Serbian horse-dealer was eavesdropping?

The actresses settled at Number 3, on the first floor—as there was no second one. They had a front and a back room, with a small kitchen between the two, and a pantry the size of a coffin where one felt like hanging oneself; they had a cleaning woman who left early in the afternoon; they made no friends with anybody in the house, received no guests and left their flat very rarely.

Clara Horváth was a straight actress, Sylvia Fátyol specialized in musical comedy. They had achieved a modicum of success in provincial towns like Kaposvár and Makó. Miss Horváth made her mark in *Monna Vanna*, Sylvia in *The Jester* and in *Childe John*. However, the manager of the company did not renew their contracts because Miss Sylvia was outrageously beautiful and charming—but nothing else. Clara Horváth was neither beautiful nor charming; she was merely overproud of the fact that her uncle held some high position in a government department. So she also proved inaccessible. The two girls shared lodgings for years; they had started to take care of each other when they were students at the drama school and they had never since parted. Miss Fátyol could never achieve a real provincial ovation though her silk undies and delicate stockings were finer than anybody else's in the company. She never wore her shoes longer than a week; then she sent them back to her Pest shoemaker. An old gentleman was waiting for them eagerly—he bought the used shoes at a generous price from the shoemaker. For it was possible that Miss Sylvia's dreamy, sometimes tearful eyes, her funny little nose which immediately became pink whenever she cried or laughed, her small ears and her delicately scented brown hair did not please everybody; but no one could fault her feet. These were exactly as the expert old gentlemen imagined the ideal feminine feet; the old gentleman and the other devotees who sometimes followed for hours a pair of well-made shoes and embraced with wild lust the more shapely feminine footwear at night, in deserted hotel corridors.

Miss Sylvia probably had the loveliest feet in Hungary at that time—but few people knew about them as yet. (The shoemaker and the mysterious old gentleman did not count.) Clara showed a decided touch of jealousy, looking at the men who followed them now and then when they took their evening constitutional along the Danube in Buda.

Clara had grey eyes, reddish-brown hair and a dreamy walk and looked into the world with a constant measure of indignation as if she had been, or was about to be, insulted. Her full nose and chin, the peculiar curling of her hair on her neck and along her ears where the reddish-brown locks sometimes billowed like a veil; her drowsy, swaying hips, her white-and-blue striped shawl she wore when she hurried round to the grocer's in the evening; her swelling bosom and neck which shaped a light fold in the tight blouse—all this gave her a Jewish look. If she forgot herself, she spoke in a nasal tone, opening her mouth wide, moistening her lips and fluttering her fair eyelashes. Her eyelids were sometimes reddened by nocturnal tears and she kept the pawn-tickets in such exemplary order that she always knew which was mature for selling off.

During the walks along the Danube, on the Buda side, under the big plane trees, she held fast to Sylvia's arm and indulged in sarcastic remarks at the expense of the Buda beaux. She abused the baldheads who wore eyeglasses with malignant joy; she expressed pity for the clerks in their threadbare trousers; as for the officers, she had a good laugh over them.

'If only once in my life I could meet a man with a delicate head who owes nothing to the barber's hand and to the well-

21

rehearsed theatrical tricks to be interesting—but whom Nature has made refined, noble, exquisite! I'd love to know a medieval knight or an ancient artist. A Florentine nobleman who thinks and feels as Dante did! Or a journalist who must be as much of a gentleman as the Doge of Venice. I'd love to give myself to such a man. After all, I am twenty-four years old. It's time I started my love-life,' said Miss Horváth most seriously, and she didn't care if the Buda people, sitting on the benches in the dusk, overheard her wish.

She looked about passionately with her ash-grey eyes for any superfluous beaux who happened to be underfoot around Sylvia's shoes; then she continued her oft-repeated song with a measure of indignation:

'I should've been a Russian girl-student. To be born in such a hole as Kőbánya!... There are still real men in that country. I could've been Gorky's mistress... or a nihilist's! My God, what complete, perfect men live in Russia! Even the old fictional characters in the books of Turgenev or someone like Oblomov all deserved a woman to fall in love with them. Their strange, dreamy lives, their endless snowy steppes, their trains which cross without a single stop, provinces as large as the whole of Hungary; the troikas, the onion-domed churches...Lord, in that country I'd have long ago started my love-life. Even from a purely medical point of view it cannot be proper that a healthy woman of twenty-four should walk around a virgin. What are all those men for in this city? God, if I could only choose among them!'

A gentleman in ducks and white shoes shuffled by, keeping rather close to them. Miss Horváth measured him with a look of cold contempt.

'A counter-jumper from Pest,' she murmured. 'Sniffing for Buda women. And there are hardly any worth looking at on the promenade.'

Miss Horváth was quite right about this.

Before Easter the people of Buda rarely left their homes.

Who could foretell the spring fashions? and the winter clothes were rather shabby. Now and then a woman-teacher hurried along the promenade in a short skirt, walking flat-footed; the winter hats passed in an almost embittered parade, soaked, as if they had suffered greatly. The melting snow had worn out the shoes; only those of the Buda folk brought some freshness, elegance, public gaiety who during the day commuted to the Pest offices and shops to work. The midinettes learned a new sort of smile which they tried out on the small river boat and later on the promenade—they had seen it on the face of a delicate little matron of Pest as she strolled past the hat shop. Schoolmasters walked about with books, and near the hotel a black-bonneted, black-veiled lady sat in mystery; she appeared to watch the Danube, but secretly she was tensely expectant.

The two actresses often spied on the lovers who eloped from Pest to Buda—their progress in carriages, their disappearance in the hotel and then their departure. The lady took the horse-drawn omnibus at the other side and while it bumped across the bridge, she watched the arches and the people, absent-mindedly and a little surprised—as if suddenly everything had become so very strange. The ships' funnels, bellowing black smoke, the chains of the bridge, rising and then swooping down, the great Danube, curving away in the distance, and the female underwear being dried on the flatboats that carried wheat from the Bácska. As if all this had never existed before!

But by the time she reached the Pest side she forgot everything; she adjusted her veil, there was a fresh smile on her lips, a dewy spring in her eyes...

Her lover would get on the tram, ask in a bored voice for a penny ticket—at which the conductor informed him that it was only valid until the bridge. 'Blast you!' he said and got off to take a hansom. The cab jogged on, the blind horse almost collided with every automobile, the reins twitched as monotonously as aspens trembled in village cemeteries; the lover blew his nose, wiped his eyes, looked and sniffed at his hands and finally lit a cigarette or cigar; apparently forgetting what had just happened, he leant back indifferently in the hansom. He would truly be surprised if on the Pest side he should, by accident, catch another glimpse of his lady as she hurried on with triumphant, resilient steps. She bought a bunch of violets on the corner and, stopping in front of a baby shop, examined the goods in the window with an expert eye.

'My God,' on such occasions Miss Horváth would say, rather loudly, behind the lady's back, 'have you washed off the pomade?'

Within a short time the two actresses acquired a fearful reputation along the Buda promenade. The beaux who, on their way from government or other offices, contemplated spring on the Danube quay with an assurance befitting Christian gentlemen (though their homes were near enough where some pleasure-loving and dissatisfied, foul-mouthed or insidiously hating, constantly tearful or always-on-the-verge-of-taking-a-definite-step civil service wife waited for them with malignant joy or suppressed fury)—these gentlemen never passed the two young ladies without receiving a deprecating remark or a sneering look. And so Buda began to know them for their superior manners, their unapproachability and their sarcastic, contemptuous behaviour.

Old departmental chiefs asked whether they could be given suitable information about these brazen-tongued girls. These two refused even the courting approaches of Mákosi, a junior civil servant who was smooth-shaven and deservedly known as the most impudent skirt-chaser of Buda. Miss Horváth promised to box his ears whereupon Mákosi threatened to call a policeman.

'I just have to give him a wink and he'll arrest you!' said Mákosi, the leading Don Juan in those days on the right bank of the Danube.

Miss Horváth was taken aback, it seemed that her sang-froid had deserted her. Mákosi immediately put on a friendly smile whereupon Miss Sylvia spoke softly (for she rarely took part in these guerilla battles):

'We'll write a letter to the *Sun*!'

Several people must recall among the visitors to the Buda promenade that slender, blue-eyed, handsome young journalist with the daring face who appeared next day on the promenade and accompanied the ladies from some distance. At the request of the women of Buda Mákosi once again took up his post to drive these intruders from Buda—whereupon Miss Horváth actually slapped the cheeky cavalier, a policeman appeared, the journalist busily took notes; in the evening the copies of the *Sun* sold like hot cakes in the quiet Buda streets. The ladies of the promenade who had suffered much from the tasteful little hats, simple dresses and delicate beauty of the actresses, rewarded Mr Mákosi very warmly. The wife of the department chief gave a tea-party in his honour; the master chimney-sweep invited him to dinner at which the sweep's wife (who owned several houses) gave an almost public pledge that she would settle Mákosi's debts; there was a soirée at the choral society where the Buda misses bestowed a fan (which they all signed) upon the junior civil servant and the hero was celebrated all over the place for having rooted those insolent Jewish girls of Pest from Buda.

The two little swallows, it is true, no longer frequented the Danube quay under Gellért Hill. No one spied any more on the women bent on extramarital adventure and no one made sneering remarks in the dusk at eventide when from the benches thirsty, forsaken women watched the cavaliers with shining eyes, and the feet were powerfully busy under the tables of the Kiosk Café. Everything dropped back into its old rut. Miss Horváth no longer prevented anybody from wearing ducks and the gentlemen could resume their placid courting of the chimney-sweep's wife (who was past her springtime) in order to be invited to a dinner or two. The plane trees sighed, the ships hooted, the sun sank behind the mountains; cats chased each other on the roofs of the old houses; the burgher ladies could dream, undisturbed, of Mákosi's yellow shoes, and in the small gardens the young ladies could wait quietly for their evening suitors; no one heard again the sneering, sharp laughter of the Pest Jewess.

Clara and Sylvia no longer risked leaving Bombardier Street for Buda where they had spent their most enjoyable evenings. Clara cut various figures from paper: men and women. With coloured pencils she provided the men with moustaches and beards, the women with big eyes and open mouths. Then she set them up on the dining table and re-enacted the Buda promenade. There was a drunk swaying unsteadily; an elderly lady, longing for love, limped along; small dogs ran about and the department chief, with his big stomach, cleared himself a path through the throng with his warning walking-stick. Clara always felt serious and some-what revengeful when she thought of Buda—of the strange houses from which strange people emerged, the clerks (in their threadbare clothes) and the poor officers who rattled their sabres so aimlessly under the wild chestnut trees.

'It was definitely wiser to leave that quarter—it smells of soot and mildew; we'd never have amounted to anything. You know that Krecsányi never frequents the promenade,' she consoled Sylvia, referring to the director of the Buda theatre. As a girl from the provinces, Sylvia loved to walk in step with the distant military music and to become soppy over the stars shiningly reflected in the Danube; sometimes she thought of King Matthias who must have walked these streets. It was possible that up in the Castle, in one of the twisting streets, a medieval king, wearing a golden helmet, would step at midnight from the ramparts.

Quarter day was approaching, time to pay the rent. Clara counted the days anxiously.

26

'Maybe it would be better if you wrote to your auntie,' she told Sylvia one evening.

'What could we do with her in Pest? We aren't with any theatre now,' replied Sylvia. 'Auntie won't part with a penny just for our sakes, without someone like Dancsfalvi or Kürtös helping us...'

Auntie was a Croatian matron living near the River Drave who had been widowed early; at home she went about in top-boots and a leather jerkin. Sylvia Fátyol was her niece and the provincial lady doted on the theatre. At home, rumour had it, she flayed her farmhands alive and roamed the woods with a loaded gun, guarding every leaf—but she was happy to spend on the art of drama. This was arranged in a special fashion. When she acted in the provinces, Sylvia asked the director of the company to put this or that costume drama on the bill all next week. The male actors would appear in yellow top-boots, fur-lined pelisses, feathered caps, clanking swords; the women would be all heroic beldames, blowing Greek fire, talking in iambics—with perhaps even the prompter wearing spurred high boots in his box.

Sylvia invited Auntie from the banks of the Drave for these peculiar evenings and the widowed Mrs Urbanovics would put on her thick gold chains, her huge diamonds, her heavy silk dress, slipped a fat wallet into her bodice and set out to have a good time in Hungary.

She had soot-black hair, brilliant eyes and her face was heavily made up. Her arrival always raised great and general expectations in the company; the half-starved actors shaved and the director sold his own box. After the performance there was a supper at the inn, paid by Mrs Urbanovics who also commanded the gipsies to play different kinds of songs. In the course of this supper she usually fell in love with one of the actors; she made him sit at her side, regaled him with food and drink, rewarded him often even with money. This love of the dark, ravenous lady lasted sometimes two or three

27

days; during this time the whole company ate and drank at her expense at the inn and in the course of these orgies Sylvia acquired handsome sums—for her aunt loved her greatly because of her innocence. Then the she-wolf of the Drave, leaving one or two pieces of jewelry as a souvenir, left town looking pale and relaxed—to return to her estate and continue to keep track of every fallen branch in her forests.

'We'll amuse her well enough in Pest, too, just leave it to me,' said Clara now. 'We'll lead the old woman a pretty dance and take away her money.'

So Sylvia sat down, wrote the letter and three days later the Widow Urbanovics actually arrived. She was festooned with such huge gold chains as if she intended to spend at least a month carousing in Hungary. Because the innkeeper was a compatriot of hers she lodged at the White Ship and hired a street porter to guide her to Bombardier Street. She shouted at her niece angrily, almost challengingly:

'What a filthy city you've lured me to! I haven't seen a halfway decent male in the street; there are as many skinned-faced comedians here as there are moles in my fields. The women wear their bosoms on their hips and their backs are as flat as a board...'

The huge matron, still in her white travelling cloak, tramped through the small apartment with a heavy, echoing tread as if she wanted to crush the whole of Budapest.

Clara knew how to speak the wild widow's language.

'Sure enough, our great Miklós Zrínyi would hardly find warriors to his liking here!'

'Zríni!' replied the lady contemptuously. 'There was only one Zríni in the world. That actor Kürtös in Kaposvár. When he cried out: "Jesus! Jesus!", my heart stopped. I wonder where that boy's gotten to?'

Sylvia became lively.

'He's in Pest. I met him the other day in the street.'

'That's very good news,' replied Auntie, satisfied, and took off her coat.

She looked around in the small flat.

'You're living pretty poorly—it shows that you haven't yet sold yourselves to the devil. But I won't ever look at you again if I hear bad things about you... True enough, the post only reaches me every third day in the forest. Let me look at you, Sylvia.'

She drew the girl close and examined her eyes critically, standing near the window; she sniffed at her mouth, felt her waist, rummaged in her clothes; finally she slapped her back in a friendly manner.

'All right. I'll bring you one day that savage landowner from the Draveside. He's got five thousand acres of forest land and he rushes around on a two-wheeler among the mountains like a madman. He's strong like a bear and chases the wild boar on foot in the wilderness. He's not afraid of wolves, either—only of women. But he carries your picture—the one with you in shorts—over his heart.'

'When will you bring the savage, Auntie?' asked Sylvia.

'Wait your turn. Master George's still my boy-friend, I can't be all alone in that wild countryside. We have a telephone—what a wonderful invention!—and in the evenings we converse across the Drave. Hey, you, red-head! Come here! I don't trust red-heads!'

Miss Horváth submitted to the examination with a certain reluctance.

'Aha!' cried Mrs Urbanovics, suspiciously. 'Look into my eyes!'

When she finished with Clara, too, she shook her head, growing earnest.

'You're ripe for it, my girl, I wouldn't dare to hold you back. Get married or find yourself some decent lover.'

'I wish I could. There's no man to my liking.'

'That's true enough. Women are becoming more and more

beautiful—men grow ugly, twisted, degenerate. My grandfather was like a towering tree. My father, true enough, was stocky but he had shoulders as broad as a mountainside. These days men wear spectacles, scrape their faces clean, cut their hair—and yet, what's finer than a hirsute, bearded, hard man's head? If I were the government, I'd send all the male children once a year to the forest, the wilderness, among the mountains. Let them grow there into a generation of fresh, strong, brave men! Let them wrestle with young wolves, climb trees to the eagles' nests. Alas, I'm fifty, I won't bear any children myself. But if I had any, I'd make them bathe every day in the frozen River Drave!'

Clara was studying the theatrical announcements of the newspaper. She knew the principles of Mrs Urbanovics.

Sylvia reclined thoughtfully upon the sofa and because she was a singer, she sometimes had quite crazy ideas.

'Tell me, Auntie, why wouldn't you like it if I fell in love once?' she asked in a pensive tone. 'Why is it all right for you but not for us?'

The Croatian lady turned red in the face.

'I've told you, I'm fifty, I'm free to do as I please. I've forests, fields, jewels, no one can give me orders any more. But who are you? A beggar. You've nothing. D'you think you have a voice? Or that you're a good actress? The hell you are! You're a young, beautiful, innocent girl—that's all your wealth. And if you've once lost your innocence, you can bawl all alone, unseen, unheard. Men will no longer want you— and if they do, it will be a different kind of desire. That small invisible line that separates you from me and the other women might be a real treasure while you possess it. Maybe it isn't worth even as much as a bit of cast-off cigarette paper. But in any case you might as well guard it, for men are most particular in these matters!'

Clara, in order to dam this flood of words, suddenly put her arms around Auntie's powerful shoulders.

'I've found him. Mihály Kürtös plays in the City Park Theatre. Shall we invite him to dinner?'

'Naturally,' replied Mrs Urbanovics and turned again to Sylvia:

'Your mother was a fool, too, that's why your father chased her away. She died in some provincial hospital. You don't know of that, because I brought you up. Your father became a ne'er-do-well, a travelling musician, he wore black glasses and played the piano at night—until he froze to death in a ditch. You didn't know that either—for I took care that you shouldn't. But I, I made a gift of my innocence to my husband and I kept my faith as long as he lived. He'd no reason to feel ashamed because of me—though I was beautiful, I was young. And he was an old man. But I kicked the men, hard—like a mare raised free kicks at the slavering wolves. A woman has only one weapon: her innocence, her loyalty. Everything else comes long after that. But I've preached enough. Where's that actor-boy?'

Clara presented the newspaper. Mrs Urbanovics took a pair of glasses from her bag, put them on carefully and read, her face joyful, her head shaking as if in surprise, that M. Kürtös was appearing that evening in *The Martyrs of Szigetvár* at the City Park Theatre.

'Is that a really good theatre?' she asked, after a short pause.

'Lovely,' replied Clara.

'Then I'll put on my silk dress. Get a box, close to the stage. Hair-dye has ruined my eyes. There must be quicksilver or devil knows what in it. My sight's growing weaker. But I can't very well appear as a white-haired old crone if I've managed to look young until now...'

Sylvia rested her head on her hand and stared thoughtfully into the air.

'As for you, don't sulk! You don't know men—but I had plenty of them. Men are good only for two kinds of uses.

Either marry one, stay at his side in faithful love, kindness, devotion until he closes his eyes, so that even in his very last moment he should think of nothing but "my dear good wife!"; or take them up for a day or an hour, then kick them out and give the room an airing and have a thorough wash. Only the baseness of women surpasses the baseness of men.'

She took a bundle of bank-notes from her wallet, caressing them one by one—as if making sure at a fair to see whether all of them were good ones—then she counted them on the table.

'I know you need this. I'd rather give it to you than some wretched man promising you money and then not keeping his promise. I don't want anything in return except that you'll behave decently, chastely. I'll come and fetch you tonight in a cab.'

Clara hid the money in the wardrobe.

'So we weren't disappointed by the old crone!' she said and began to hum. 'Lordy, wouldn't it be fine to be rich and make a far journey, to find a real man, the most handsome, the kindest, the wisest! Or maybe even that wouldn't be necessary—if only he were delicate like an antique ring, noble like the verses of Dante and brave like a Toledo blade. I'd like to resurrect a medieval knight, a young Pope or a mere Cardinal, a condottiere or a robber baron who'd read poems to me at home, in front of the fire while he sipped cool red wine from a golden goblet. A man who'd never have an ignoble thought about me, who'd caress my hair with his thin, gold-ringed white fingers, who would use words sparingly, almost like gifts—if he said only: "You, carrot-top!" I'd know what he thinks deep down... My God, shall I ever find such a man—for whom it would be worth dying and rotting!?'

Sylvia sat down at the piano.

'My mother must have found him surely if she deceived my father...'

32

'What was your father?'

'I think he played in a theatre orchestra,' replied Sylvia and they both fell silent. Maybe they thought that there was little lovable in a theatre musician.

Sylvia hammered out the waltz from *Rip van Winkle* on the piano, now and then letting her voice rise; then she suddenly jumped up and embraced her friend who was taking some little bits of lace from a drawer.

'Clara, I'm terribly miserable!' she cried.

The straight actress laughed.

'We'll get an engagement somewhere again and everything will be all right.'

'There are no such two foolish girls in the world as we are. I've been in love many times in my life and have always commanded my heart to keep silent...'

'Lord, if I could only fall in love once!' replied Clara with a gay look. 'I wouldn't care a brass farthing what that old whore, Mrs Urbanovics, said. Or what would happen tomorrow or the day after!'

'You're a dreamer! You expect Prince Borghese, the Papal Chamberlain, to leave his tomb of three centuries and knock at the door in full ceremonial dress...'

'Or at least ask me for a rendezvous in that little pastry-shop in Buda where those strumpets from Pest meet their little lieutenants or budding barristers! I wouldn't cross that threshold for anybody less than a real cardinal!'

'You've always been much too ambitious, Clara. They made fun of you often enough in the company because of it...'

The red-headed *ingénue* bridled like a thoroughbred mare.

'What of it? Why the bloody hell shouldn't I be? Should I've thrown myself away on some third-rate barnstorming clown?'

Sylvia laughed. She always laughed whenever Clara swore. And Clara was quite an expert.

For a second or so they looked at each other with the old

33

gaiety. But Sylvia was in a restless mood. Her aunt's visit had made her rebellious.

'Love doesn't ask whether a man is an orchestra leader or a cardinal. It's easy for you. You make your own dresses...'

'Because I learned dressmaking while the others promenaded with their gallants after drama school classes...'

'No one can do laundry or pressing as well as you...'

'That's easy. All it needs is to get up at dawn.'

'You're a good sleeper...'

'Like a cook.'

'You're the best, finest girl I know. What shall I do, whose only talent is a bit of singing—and Auntie denies even that!— a weak girl, often anaemic, that's why my nose is pink whenever I laugh... I can't trust myself, because I get palpitations at night and I'm afraid in the dark. I'm twenty years old and I've been in love maybe twenty times already. I can't live alone, without love, without a man.'

'And who were all those men?' asked Clara with serene superiority while she went to look for the iron in order to press the crumpled bits of lace.

Sylvia sat on the piano stool and pressed her head against her arms as if she tried to embrace herself.

'I could better tell you at night—for then I remember them all. They come to visit me, they caress me, some sit on the edge of my bed; one of the hussars knocks on the window, the other fetches the gipsy band in the winter night. Cseres, our stage manager... once I even went to his room; he lived far out, on the edge of town, next door to a cowshed. The front of the house was occupied by a wine shop called the White Rose and the girl-cashier had lived in Cseres's room before him; the air was still tainted with her cheap scent and with the smell of dirty linen, I kicked over an empty pot of rouge, the sort the girls in the chorus use; and that's perhaps why I didn't yield to Cseres who was, I must say, a good-looking, sad boy. After that he always called me a trollop...'

34

'Any more?' asked Miss Clara, bending over the bits of lace.

'The hussar begged me to visit him in the barracks for he couldn't come to my place. I lived with a saintly Jewish family; they slept on the porch, the windows had iron bars. I think he was a full lieutenant... He had brown hair, big eyes, a delicate walk, he was a most elegant young man with a white scar on his forehead—he got it in a duel he fought over an actress. Oh, how I loved him! I waited for him every night; the snow was coming down heavily and the dogs howled as if they felt the nearness of wolves in that big town of the Plains. I opened the window and the cold of the fresh winter night poured into my tiny room. I remembered a very distant, nearly forgotten Christmas Eve; my father sat at the table with a big bottle of wine in front of him, smoking a long-stemmed clay pipe; I stood with my mother at the window and somebody passed by. "Close that window!" While I waited for my hussar at my window every night, I often wondered whether my father, if he sat there at the table, with the square pint bottle in front of him, would say the same thing?'

'To be sure!'

'Then the hussar came. The snow was deep but his spurs were still clinking as if a little angel with a silver bell had flown in front of him. I'd already stretched both hands through the gaps in the bars and he bent silently over them. There were white snowflakes upon his thin moustache but his lips were hot. Then *he* put both hands through the bars and caressed me where he could reach me. I can't recall him saying anything—he smelled of wine but even that was very nice. Often I caught a bad cold and was hoarse the next day— but I was very very happy...'

'And where was I all this time?'

'You? Under the eiderdown, deep asleep; I put a shawl over your face so that the cold air shouldn't wake you. He

35

was a hussar in a blue uniform and he always pleaded me to come to the barracks!'

Clara laughed as she turned over the flat-iron.

'Wasn't that at the Kleins' where we slept under such huge blue and red quilts that even the tips of our noses were hidden? I dreamt about mountains of gruel, trying in vain to dig my way through them. I bought lead soldiers at Christmas and put them on the window-sill. One of them vanished, too. And yet the Kleins were honest people...'

'It was my hussar who took it—for a souvenir.'

Clara lifted the piece of lace (which she was planning to wear on her shoulders in the evening) and examined it attentively, bit by bit, to make sure there were no tears or spots on it.

'Mhmhm,' she mumbled. 'My lead soldier?'

'He took it. Didn't ask whose it was.'

'I never had a doll—nor a toy sewing machine. So I bought myself a box of lead soldiers that Christmas. I was much amused by those miniature warriors. The captain had a red nose.'

'Like mine, wasn't it?' asked Sylvia suddenly and gave her friend a sly look.

Clara didn't answer. Humming, she bent over the iron.

For a second Sylvia looked at her friend in silence. A cuckoo clock was ticking very loudly in the room. It was a clock that accompanied them on all their wanderings. They had become used to its ticking at night; how often their eyes were glued upon it hopefully—if they could only spend another ten minutes in lazy comfort before the morning rehearsal! The clock gave an asthmatic cough whenever it reached its little halts, the quarters. But at the terminus of XII, a cuckoo popped from the little door and bobbed its head rhythmically, saluting the ladies like some miniature station-master on a tiny platform of life's endless journey. They had to go to the theatre; a servant girl carried the clothes-basket with the scented costumes, covered with a fresh white cloth. The bluish eveningtide had already descended upon the snowy streets; under the bridge the ice was still steely grey and the boys, on their single-edged skates, darted ahead and in circles as fast as if they were terrified of the moon that was wandering behind the bushes of the steep banks, covered with rags of snow. The theatre of the small town stood in the middle of a large, bare meadow—during the great cold spells perhaps even wolves roamed here. In another little town the theatre occupied part of the Municipal Assembly Hall and the actresses hurried along the narrow promenade with their servant girls carrying the clothes-baskets. There was a chestnut vendor on the corner, standing under an umbrella and when the lid was lifted, the narrow street was filled with the smell of roast chestnuts. Further along the street the bookseller displayed lovely English calendars which the whole town admired. The fox was hunted by gentlemen in red tail-coats; on another the characters of Mr Dickens travelled by stage-coach; everybody could recognize the plump Mr Pickwick (known for his excellent appetite) in his swallow-tail frock coat, not to mention Mr Weller, and the inn was named after one of the Georges. While our actresses passed with indifference the jeweller's diamonds, bedded in blue velvet, and gave only a hooded glance to the flowering palm tree of the florist shop, they always stopped at the bookseller's. On the boxes of stationery, My lady was taking a fence on her hunter or My lord's ancestral colours were waving on the flagpole of an old Scottish castle. Once it was an autumnal woodland full of rooks...

'Remember,' Sylvia said, 'how many rooks we saw during those two weeks...?'

'It must have been a sad autumn evening on some nobleman's deserted estate; the squire must have taken to the road because he was crossed in love and only rooks remained on the land,' replied Clara softly, with an understanding smile as if she knew in advance how a sentence would end, how the half-dreamed dreams wold be completed.

The salute of the miniature station-master was no warning of any urgent engagement this time. The wide gaslamps, shaped like champagne glasses, were now lit for others in the Municipal Assembly Hall; the orchestra was softly tuning up in the pit while in the half-illuminated stalls only the white bows of the usherettes gleamed. The propman knelt on the grey planks of the stage, using inch-high candles to paint an ancient royal portrait for the throne room. The dresser opened and slammed the iron doors of the dressing-rooms stormily as he rushed to and fro to fetch beer, white waistcoats and patent leather shoes for the comedians.

'I should've known at once... Those Kleins were most honest people,' said Clara after a long while, having pondered for a considerable time. 'Why didn't you give him your own lead soldier—not mine!'

Sylvia, as if she had been rudely jolted from her reveries, gave her friend an indignant look. It was on the tip of her tongue, the crude reminder that for years she had shared with Clara all she had—but Sylvia was a gentle, refined creature. True, Clara's grandfather had been a fairly high-ranking civil servant—while her father had been a plain night watchman in Máriapócs. Who could tell, who was able to recall how Clara appeared at the drama school?

Sylvia sat down at the piano, threw her head back and the waltz of the *Royal Capture* came tripping from under her fingers while her thoughts still roamed the past when (so she now believed) she had been happy—as happy as she would never be again.

...She had a blue velvet cloak that reached to her heels and in which she conquered the whole town. Her hat, trimmed with ostrich feathers, bobbed elegantly past the mirror of the florist's, a small snowflake had landed on her shoulder, the lamps were hiding in blue circles within the descending fog

38

and the tall, distinguished officers of the promenade, the captain with his gunpowdery face (wearing a braided tunic trimmed with back fur) and the cadet in his tall cap all saluted ingratiatingly:

'We'll be at the performance!' they called after her.

"My God, how unhappy I am!" thought Sylvia and laid her sorrowful dark head upon the top of the piano.

'Your aunt's here!' Clara said coldly behind her back. (She still hadn't forgiven the theft of the lead soldier.) 'Get dressed. We're going to the theatre. Look at the carriage Mrs Urbanovics is driving up in!'

The most elegant hackney carriage of Gisella Square was turning into Bombardier Street. The young coachman wore a light grey overcoat with big mother-of-pearl buttons and he deftly spread the yellow-chequered blanket upon the horses. The carriage lamps shone like crystal. Auntie panted so loud when she climbed the stairs that the girls opened the door in considerable trepidation.

'What's happened?' asked Sylvia.

'Nothing,' replied Mrs Urbanovics though she was so tightly laced that she couldn't even sit down. Her face was painted carmine, her eyes shone amazingly; there was a fresh tea-rose pinned to her yellow silk dress and her diamond earrings were the size of walnuts.

'True, this is no longer fashionable,' she said, facing the mirror. 'Who on earth can spend three thousand forints these days on earrings? Fashion's conforming to the taste of poor, penniless people so that everybody can afford to buy earrings; they are made of splinter diamonds. I am a country woman,' she added in a bragging tone. 'A peasant woman. I know nothing about the fashions of the Pest clerks...'

Clara admired her in proper fashion though secretly she hated heavy, chunky jewelry. (She would have liked to wear a very finely wrought gold chain—perhaps with every link the shape of St Peter's keys—under her shift, with a flat medallion on the chain, decorated with barely visibe etched patterns and inside the medallion the portrait of a pink-faced, blue-eyed, delicately-blond man, dressed in red. She desired no other jewelry.)

Mrs Urbanovics pointed to her thick black hair.

'This is all my own. I won't wear any false hair. It's only the fallen women who patch and eke out their hair with all sorts of tresses, which may have been cut from the heads of strumpets who perished in hospital. True, I'm dyeing my hair—I don't want to look like an old woman yet. Am I not right?'

'You are, ma'am,' replied Clara who was helping Sylvia with the agility and silent efficiency of a theatrical dresser to deal with hooks and buttons. Actresses, on the whole, are fast dressers; by the time Auntie began singing the praises of her unlined temples, admiring herself in the looking glass, Sylvia had already slipped into her evening cloak, trimmed with swan's down.

Mrs Urbanovics measured her niece from head to foot.

'What pretty feet you have!' she said finally.

'The loveliest feet in Hungary,' said Clara Horváth matter-of-factly. 'Everybody knows that.'

The coachman with the mother-of-pearl buttons doffed his round hat with a low sweep in front of the ladies. He helped them skilfully in entering the carriage, then vaulted to the box and directed the short-tailed horses towards the Andrássy Avenue.

The drive had a definitely improving effect upon the ladies' temper.

Clara who had powdered her reddish-brown hair had kept her grey, deep-set eyes closed for a good while as if she were still thinking about the lead soldier, but now she revived suddenly under the brilliant lamps of the avenue and watched the evening parade with a sneering pout.

'You won't believe it, ma'am, how many elegant ladies

promenade here now who don't know yet where they will sleep tonight...'

'I know. The women of Pest are rotten...'

'And these gay, smooth-shaven gentlemen—maybe they are planning a burglary or robbery with violence or murder...'

'Out of every hundred men ninety-nine ought to be shot to death to restore order to the world,' replied Mrs Urbanovics zealously.

Suddenly, on the outer Andrássy Avenue, past the Circus where the streets were quieter, they heard a great cracking of whips and the thunder of approaching hooves. The coachman pulled his horses to the side.

Six richly caparisoned, long-tailed bays thundered past them. An outrider, dressed in white breeches and a velvet cap, sat on the tracer, the coachman sat enthroned almost a storey high on the top of the huge coach which was painted crimson; its lamps cast broad swathes of light a good distance ahead. Maybe this was how British peers travelled once from Wales to London before the railways were built. The huge wheels turned solemnly and the footmen stood stiffly on the steps. The coach was lined in yellow and white; in the back there sat a gentleman with a bold visage, a black beard and a Tartar cast of features. His eyes that seemed to be blinking half-closed flashed now like an electric bulb as he caught a glimpse of the actresses rolling past him.

Beside him there was a lady in a furcoat and a small circular veiled hat, her expression one of bored indifference, her eyes violet, her hair an Anglo-Saxon reddish-blonde. She was like someone out of the pastel pictures of old Scottish hunting lodges.

The searching look of the black-bearded Tartar khan caused some sensation among the ladies. Mrs Urbanovics did not exercise any restraint. She signalled to the coachman by knocking with her ringed finger on the window.

'Whose was that red coach?'

41

'His Excellency Mr Alvinczi's.'

'Drive on,' she said sourly for this didn't mean anything to her.

Sylvia later spoke softly to Clara:

'That woman with the violet eyes looked familiar. Lottie Stümmer had such eyes—she was with us at the drama school...'

Clara made a contemptuous gesture.

'Our classmates have ended up in strange places—even as cashiers in cheap night-clubs...'

II

THE ACTRESS AND HER FOOT

The old wooden music hall in the City Park was little more than a barn, but Sigmund Feld, its owner, loved to call his establishment a theatre though it barely deserved such a distinguished name. In the summer evenings its windows were open and the people of the neighbourhood gathered in groups outside, under the big trees, listening to the lilting music of the orchestra.

It was a lovely world. Many of us, I am sure, recall with deep emotion the City Park Arena, our youth, a beautiful submerged island that disappeared, traceless, under the sea. The young rebellious journalists who already swore by Sardou, Dumas and the Hungarian Gergely Csiky in the art of the drama, gathered in summertime in Feld's theatre or its neighbourhood. The more serious of these youths earned 'the unsalted bread of political journalism' by working for clerical or conservative papers; they mostly frequented Buda and were fervent partisans of the musical comedy stars. The brief tarlatan skirts of Miss Bárdos had created a considerable upheaval beyond the tunnel that led from the embankment into the heart of Buda; while the square-built Mr Németh was a tenor of whom the middle-class misses of Buda dreamt with longing. Mistress Hadrik represented the modern trends in drama; her beautiful sad eyes were constantly fixed on the door leading to the stalls, hoping that the fat, all-powerful critic (a doctor of philosophy, no less!) would enter and then publish next day a review that would rescue her from her present situation. Miss Flóra Fái bounded on the stage in her magnificent tights like the very personification of the laughter rolling from the shell-like lips of warm, plump amoretti, of the rosy joy on their cheeks; between the second and the third acts the secondary school boys emerged looking pale from the bushes of the Horváth Park that surrounded the theatre. The manager, Mr Krecsányi, lingered solemnly, with a somewhat precious manner, appearing to be quite moved; with his grey hair he looked like an ancient Thespian of London Town who had acted Shakespeare at Queen Anne's court. It was here that the more serious-minded young men grew up—the kind of men who later professed the principles of Ferenc Deák (liberal and moderate) in politics, who preferred to deal, in journalism, with economics and sociology, in the legal profession with summary actions and representation of banks, who frequented the fashionable cafés and courted the ugly daughters of influential fathers. One or two managed to get jobs in the ministries and perhaps rose to the rank of supernumerary clerks because they always helped the department chief into his overcoat.

But let us return to the attractive revolutionary party, to the noisy Jewish boys, wearing red carnations, the long-haired cub reporters who called everybody they didn't know personally scoundrels (on principle) and who applauded poor Mary Csongory wildly because she wore a sad, delicate smile on her face and her garters were virginal white ribbons like those of dead convent-girls. Their favourite entertainments were the silly, upside-down French operettas and the burlesque, excruciatingly stupid but gay and, for our youth, side-splitting comedies. Mr C. Sziklai danced in female apparel and the actresses, young, pink, snub-nosed, smiling little lambs, had a passion for wearing tight panties on the stage, with or without an excuse. In the courtyard there was cigarette smoke and the smell of oranges. Irene Feld, her face like a cameo, crossed the yard with the long stride of a holy priestess. Now drama moved far away, and you couldn't act *A Doll's House* before the next rainy season. Under the eaves of the arena the couples settled early in May; young journalists promised their girls they would get them employment in the serious brick-and-mortar theatres before winter. These young ladies had only stepped across the threshold of a janitor's flat a day or so ago, or had come from under the trees of the Park where they sold soda-water or flowers on dusty Sunday evenings—and perhaps had never loved before. The grey top-hat of Mr Báttaszéki, the editor, appeared exactly on time in the evening dusk; for he was famous for having seen fifty performances of *Charley's Aunt*, sixty of *Sami Goldstein* and innumerable ones of the *Three-Legged Captain* in the wooden summer theatre. The management received the noble friend with distinct cordiality, perhaps if it had been possible to smoke and drink beer on the spot he wouldn't have left his seat at all even during the day. This was also why the gay editor now and then missed an act or two of the repertory, indulging his secret passions—women or leisurely champagne suppers (though the directors of the theatre believe to this very day that the gentleman in the grey top-hat was a zealous and enthusiastic addict of nothing but the performances). It was the poetess Gizi Király who represented her sister-Sapphos at the theatre; her aristocratic face expressed classic sadness even when she was watching *Charley's Aunt*.

In those days such were the amusements of the young newspapermen. In the editorial offices, according to the changing seasons, it was the tradition to worship Klári Küry or the provincial nightingales of the airy summer evenings. Just as the caps of Oxford students are marked with coloured ribbons when they enter university life, to indicate their rank and descent, so the journalist of Pest passed his entrance exam when he sat in judgment in his column over the lovely

45

Klári, either for or against her. He was given a badge and Dr Béldi, one of the leading critics, was able to muster his forces with satisfaction at the feverish evenings in the People's Theatre. They were numerous enough to have carried the fortress of Buda by assault. If the troop keeping account of Madame Aranka Hegyi's trills was smaller, it performed its duties with a more dedicated enthusiasm. The leader of this Brigade of Guards was the brilliant Béla Ágai—a man who probably had never once visited the theatre since those days. Lord, where did the huge flower arrangements, the showers and battles of bouquets go? Holy ecstasies, confessions, beliefs! There were quite a few people worshipping Buddha in India—but Küry's admirers were even more numerous. When she made her entrance, her smile which was new and bewitching flowed like a warm wave of blood between the shabby seats of the stalls.

Winter was followed by summer; Klári Küry by the larks of the City Park and the Buda side of the town. The summer had decimated to a considerable extent the phalanx of fans attached to the People's Theatre; even the poet hiding behind the *nom de plume* of Satanello changed sides, though he had already decided to write an operetta for the establishment. The hansom of Sándor Bródy, the brilliant playwright and novelist, was often seen outside the *Political Cobbler* and the ladies of the troupe from Temesvár had no hesitation in drinking vast quantities of summer punch. The National Theatre was closed. Not even Miss Márkus, the 'blonde miracle' was to be seen. (It was summer, the season of love, the true poet frequented the Buda arena to enjoy *Rip van Winkle;* after the performance the valses of Lisbeth whirled wildly around in half-intoxicated heads. And how wonderful the scent of the acacias! The narrow alleys were dark... In Lógodi Street someone strummed on a mandolin at midnight, behind a darkened window. It was the fashion to take the actresses of Buda under this window and tell them on this spot something they knew very well already...) The daring gambler, László Beöthy, was only a simple stagedoor johnny (though a formidable editor), frequenting the dressing-rooms where the fireman on duty, with the calm of an ascetic friar, rested his hand on the faucet of the sprinkler. Andor Miklós, destined to be the Joseph Pulitzer of Hungary, was writing lyric poetry under the pseudonym of Armand and the usually severe critics forecast a promising future for the young minstrel. (I wonder whether he has written any poetry since he became a tycoon?)

And all those young, nameless journalists! Without an actress as a mistress no one could be considered a serious and important newspaperman. Was it an epidemic? or a fashion? In the desk drawers where these days the cub reporter keeps his English grammar, there were, in those days, portraits of actresses. *That* generation knew more about theatrical intrigue than covering a story. To hum the operettas of Konti from the first to the last beat was easier than to secure an interview. As if in those days the future would have been a mere utopia—the immediate approach of another generation that no longer worships actresses but has gathered into its travelling bags all the knowledge of Cambridge and Oxford, the diploma of the Sorbonne and the brilliant talent of poets —the splendid young journalists who, showing the full mettle of their talent, have recently begun to produce the finest newspapers of the world in Budapest. Our age could be also called the decline of the actress. As far as I know these days it is no longer the custom to fight duels for the sake of actresses in Mr Fodor's famous fencing school. No one has ever died with the name of Sári Fedák, the great primadonna, on his lips on these premises. The sabres are at rest, the pens at work. Instead of Mrs Fodor—whose given name was Aranka—the youngest generation dreams of Japan which they would like to visit on a study trip; though this is by no means justifiable.

It was May, the principals and the bit players had already held their informal weddings under the old poplars of the Park; the thwacking of the big drum could be heard as far as Stephania Avenue where young lovers sucked the scent of May from each other's lips, the lamps shone beautifully in the theatre, the season started early; spring roamed like a young and pretty flower-girl around the Arena and the osier baskets of the actresses were hefted by chivalrous City Park scoundrels from the girls' lodgings to their dressing-rooms in time for the evening performance. The maid of Miss Csongory was courted by three barkers of the City Park giant swings. This unavoidably meant trouble. The three young men fought for the basket containing the costumes, their eyes bloodshot with jealousy. An ancient peer's silver head often appeared in the Number One box; he praised the plays while from the opposite side the famous Adonis, a cavalier celebrated for his fine horses and gilt carriage, fixed his binoculars upon the battlefield of the stage. The journalists had already settled down in their seats; and from the middle rows one could hear the bubbling, malicious laughter of those female members of the company who did not happen to be in tonight's perform-ance. The bewigged conductor turned his back to the stage as soon as the *entr'acte* medley was finished (it was music from *Gasparone*), the bass-fiddler took a secret swig from his mug of beer and a fair-haired, bespectacled young musician read a crumpled letter for the third time. (Who could have written it? Did it contain joy or unhappiness?)

Mrs Urbanovics, in her brilliant finery, deposited her swell-ing bosom on the edge of her box. Sylvia sighed: 'Lordy, I'd be quite content to appear even in this place—but Cson-gory monopolizes all the roles!' while Miss Horváth, purely for practice, cast melancholy, prim or dramatic glances at the fireman standing behind the boxes and was perfectly con-tent when he began to shift his weight from one leg to an-other.

'I like the fourth act best,' said Mrs Urbanovics, peeling an orange, 'when there's the sortie from the fortress and they cry "Jesus!" three times!'

Miss Horváth nodded understandingly.

'I really don't know why old Feld bothers to put on the other acts? He ought to repeat the sortie and all that Greek fire four times...'

The front of the boxes was decorated with rustling pink playbills, small oranges shaped like the breasts of virgins, boxes of sweets ornamented with colourful bouquets of flowers, gilt glasses, scented white gloves (shaped delicately as if cut from the inside of feminine arms), marabou fans (like the swaying plumes of funeral horses drawing the hearses of men who had died for the sake of women), all sorts of perfumes, elaborate, slightly powdered feminine coiffures, female faces looking feverish in the evening illumination, shining eyes and fresh white blouses. Past this display a tall, brown-haired, walnut-eyed, pale-faced young man, distinguished by a clipped moustache and a dark suit, passed in leisurely fashion. He held his hat in his hand and nodded respectfully to Clara.

Clara, however, was otherwise occupied and did not notice the salutation—for the leading dramatic actress of the theatre was busy on the stage.

'I know this Újhelyi,' she said softly, without taking her eyes from the stage, adopting the manner actresses used to criticize their friends during the actual performance, their lips barely moving. 'She never learned her lines and of course she doesn't know them now either, because her mind's always set on men. She's the most amorous actress among all the dramatic ones. Even at the academy she was always flirting with the old professors. She kissed Újházi's hand, almost swallowed Gál with her eyes—though *he* didn't like her very much, because he didn't consider her talented enough. Jászai once told her: "Miss, only chambermaids act like this, you'd

49

better take yourself off to the domestic agency." But nothing helped her. She came to the academy from a commercial college. And those girls learn impudence at an early age. She had learned shorthand and she wrote her love-letters all in shorthand to the boys. I love you, I love you, that's what she wrote to all of them—and every boy at the academy knew the shorthand for this. They said she didn't like clean under-clothes. Even now I find her lace-stockings most suspect—however hard she tries to imitate our great Jászai...'

Clara delivered this speech very fast, as if arguing with herself. Then, under the well-known suggestive power of the theatre, she at last noticed the melancholy cavalier who had greeted her, and returned his salutation in a lively fashion.

'Who is that?' asked Mrs Urbanovics whom nothing could escape.

'Mr Rezeda, the editor,' replied Clara and started an intense ocular combat with the sad-looking gentleman whose haircut and poise of head were both slanted. He looked as if he had fallen a-dreaming some autumn evening in front of the first fire lit in the stove, burning the tokens of a past love, letters, locks of hair, little flounces, maybe even a garter—as if he were still holding his head in the same pose he had taken when he gazed at the feminine letters going up in flames. 'What's he doing in Pest?' continued the *ingénue*, addressing her own white gloves.

'I'd really like to know,' Mrs Urbanovics remarked sharply, 'why you don't introduce your acquaintances to us? I believe that anybody *you* know, we might be allowed to know, too...'

Clara lifted her ash-grey eyes; a lively smile lit up her face—like the sunshine scurrying through the window when the shutters were opened.

'Mr Rezeda was a journalist in Debrecen and adored me. I find nothing remarkable about in this fact...'

50

But she had already signalled to the gentleman, as he dreamed about the fancies of the past, gazing after the clouds of yesteryear's spring; he immediately rose from his place and, taking long and shamefaced steps, moved to the box. He seemed to be blushing constantly because he had grown half a head taller than normal-sized men and his stride was long (though he knew that in dancing school twenty-four inches was the maximum allowed).

The widow from the banks of the Drave shook the journalist's hand vigorously while, according to her custom, her glance passed down the waistcoat buttons of the newly-introduced person.

'Reseda,' she said, 'is a scented flower. The flower of provincial girls. When I was full of dreams in my girlhood, my garden, too, held many resedas and hollyhocks.'

'He's a talented poet!' remarked Clara, her eyes flashing.

Sylvia gave Mr Rezeda a sidelong look as if she intended to count the hairs on his head, or his teeth. Her funny little nose blushed quietly and she breathed as softly as if she watched the course of some extraordinary event or spied on the continuation of a dream while half-asleep.

'I, too, was always praised by Mr Rezeda. When I appeared in *Rip van Winkle*, he wrote that my voice was like an estate in the Banat, growing golden wheat,' remarked Sylvia in a low voice, enunciating each word very clearly, as if she herself felt the importance of these things. 'And he never asked to be introduced while we were in Debrecen. Why not?'

'Eh, whatever for?' said the journalist. His voice was like the tone of a violin with slackened strings, as if he had become exhausted from too much unnecessary talk. It wasn't worthwhile to speak—to whom, what for? Words didn't count; actions did.

And he raised his childishly soft glance—mirroring the image of an October dusk, with a streamlet wandering from town under dwarf willows, forsaken little bridges and lonely gardens—he lifted his eyes from Sylvia's gently swelling bosom to her neck so that he could see as much as his curiosity desired of her delicate, firm chin and her noble neck that was as shapely as the necks of ancient aristocratic English ladies.

'Whatever for?' said Sylvia and there was amazement in her voice. 'So you shouldn't always enthuse about long-gone actors in your similes!... I remember your pieces in which you said about an old operetta that since Mrs Szalkai no one could play the lead; you declared that Mrs Ilonka Tiszai *née* Ellinger was inimitable in *Die Fledermaus*—while the whole town and district worshipped at the altar of Zelma Margó! Sir, I know every word you have written!'

'Mademoiselle,' replied Rezeda as much moved as the sentinel of the Holy Tomb on resurrection night, for he wished to be extremely cynical, even sneering, 'the Muse of Musical Comedy last visited the provinces when the plump lady-singers were not ashamed of their white panties. In the days when it was still fashionable for actresses to powder their hair; when their attractions, generally demanded of actresses in the provinces, consisted of black stockings, low-cut patent leather slippers and white petticoats which they washed snow-white every night with their own hands. Eh! Mrs Tiszai was like a small bird's nest woven in a round shape from long-stemmed, late summer grass.'

And now he lifted his gaze completely and gave Sylvia's dewy eyes a quick, exploratory look. Her eyes held a sincere melancholy which seemed to be eternally saying: "How unhappy am I, nobody loves me, you don't love me either, do you now?"

The journalist emitted a hissing sound:

'Because I was Don Quixote... Plip-plip!'

He produced a peculiar, plopping, snapping noise with his lips. Clara hit him on the shoulder with her gloves.

'What sort of awful habit is this?' she demanded with aunt-like severity.

'Excuse me, I thought you ladies were already familiar with the latest Pest fad. Plip-plip! Forgive me. Plip-plip!'

Thus spoke Mr Rezeda, with a malicious smile, as if laughing secretly at the fact that the ladies thought him a most vulgar fellow in this moment... He happened to look at Sylvia Fátyol—as if he might conceivably be interested in her opinion, too. The singer's gaze remained stubbornly and tenaciously sad, as if she were intent on staring at a portrait until it came to life.

'Plip!' said Rezeda as mournfully as if he had really said, "I'll make a fine corpse by the morning, for I'll do something tonight to turn myself into a fine corpse. Will you come to my funeral, ma'am?"

'Tell me, darling, how the devil did you get here?' Clara spoke in a superior tone as if she knew anyhow that she just had to lift a finger and the gentleman would dive into the Danube for her sake.

Mr Rezeda was certainly responding with complete emotional attention to the reddish-brown girl as if he touched a very tender, very dear, small and unhappy memory: a revolver bullet or a feminine portrait.

'I'm a Pest resident now.'

'Ah, so you're no longer a journalist?'

'I am, too, but in Budapest, with your permission. I have three weekly papers, no less.'

'Excellent,' Sylvia interposed. 'A king of the press.'

'Only a prince, milady,' replied Mr Rezeda with slightly false reverence.

'And which are these charming periodicals?' continued Sylvia.

Rezeda gave a slow wink as if he were about to tell the funniest joke in Europe.

'One is called "The Good Wine Merchant".'

Sylvia clapped her hands.

'Incredible!'

Mr Rezeda now closed his other eye.

'The second is named "Journal of Christians". And the third...'

The newspaper tycoon now closed both eyes as if he were himself afraid of the devastation caused by his explosive joke.

'My third paper is "The Lantern".'

Miss Horváth knew Mr Rezeda rather intimately, so she was forced to nod.

'Of course, it is the house organ of lamplighters?'

'Oh no. It is a revolutionary paper, my very own, of which I write every word myself,' replied the editor with an insidious laugh. 'It is the funniest paper in the world—but only would-be suicides read it. Its motto is: "Better die than live!" Isn't it amusing?'

Mrs Urbanovics turned back:

'Children, amuse yourselves a little more quietly. You're already being watched from the stage...'

'We've paid for our box though Feld would've given us a half-price one as it's due to actresses,' replied Miss Horváth, very fast, indignant. 'And you can't upset that cow in her role because she hasn't learned it anyhow...'

Still, for a few minutes they were silent in the box. Mr Rezeda smiled a self-absorbed smile—as if he found the thought of himself as a most amusing man truly entertaining; for tomorrow or the day after he would certainly hang himself...

'The Lantern!' said Clara absent-mindedly. 'Do you write about actresses, too?'

'Naturally. Actresses are fond of my paper.'

'Well, well. So we haven't forgotten the principles of the provincial journalist? A small pleasant lie in the press is worth more than even the finest bouquet of flowers! Are you still trying to be cock of the walk, my dear editor, behind the scenes of the Budapest theatres as you were in the provinces?'

Mr Rezeda gave such a strange laugh as though he were a long-dead corpse, floating downstream in the Danube, accompanied by a black fish. The fish would keep him company for a long time—until he became tender enough to eat.

'However,' he began and he adjusted a twisted curl on his forehead. 'However, I don't think I would be riotously popular in the environs of dramatic art. Nor would I unduly frequent or wallow in them...'

'Rezeda, you used to be a serious, soft, sad and dreamy young man in the provinces. You sat in the theatre with a transfigured face like a poet...'

'Whenever you appeared...'

'You wore a frock-coat.'

'That's how editors dress in the provinces.'

'In the forenoon you discussed theatrical affairs with the Mayor during his promenade...'

'Telling him how brilliant you were in *A Doll's House*.'

'You wore sideburns, too...'

'My God!' sighed Sylvia suddenly and swiftly looked at the stage.

'Well, what d'you usually write about actresses in your Lantern?' demanded Clara.

'In the last issue of my paper I took the liberty to refer to the mouth of the most respectable and honourable lady who acts grand ladies on the stage—describing not its shape but its odour...'

'Ah, splendid. So you became a blackmailing hack?'

'Anarchist, dynamiter: as you command me. In my little gutter paper I keep track of the lovers of actresses, and of their rich patrons; I record the course of the moon and bestow first and last names upon the children whom the black skipper, sailing the Great Sea, has carried to the country of the Great Beyond, there to spend their lives—those children who had already a right, but barely an opportunity to taste the ways of this world...'

Miss Horváth shook her head.

'Pity you forsook poetry. I'm sure your Muse doesn't wear clean underclothes...'

'My Muse, ma'am, poor soul, goes barefoot, her wreath is of immortelles and she suffers from the disease of pyromania.'

The performance was over; there was scattered applause, the gatekeeper, dressed in street clothes, opened the portals of the lobby.

The ladies gathered their bits-and-pieces. Clara helped Mrs Urbanovics while Rezeda held Sylvia's swan's-down-trimmed theatrical cloak ready—the kind of cloak only provincial actresses and real-life princesses wear. Sylvia stretched out her small hand which was as warm as a bride's pillow and pressed the journalist's under the folds of the cloak.

'Send me the Lantern!' she said, whispering, as if communicating a great secret.

Then she asked, aloud:

'Are you coming with us?'

'We're supping at the White Ship. Didn't you tell Kürtös about it?' Mrs Urbanovics said. Her face mirrored sincere and deep emotion as if she had just come from the funeral of her lover at the end of the performance.

Outside the arena a gentleman with a grey top-hat had taken up his post. His grey *redingote* was brightened by a flower, his face wore a dazzling smile: he was recruiting company for supper.

'Any decent person eats at Vadkerti's,' he proclaimed loudly, for this season it was this particular restaurant that was the 'theatrical' gathering place.

'Pity we've already promised to go to the White Ship!' said Mrs Urbanovics apologetically, addressing herself in a certain measure to the gentleman in the grey top-hat, for she felt, on account of her niece and Kürtös, some obligation to theatrical traditions.

56

The dazzling young man shrugged as if he couldn't understand the words of the elderly lady. At this moment two young little actresses appeared in the dusk like hungry sparrows, trudging home supperless, looking wan and wistful.

'Girls, you're my guests!' shouted suddenly the gentleman, who could have well been described as an evening rainbow. 'I've won a prize on the lottery!'

Mr Rezeda accompanied the ladies to their carriage.

'Who was this magnificent nobleman?' asked Mrs Urbanovics whose curiosity was all-embracing. (She didn't like to waste her time in the capital.)

'He isn't a nobleman—though he can almost be called that. It's Mr Bátta, the patron of little actresses,' said Mr Rezeda with a certain respect. 'He drinks French champagne every day.'

'We'll expect you then, maestro!' cried gaily Clara from the carriage as there was no place for four in the fashionable hackney cab.

Mrs Urbanovics waved graciously like a queen and leant back on the seat.

At the White Ship the music, played by gipsies from the Nyírség, sounded beautiful; mirrors shone on the walls. Gaslights flamed in an ancient chandelier and the floor was covered with a red carpet.

'There's a finer inn at Kaposvár; it's called The Stag,' said Mrs Urbanovics in a deprecating tone. 'Hey, mine host!'

Kürtös, the actor, arrived promptly; he had only removed his make-up. He was an ordinary, brown-haired, rather impudent-eyed young man who had no other talent in the world except to shout heroic words on the stage.

Rezeda also arrived; he cut the actor dead, trying to signal in every possible way that he ignored his presence. At first Kürtös blushed red, but later did not pay any attention to this insult, devoting himself to the entertainment of the aunt.

'Do you remember, ma'am, Dancsházi? The character actor, Dancsházi?'

'I don't,' replied Mrs Urbanovics who loved to eat well in preference to everything else.

'Well, what's happened to him—he's lost his mind. He didn't tell a word to anybody in advance. Just went cuckoo. Magnificent, isn't it?'

Auntie nodded kindly to her favourite; then, while waiting for the second meat course, she began to roll the breadcrumbs into pellets.

'What a pity,' she said with a sigh, 'that the Hungarian national costume has become unfashionable. How different men would be if they sat at table in flowered tunics!'

The journalist sat silently between the actresses. Sylvia must have been pondering some sad subject; Clara competed with the aunt in torturing the bits of bread; Mr Rezeda always grew serious when a wine-glass was placed in front of him. He drank tenaciously, wordlessly, and immense quantities. He took a mouthful of wine with due ceremony, after examining its colour and bouquet. Of the mineral waters he only used those which bore feminine names to mix with his wine. For years he had favoured those called 'Margaret' and 'Ilona'. Yet he wasn't even thirty, all told.

'Do you know who has the loveliest feet in Hungary?' Clara asked her taciturn companion suddenly.

'You.'

'Oh no. Sylvia.'

Mr Rezeda turned up the tablecloth.

'Let's see,' he said. 'Pull up your skirt, my dear. I'll write about it in *The Lantern*.'

Sylvia did as she was told.

Her delicate ankle to which the silk stocking clung with fervent passion, her tiny patent leather shoes decorated with a ribbon-bow were certainly worth inspection. Her feet never let her down if even the slightest expertise was present.

Her small nose became pink as she waited eagerly for Mr Rezeda's judgment.

'Neat,' the journalist said. 'I approve specially of the fact that above your ankle, in the middle, your leg starts to swell suddenly. One would never believe it! So mademoiselle is plumpish, if I am not mistaken!'

'Excuse me,' Clara intervened, 'only Auntie has the right to talk about off-colour subjects.'

'Alas, with me, too, it is only just talk,' replied the journalist, brightening, 'for in practice I've never vaulted across the window-sill of any actress—though in the provinces, where watchdogs bite in earnest, this is the custom, isn't it?'

'We know nothing of this custom, my dear sir,' replied Sylvia with a certain measure of self-respect.

'Pardon my daring!... In the old days, sometime before the Napoleonic wars, when I worked for a local paper, I willy-nilly discovered certain theatrical news. No night passed in summer—or even in winter—without the lady-members of the company being serenaded! It was no great effort to loosen the window-catch; the gipsies trudge off, the bass fiddle is carted away as if it were a dead member of the band and the violins, slipped into sacks, are always surprised that their masters never lose them when they are drunk—though they would find their own way home. At last, the chance to push the window open has arrived! The dreaming dawn wanders wetly among the acacias, with the greyness of spring waters and in the room perfume and nocturnal scents hover above the bed of Miss Catsup or Mademoiselle Dogberry. "Is it you, Henry?" the languid question is asked. "No, I'm Steve!" Alas! That I never had the chance on such a night to say that I'm Mr Rezeda!'

'Your chance might very well come yet!' replied Clara.

'Don't dazzle me, mistress mine! I have played Don Quixote long enough for your sake in Debrecen and Várad. I walked into the café and people greeted me: "We know already that Miss Horváth is the finest *ingénue* of Europe!" In the pastry-shop the young ladies offered me vanilla liqueur, though before they used to pour more masculine drinks into my glass. "We know already..." they said with a wry smile; after all, they could have expected from their daily guest that I would hang myself in the public gardens for the sake of one of the misses belonging to the establishment. The shop windows, the signs, the loitering hound-dogs all "knew" about it. I fled to the woods. The oldest poplar bent down and whispered into my ear: "We know already that Miss Horváth..." At night my pocket-watch ticked the same message. I cocked my pistol. S'help me, it already knew about it. You never had such a faithful squire, milady.'

'I hope you won't desert me in Pest either, sir?' asked Clara with a special emphasis and gazed with grey eyes deeply, penetratingly, then humbly at Mr Rezeda.

'That's still a riddle to be solved. I'm a riddle myself, Dr Samuel Riddle of Riddleburgh. Don't ask me, princess, anything that doesn't depend on me. Promise me, for instance, a small gift for every day—as Alvinczi, the gambler, promised them to Clarissa Montmorency.'

Mrs Urbanovics pricked her ears though it was no easy matter to free herself from the actor's hypnotic eyes. ("It's that necklace our great artist is trying to hypnotize off!" thought Mr Rezeda.)

'The owner of the crimson coach?' asked the Croatian beldame. 'He's a most interesting, distinguished gentleman,' she added with a deep-felt homage as if there were someone present who would early next morning hammer on Alvinczi's door and report the statement of Mrs Urbanovics.

'Certainly, Alvinczi is a very striking character!' replied Mr Rezeda. 'A great crusher of hearts. An ardent womanizer.'

The actor glanced with a certain jealousy, frowning, at his lady because of this sudden interest she showed. He nodded at Mr Rezeda with a sneer.

'You, too, pal?' he asked half aloud as if he had caught the journalist in some shameful action. He pursed his lips contemptuously and looked around as if searching a different company.

Rezeda simply obtained satisfaction by casting a look at the actor's carefully curled locks. "Jesus!" he thought, repeating the silent ejaculation three times.

'Tell us, tell us!' cried the aunt and pressed her bosom against the table.

'This old sow,' said Mr Rezeda softly to Miss Clara, 'thinks I'm here because she'd pay for my dinner.'

'For a long time now I'd have liked to meet Alvinczi,' said Mrs Urbanovics most emphatically as if she would meet the aforesaid gentleman at least every morning, riding in the Park. 'He's a great character. And I wouldn't cost him any money—unlike the other women he knows.'

'You five-hundred-year old crone, you outworn red petticoat!' grumbled Mr Rezeda.

Clara finally produced her dreamy look which was like an early spring evening in a hilly, wooded landscape where a soft mist hovered over the meadows of the plain, like a dream of the fields.

'Don't be wicked, Rezeda. Tell us about Alvinczi.'

'I will—if the actor changes his place. I wouldn't like the young man to think that I'm talking to *him*.'

Clara immediately settled the matter.

'Kürtös, sit on the lady's left side.'

'Why?' asked Kürtös, sneering. 'Are we being seated according to rank?'

The journalist emptied his capacious glass at a single draught, without swallowing.

'You see, I learned that in the provinces, too. In Pest they can't drink this well,' he murmured and fixed his sorrowful eyes on Miss Horváth. 'I've become a drunkard now—that's why women no longer love me.'

61

'I couldn't love a man with cold lips,' Clara reassured him.

'That's right,' replied the Croatian widow from the head of the table. 'A man should drink, smoke, play cards. No one is a real man who's never been drunk in his life. Whether drunk on wine or on love...'

'Love?' asked Rezeda loudly, then added *sotto voce:* 'You ought to be burned alive, you old witch!'

III

THE HARVEST WAS BAD IN INDIA

Edward Alvinczi, the owner of the crimson coach, was the scion of one of Hungary's most ancient families. A descendant of Alvinczi of Gut-Keled, Margrave of Temesvár under Louis the Great, and of Palatines of long ago, he was the proudest man in all Budapest. He was proud of his ancestor, one of the conquerors of Hungary, who wore a chieftain's feather on his bonnet; and he was proud of the fact that if the nation once again were gathered in the traditional field of Rákos to elect a king, his descent would establish his clear title to the royal crown. In the days when the sons of the Gut-Keled clan were margraves and commanders of fortresses, the Hohenzollerns were still goa-therds. According to the opinion of a learned Moscow historian the princely Gut-Keled obviously was descended from the royal tribe which had ruled far in the east, over the lands of the River Don and the whole clan had lived on horseback. (Mr Alvinczi was so gratified by this that he wished to send a whole herd of cattle to the professor in Moscow; his herdsmen were already set for the great journey which would have to be made on horseback. But then, being a capricious man, he changed his mind. He ordered a hundred cigars from Messrs Diaz Hermanos y Co. in Havana, the best and most expensive cigars in the whole wide world, and sent them to the historian accompanied by a gilt-edged letter.) In his youth Edward

Alvinczi naturally rowed in the Oxford Eight; then he was attached to the Austro-Hungarian Embassy in Paris. He produced thirty-three ancestors to obtain the rank of an imperial gentleman-of-the-bed-chamber though fewer would have been quite sufficient. Thirty-three ancient barons and commanders supported his claim at the Court Chamberlain's office in Vienna so that the two buttons marking the high court rank could be attached to the diplomatic tail-coat he wore as an attache in the French capital. (In his dreams Mr Alvinczi must have clearly seen how Miklós, the Margrave of Temesvár, banged with his mace on the gate of the Viennese Hofburg: 'We are not petitioners, we demand our rights!') In Rome a fabulous Italian countess fell in love with the descendant of Kirghiz-Tartar Khans, but this passion proved to be bad luck; in the Club of Nobles he lost in a single night the hundred thousand florins which his mother (a great lady indeed) kept in her lavender-scented wardrobe for some serious domestic emergency. The splendid woman did not shed a single tear; calmly she sent the hundred thousand to her son, though in those days it represented an immense fortune; you could buy three counties for such a sum. 'My son, we have no more money now,' was all she wrote. So instead of the hand of the Italian countess Edward Alvinczi picked up his Indian idol which he always carried with him, and had himself transferred to St Petersburg. Amor, however, followed the young diplomat and a lovely, sad Russian dancer cast her dreamy eyes upon our Edward. The dancer was also admired by the French Ambassador; seconds met in the Traveller's Club and then the gentlemen fought a duel—they only sent to their lodgings for silk shirts. The Cossack of the Casino sharpened and tempered the rapiers in fire; at just about the same time that her horse-driven sleigh carried the ballerina along the Avenue of Alexander Nevsky to the Opera, all its bells jingling gaily, in the fencing room of the exclusive club Alvinczi's épée pierced the French Ambassador's chest, three fingers' breadth above the heart. A red spurt of blood, blanching face, faltering knees and the pale sun of death cast its northern light upon the Frenchman's forehead. An hour later the express was due to leave for Nice; three versts from Petersburg the brown-coated waiters of the railway company laid the table for supper. Alvinczi enjoyed his elaborate meal, then slept peacefully in his berth and could hardly wait to resign his position at the Ballplatz, the Foreign Office in Vienna. He came back to Budapest, having had his fill of diplomacy. He settled down in the ancient Golden Eagle inn where he used to live as a university student; then he had had one room, now he took two so his man could sleep there, too; at night he had to be undressed, his feet and hands had to be massaged, he had to be tucked up and someone had to say goodnight to him—just as at home in Ung County, in the ancestral mansion where the fields, the meadows and the streams had remained Alvinczi property ever since the first conquest. The Ung copses rustle, rebels of two centuries hide in them, the mountains, marking the frontier, stand like snowy ghosts above the landscape... What a pity one couldn't keep a village *komondor,* one of those huge white sheep dogs, in the Golden Eagle, to bark for Edward Alvinczi during the night.

(When the distinguished editor of *The Lantern* reached this detail of his tale, Miss Clara Horváth gave a barely audible sigh: 'My God!')

A few days later Sylvester, the old man-of-letters, called at the Golden Eagle.

Sylvester was such an old writer that he still used a quill; he was proudest of the fact that Sándor Balázs, the playwright and translator of Thackeray, had bequeathed his cloak to him when he committed suicide. The first person Sylvester met in the corridor was János, the valet, who was just as proud of his small gentry ancestry as Alvinczi was of Ilona Zrínyi, one of the great ladies of Hungarian history.

'Is the Prince awake?'

'You must cough outside his door. We know you by your cough, sir.'

Sylvester coughed and was rewarded by a tired, indifferent 'well?' from inside. This single word seemed to cost the owner of the languid voice as great an effort as if he had delivered a long oration.

'Sire, I came to wish you the top of the morning,' said Sylvester.

Alvinczi sat on the edge of the bed; he always sat on the edge of the bed since leaving St Petersburg, his feet slippered, a silk caftan over his red open-necked shirt, in the traditional garb of Oriental princes. He wore a round white hat; his black eyes gazed with alert attention not unmixed with a certain melancholy at his visitors. The riders of the Great Plains exhibit such a gaze when staring into the distance bathed in mist and cloud. Alvinczi gazed towards the East where his ancestor had been king. There were some French papers at his feet. Sylvester picked up *Gil Blas*.

'Tonight they're performing a sketch called *Gil Blas* at Madame Louise's. I wrote it.'

The Prince looked boredly at his morocco slippers.

'A small sketch,' repeated Sylvester. 'Very short,' he fibbed.

Alvinczi lifted his head and gave Sylvester a haughty look. 'Well?'

'Sire! Do not be angry. I'd like you to see it...'

Alvinczi rose, shrugged his shoulders, then crossed the room and stared broodingly into the fire flickering in the porcelain stove that stood in the corner.

The snowy white of the china framed the vivid red of the flames. Alvinczi picked up a couple of small logs which he had had sent from the forests of Ung—the same sort of wood his ancestors burned—and threw them on the fire. He rubbed his very delicate yet powerful hands. He glanced down at his

66

slim fingers which were better suited to hold swords or reins than grasp the hands of women. Then he reached into the pocket of the silk dressing gown and took out a few gold pieces. He placed them on his palm and said softly, in evident boredom:

'The English are the most solid people. Their beef is just as good as their money. English gold is the best gold. It is really worth as much as its nominal value. Here, Sylvester, try them!'

He presented the old writer with a few sovereigns bearing the profile of Queen Victoria. The gold pieces disappeared as if by magic in the neighbourhood of Sylvester's red waistcoat.

'Gil Blas!' he said quickly, instead of thanks, because Alvinczi always took his gifts back if someone showed gratitude.

'I'll see. If I have nothing else to do, I'll look in at Madame's.'

'There will be a party, sir. A soirée...'

'Don't care. And don't use foreign words when we have good Hungarian ones. That's why this nation doesn't get ahead—because it has authors like you. During the time of my uncle, the poet Jeromos Alvinczi, people took good care to preserve the purity of the language. Anyhow, give my greetings to Madame Louise, our old friend...'

The man-of-letters whose red face competed with the colour of his waistcoat, adjusted his cloak—as a dancer adjusts her veils. (He always wore a cloak, the cloak of his dead friend. Alfred Musset used to have a similar cloak.)

Alvinczi picked a small white basket from the floor. It contained tropical fruit. 'Got it from Naples today. Our lady-friend likes such delicacies,' he said and smiled strangely, an Oriental prince smiling tolerantly at the foolishness of women. His room was, in general, like an antique shop. A good many old paintings were leaning against the walls—but the

67

Prince could identify them all from the signs on their backs. There were ancient sabres, pistols, Asian carpets and Hindu idols. Above the simple, almost barrack-room bed a small silver crucifix: Marie Antoinette's last kiss had touched it. On the bedside table a short, stumpy little gun which looked like a bulldog's head. Then a small, very old prayer book which used to belong to a medieval French princess. The letters had faded—only the capital initials shone with a noble Flemish red and the inscription on the front page had faded into light-brown as if written in blood: '1557. Noel Henry'. And the delicate binding was decorated with the winged fallow-deer coat of arms of the Montmorencys. Scattered elsewhere, pastels of famous jockeys and race horses which were usually bought only by English gentlemen who loved horses almost as much as Lord Derby himself. In the drawer of the night table there was a yellow pile of gold coins mixed with love letters and small, forgotten notes. A rosary which had been Catherine de Medici's and an oblong Hindu idol, shaped like a phallus, its ugly red head staring with a broad grin into the world... A martial halberd on the wall which some Alvinczi had captured from the Pasha of Temesvár— and on the desk cables and letters from every part of the world. The Prince spent most of his day sitting on the edge of his bed—but he knew everything that went on in the world. (During the years he spent at the various embassies he had acquired many acquaintances and friends.)

Before Sylvester could leave the room, with the basket under his cloak, Alvinczi suddenly became livelier. He rose quickly and picked up a long envelope from the desk.

'Wait, Sylvester, let me give you something else. Something that's still a secret. In the British Colonial Office they are about to compile the report on the Indian harvests. Well, the harvest was bad this year in India. The report won't be issued officially until next week. But you already know. Sell your secret...'

Then he dropped the letter, sat down wearily on the bed and stared into the winter dusk for a long time. There was a depressed fold around his narrow lips.

'It's evening already!' he said softly, for he hadn't even noticed that Sylvester had left the room.

His valet entered with military formality.

'What news, János?'

'Let us dress, Your Excellency. I've already ordered supper at the Casino.'

Alvinczi stretched out his legs lazily and turned on his side as if trying to postpone getting dressed.

'What did we order today, János?'

'Iced melon, Polish soup, turkey and boiled beef in their special sauce. Your Excellency would prepare the salad yourself. Mrs Boldva is making your special kind of fritters...'

'Fritters! Do you remember, János, there was a cook at my grandfather's house in Ung. What wonderful fritters she made! They kept a fine table, the old ones!'

'The best cooking in the whole world is in Ung,' said János with solemn conviction. 'What terrible lunches we had in Rome until your dear mother sent Mrs Ripka after us...'

Alvinczi became pensive.

'Tell me, Kerék, what's happened to Mrs Ripka?'

'She married the coachman of the old master of Bajnóc when her first husband died.'

The Prince stared into the past.

His man placed the rubber tub in the middle of the room and fetched hot water. Alvinczi sat like a Turk, his legs crossed under him. Suddenly he jumped down and noted some idea with his long, angular script in a book. It was a date and a name. Then he allowed himself to be dressed by his valet.

He examined his eyes and face thoroughly in a magnifying mirror, sprayed some hay-scented lotion upon the silk of his dinner jacket, tested the fit of his shapely shoes several times, then stuffed the wallet and newspapers scattered on the bed into his pockets so that they bulged. He picked up a short cornel-wood stick, with an iron core; under his arm he held a bottle of champagne which seemed as ancient and noble as the missal of an abbey. It had come from the cellar of the Prince of Wales. He filled his huge cigar-case—almost as large as a travelling bag—from various boxes, taking the same care as some apothecary mixing a magic potion. The wonderful cigars, decorated with bands like the cinctures of bishops, bearing the signature of the President of the Republic of Cuba, were dispersed over the room as generously as if Mr Alvinczi had been the foremost tobacco-grower in Havana. 'Alvinczi's cigar' was an institution in Budapest. It meant the most expensive, the best, the noblest weeds.

After the banquets at the Casino these cigars were pocketed by journalists and dukes. These were delicate and popular souvenirs of Mr Alvinczi's luncheons which you preserved just like rare geological specimens. Sometimes they were passed on to the family doctor, to an important critic, even to a judge... One of Alvinczi's cigars, sealed in a glass tube, wandered from hand to hand for about two years in Budapest until a drunken Negro dancer smoked it. This was a definite depletion of the national wealth.

Once the Archduke omitted to gather some loot after a lunch; thereupon János, the valet, slipped the Havana into his pocket.

'What is this?' asked the Archduke (who was also a high-ranking officer) in some alarm.

János Kerék's goodwill did not falter as he helped him into his officer's cloak.

'Keep it, Your Highness. It'll come in handy at home...'

...Then he scooped up a bunch of unanswered letters, put a rubber band around them and slipped them into his inner pocket. At night, stretched on the sofa of the Casino (after he had changed his usual thousand-forint banknote to pay for the meal and the butler had brought the change on a silver salver), Mr Alvinczi took his newspapers and letters from his pockets. The wide leather settee became cluttered with letters and cables. Using his gold pencil he made notes in the corners of the letters as guidance for Sylvester who would write the answers next day. The night was long, so he also took a volume of Carlyle along. The one which told of the Night of the Pikes and the Rising of the Women.

'If I don't come home before morning, you'll get a bonus of fifty, János!' he said with princely caprice. The overheated room, smelling of cigars, hot water and hay—the study, in which the Duc de Richelieu had studied the important government documents, must have been similar—was now invaded by the maids of the hotel. The anaemic-looking floor housekeeper, in her white apron, her gentle head crowned with a matronly hair-do, walked soundlessly along the red carpet. 'I kiss your hands,' she greeted Alvinczi, and disappeared with her softly clanging keys.

The Prince stopped, smiled—maybe Daudet's Pope had smiled like this in Avignon, looking after the light-footed Provence women—and said languidly:

'János, you'll get five gold pieces if you seduce this saintly woman! Five sovereigns!'

Thus he addressed the valet who followed him with the bottle of champagne.

Another moment's liveliness; his eyes brightened with an enchanting smile.

'Sylvester,' he added in his weary yet slightly more sonorous voice, 'Sylvester I would pay ten gold pieces for the same thing. You can tell him.'

Inside the carriage which smelled of cigars and perfume—it had been waiting outside the inn all day with its long-legged Russian horses—he settled himself as if he were setting out on a very long journey. He wrapped himself in his overcoat, pulled the soft hat onto his forehead. He placed the champagne bottle at his feet, thinking of the golden bubbles he would pour into a crystal glass when he supped.

'Good night, János.'

The carriage door was closed. The horses set out in a long-paced trot towards the Casino which was exactly fifty yards from the Golden Eagle.

('My God!' said Miss Horváth again and put her hand on her forehead as if she felt feverish.)

That night Sylvester caroused with provincial gentlemen in the Golden Eagle. Radics, the gipsy king, played for them and the party lasted until midnight, at a hectic pace. (The old gentleman with the red waistcoat preferred such entertainment which began with poetry and then turned into hard drinking and wild bragging, to amorous dalliance.) Madame Louise, alias Donna Juana (she was also called the Lady of the White Camellias), gathered actors and writers in her palace—provided her regular visitors, the counts and dukes, permitted this. At the literary evenings it was discovered that Donna Juana was a brilliant actress who could perform whole sketches or short acts alone. She seemed to have stepped from the pages of an old romantic novel... We shall speak again of the Lady of the White Camellias; it should suffice now to say that she acted both male parts and the single female one in the *Gil Blas* sketch and, in the name of her guests, it was Ödön Salamon, the author, who eulogized the artistry of the hostess, using the classic French of M. Sarcey. By then Mr Sylvester had escaped from Madame Louise's having received news that Mr Dapsy, the Chief Constable of Pest County, was at the Golden Eagle. A snowstorm roared above the Inner Town, the gaslamps danced in fright, the barber's sign creaked in protest—just as on the night when the young writers Kálmán Lisznyai and László Beöthy roamed the town and rattled with their sticks on the steel shutters of the Heckenast printing works—a firm they considered hostile. Sylvester wrapped himself in Sándor

72

Balázs's cloak, took deep breaths of the snowstorm and thus he soon succeeded in forgetting the perfumed party of the Lady of the White Camellias at which the writers, the authors of today, took tea in full evening dress. By the time he reached the Golden Eagle, he tilted his small pert hat to one side and he remembered an old, ribald song of Pest County... (The same song was the reason why the carousal lasted so long.)

It was past noon when Sylvester appeared in a mood of serf-like humility in the presence of his friend, patron and feudal master, Mr Alvinczi.

'Sire, last night I drank more than I ought to have...'

The Prince stood in front of the tiled stove and smoked a cigar from a long holder, a serious and deliberate occupation. The thick, brownish-white smoke and exotic perfume of the weed of distant isles filled the room. In the clouds of smoke one could see Spanish planters in broad-brimmed hats, green fields of tobacco and Negro women; the three-master just sailed out of the harbour, the white sails billowed in the wind as the ship set out for distant seas, laden with boxes of cigars ornamented with blue decorations. (The products of these distant seas reach us in strange boxes. Who had failed to examine the tea-chests and fig-boxes with their peculiar figures? As if the goods of fantastic lands would carry with them the strange peculiarities of these faraway countries. The Chinese dragon and the Japanese geisha, the coffee of Cuba which scents the harbours, and the Asiatic carpets, carried on camel-backs; all these make you think of great journeys in your solitary room.)

The Prince inhaled deeply. His red silk shirt and gold-embroidered waistcoat glittered in the winter sunshine pouring through the window.

'I don't like drunkards!' he said contemptuously. 'On the other hand, this bad year in India kept me awake last night. This is a very important matter, Sylvester. The famine in the treasure-house of Great Britain affects not only their lord-ships and the brewers but European commerce as well. One could say that the whole globe must be interested in how many tons of rice are shipped to and from Bombay... It was sunny this morning and I took a short walk in town. I saw somebody... A strange little girl with violet eyes who seems to be the harbinger of spring...'

Sylvester immediately donned his cloak.

'I'll inform Madame at once. The little girl with the violet eyes must be found. It is the Seigneur who com-mands it.'

Alvinczi gazed into the cigar-smoke.

'No,' he said reluctantly. 'She isn't destined for the tender hands of our lady-friend. She's different, she's out of the ordinary. Like a noble pastel created by an English artist. All delicacy and charm. She is slim, strong and tall. If I had met her in Wales in the great hall of a Queen Anne castle, after a day with the Monmouthshire Hunt, maybe I'd have been less startled by this vision. Her reddish blonde hair shines like the summer sun on the wheatfields. I must say,' added Alvinczi most seriously, 'I've conceived a deep admi-ration for the young lady.'

The old poet became excited—as good friends should under such circumstances.

'I shall write a poem about her.'

'No. She isn't that sort of girl,' replied Alvinczi quietly. 'She's as young as the month of March, standing on the threshold—and yet, recalling the colour of her face, one thinks of ancient jewelry, strange precious stones and gold, burning in a rosy glow—like the crown of St Louis. Or a summer morning in the Alps, with the virgin peaks covered in reddish snow, down in the depths the blue tarn and in the woods purple lilies of the valley...'

'Why, the poem is finished!' exclaimed Sylvester.

Alvinczi made a gesture of refusal.

'No. This lady is not a subject for your pen, Sylvester. You go on writing parts for Madame Louise and a drinking song for Chief Constable Dapsy. My ancestor Nicholas the Third was the Governor of Naples in the days of King Louis. I would say that the young lady would be best fitted for a Queen of Naples... Bewitching! I cannot forget her since I saw her.'

'What's her name?' asked Sylvester.

'Clarissa... At least that's how I named her for myself as I followed her in the street, keeping my distance. An old lady accompanied her and they disappeared in Mikado Street. A pity we don't live in the Middle Ages and in Madrid where in my present situation a few friends, good swordsmen, could aid me. The sedan-chair would stop in the dark night and I would quickly kidnap Clarissa while my friends would keep the men of St Hermandad at bay with their fine Toledo blades.'

'Sire, the tongue of Madame, our friend, is far keener than the finest Toledo blade. She had helped many a fresh little spring flower into the arms of gentlemen with wintry heads.'

'I'm still young, Sylvester. I would not consider it worthy of myself to spoil the bloom, the honey and the perfume of this unexpected adventure with hands holding a purse of gold. Sylvester, I have far greater respect for Miss Clarissa than you can conceive. Yes. I respect her. This is the right expression. For example, I would be most happy if I could provide for her education, her future.'

'I believe you will succeed in doing so, sire!'

Next day Sylvester roamed the Buda hills. There was a large rock and a bush on János Hill where he used to heal himself. Here, lying in the grass, he purged his soul, coupled with his Muse and preserved the fruits of their union on innumerable bits of paper which filled all his pockets. After his hermit-like excursions to János Hill he returned almost purified and rejuvenated to the human herd: he would no longer drink or roll dice; instead of drinking songs he would write a long historical novel and start a small journal in Buda in support of local interests which would bring him at least eight hundred lovely crowns a year. He tilted his little hat with the curly brim to one side and descended the hill, whistling.

"From now on I'll pay the grocer by advertising space," he thought while the idea of the Buda journal took firmer shape in his mind.

It was only on the third day that he knocked at the door in the Golden Eagle.

'His Excellency?' he asked the valet.

'He's already dressed.'

The Prince stood in the middle of the room, ready to leave. There was a quiet, playful smile on his face.

'Sylvester,' he said softly, 'if you like, you can come with me.'

They dismounted from the carriage at the office of an ancient public notary. His sign was as old as if it had been put up during the years of the Turkish occupation, a couple of centuries ago.

In the narrow and close office where the ever-growing and bulging filing cabinets, the bulky writing desks and shelves displayed such a biblical plenty as if all the stamped paper of the country had been amassed here and where the last wills and testaments exuded a smell of coffins and wax candles, there was no space left for the notary's clerk to acquire even a modest amount of avoirdupois.

The notary, on the other hand, was a fat, bespectacled man. In former days he used to play a lot of billiards at Kemnitzer's café so he recognized Sylvester at once.

'I've turned a Philistine,' said the old writer to forestall the notary.

Then they entered together the carefully locked adjoining room.

On the part of the wicker sofa which was left unoccupied by the mass of papers, there were two people sitting. A gentleman wearing a black frock-coat, his greying Spanish-style beard giving him the appearance of the president of the Veterans' Association (in those days the veterans of former wars were the favourite targets of jokes in Budapest)—and a matron with frightened eyes and mallow-coloured skirts.

Ladies of the middle class wear more or less the same expression at funerals, weddings and even at the conclusion of bills of sale if—these involve considerable property. One could never tell in advance at which point they would laugh or cry, for both of these were equally probable. On the other hand, the gentleman with the Spanish-style beard greeted Alvinczi with the solemnity of a churchwarden, in an earnest, dolorous voice:

'Good morning, Your Excellency.'

Then he sat down again, caressed his beard, buttoned and unbuttoned his frock-coat as if he were pondering why he had omitted to buckle on his veteran's sword for this festival occasion.

At the side of the desk, on a chair drawn to the middle, wearing a small hat with a lilac veil and a simple, well-cut dress, her gloved hands in her lap, Clarissa had taken her place. Her violet eyes, her golden-red hair, her arched foot, her delicate posture made her look a duchess who had accidentally dropped in at the notary to sign a contract with her tenants.

Sylvester immediately kissed her hand while Alvinczi nodded respectfully. There was a moment's pause. The matron produced her handkerchief.

The fat notary read at a fast pace:

'There appeared in my office Mr Péter Stümmer and Mrs Péter Stümmer, both residents of Budapest One, Castle Ward... the minor Lottie Stümmer, student at the Academy of Dramatic Art... on the one part... and Mr Edward Alvinczi de genere Gut-Keled, Imperial and Royal Chamberlain, landowner...'

Sylvester leant against the wall. He felt dizzy.

The document which the notary prepared contained nothing less than the statement that Alvinczi, descendant of Eastern kings, considered from this date Miss Lottie Stümmer as his fiancée, undertaking to provide for her education and her future maintenance, granting her parents an annuity, in consideration of which they undertook to bring up their daughter in chastity and innocence... Miss Stümmer, if she wishes, shall pursue a career in the theatre...

There followed the signatures.

Sylvester's writing had never been so hesitant and shaky.

Alvinczi stepped to his betrothed and kissed her hand.

'Do not forget, Clarissa, that you are my fiancée.'

'I shall not forget it,' replied a quiet voice.

Alvinczi reached into his pocket and took out the little prayer book of the Montmorencys, the small volume decorated with the coat of arms of the winged hind which French princesses, long turned into violets, had used for their devotions.

'Here is my betrothal gift.'

The magnate shook hands with the old people.

'Mr Stümmer, bring up your child in purity. I shall visit you sometimes. Let us go, Sylvester.'

At the Golden Eagle he put on his Eastern robe again... He poked the fire in the white stove, rubbed his hands as if he were cold. He fell a-brooding and in a voice people use in their dreams to address a vision, he said softly:

'I often thought that I have nobody. I live aimlessly, vainly. I loathe politics, I'm not overfond of society, I like to be alone. Now I'll have somebody at least to talk to sometimes, whose fate shall be hitched to my star. Maybe Clarissa bears in her violet eyes my good luck star. I shall have her study French and English. She shall read beautiful and good books. Perhaps I shall find much joy in the little girl. In any case, the whole business promises to be most entertaining. Tomorrow we shall begin the guardianship. Sylvester, you shall secretly accompany Clarissa every day from Buda to Pest and from Pest to Buda; but she must know nothing of this. You shall watch over her as if she were the apple of your eye.'

'Very well, sire.'

An hour later János, the valet, rushed into the room.

'Your Excellency, the sailor's here.'

'What sailor?'

'Well, that officer. The ship's officer.'

'You're an idiot, János. He's a sea captain.'

'He's still a sailor 'cos he travels on water,' replied János with a shrug.

The retired sea captain always bowed his head to Alvinczi with deep emotion. The gold pieces of the Prince eked out amply his small pension. His moustache was like a German robber knight's. His beard jutted forward in a point.

'Captain,' began Alvinczi, 'I know that you are a reliable man. My friend and secretary Sylvester has been behaving strangely for several days. I would consider it a favour if you observed him closely and reported to me about Sylvester.'

The sailor clicked his heels and, having received a good many gold sovereigns, departed.

János again invaded the room.

'You rang, Your Excellency?'

'János, the captain has to be watched. I'm curious to know what he's doing all day.'

'Very well, Your Excellency.'

In the evening Alvinczi's carriage stopped outside Madame Louise's mysterious little mansion.

The broad-eaved house stood in an old street in the centre of the town. It had pink curtains, its windows were resplendent with electric lights and decorated with flowering miniature Japanese trees. Its front door opened softly, as if at a signal, as soon as Alvinczi emerged from the carriage.

The elegant lady with her sentimental face, gentle and dreamy eyes, dressed in light white silks, received Alvinczi with a deep curtsey just as if he were a sovereign.

'At your service, Milord Monte-Cristo!'

(In this house all visitors had pseudonyms. Their true names, known only to the mistress of the house, were never pronounced in front of the servants or the other guests.)

'My dear friend Louise,' said Mr Alvinczi, settling down on the divan where one of the richest magnates of Hungary used to take his afternoon siesta, his silvery head reposing at the only spot where he was able to sleep. Madame Louise read him the headings of the news-items in a popular daily; the Duke commented on them until he dozed off and Louise took over his commentator's role, too. *Seamstress Badly Burned...* Who the devil wants to know? Why didn't the strumpet take care?

'At your service!' replied Madame with humble, deep emotion for no one knew humanity better than she did. She carefully closed the white double doors leading to the small drawing-rooms on the left and right in which kings, cardinals and ambassadors were wont to sit on the flowery silk cushions.

'My dear friend Louise,' began Alvinczi again, growing serious, with a strange quiver on his pale, yellowish face, 'My valet János Kerék has been serving me ever since my childhood. I have an important reason to discover how my valet János Kerék occupies himself. Can I have a glass of water?'

Madame served the water on a silver salver. Then she placed two fingers on her lips and looked most attentive.

Alvinczi put a handful of Victorian sovereigns on the silver salver, then rose comfortably and well-satisfied from the divan whose cushions had been embroidered by Madame Louise herself.

*

…Miss Horváth who had been listening to all this in a dreamy mood, now caught hold of the editor's hand.

'Tell me, who is this Madame Louise? Does one visit her? I'm going to.'

Mr Rezeda shrugged his shoulders.

'I doubt whether you would do so. Madame might not receive you at all. She does not admit strangers to her house.'

'And if you took me under your protection?' asked Clara with a humble look.

Mr Rezeda shook his head for once in refusal.

'Madame Louise is a very amusing lady, but women do not pride themselves on frequenting her house. Naturally I mean women who still intend to get married.'

'Strange,' murmured Clara and fell a-thinking.

The orchestra of the restaurant must have sensed that Mrs Urbanovics was a generous patron who would throw her gold bracelet to the leader of the band if he plied his bow to her liking; now they showed their real mettle. It seems as if musicians, waiters and cab-drivers had their own special language. Sometimes a gesture is sufficient to indicate something. Beggars and thieves characterize whole towns by crossing straws in certain ways at the milestones marking the city limits. The gipsy *prímás* was playing for nobody else but the thick gold chain hanging from Mrs Urbanovics's wrist. The songs chased each other. Dreamy and sensuous, silly American songs and French *chansons*. Finally the second violinist, seated at the back, behind the *cimbalom* (his moustache was dyed, his eyes bulged, his face showed such exhaustion as if he had not slept for generations) began to pick out the strains of the *Valse de Moscou*. (Perhaps one of his ancestors had

81

kept vigil with his fife in Prince Rákóczi's camp, a couple of centuries ago.)

Mrs Urbanovics actually lifted her head and glanced towards the gipsies.

It was a long time since she had heard this waltz. Some Uhlans had been quartered at Fehérvár. The officers gave a ball. The captain's name was Heinrich.

The young misses also grew dreamy over the old waltz. 'It is winter, sleighs with bells glide along the snowy Moscow streets, the gilt cupolas of the churches gleam here and there under the snow-cover and under the silver-clawed sleigh robes the women's steel-grey eyes show endless melancholy. Pushkin is carried home from his duel, bathed in blood... Or the French attache... The Tartar Khan, Edward Alvinczi, enters his sleigh outside the embassy and drives to the station; the long-tailed horses disappeared in the falling snow at a gallop... The luxurious brown carriages of the express train are already bathed in a flood of electric light at the station and the compartments are filled with the odour of leather suitcases...'

It is not hard to guess that these images were invoked by Clara Horváth, straight dramatic actress, while she listened to the *Valse de Moscou*.

*

A few days later Mr Rezeda took *The Lantern* himself to Bombardier Street, the flat of the actresses. Sylvia saw him coming down the street and awaited him in the narrow hall which had barely room for anything except the picture of a stag hunt on the wall. The coat rack was set high as if the hats would have liked to gaze into the street through the transom of the hall. To be truthful, no one visited the girls.

Sylvia wore a linen wrap, red with white spots, her arms and neck were bare, her hair was fastened with a single twist into a bun and her bosom had a youthful, fresh perfume. The tiny patent leather shoes peeped pertly from under the short dress.

'You've brought it?' she asked in a very warm voice. 'Is it already printed... I mean, about my feet?'

'Do you think, ma'am, that my paper is published daily? Not at all. Only weekly and even that isn't regular. Maybe I can find space in the next issue for a few fireworks about milady's feet—provided we are still bringing out the paper!'

'Well, I thank you in advance,' said Sylvia and almost embraced Mr Rezeda's neck as she put her hand on his shoulder. Her fresh face which had such a lovely scent of cold water and perfect health as the morning dew in the calyx of a white rose, touched Mr Rezeda's sad cheek as if by accident... Her pensive eyes, lost in distant dreams, directed his gaze again to her tiny shoes, her openwork stockings decorated with golden arrows, as she stood in the narrow hall with her legs peeping out from under the red wrap.

'I know, I know,' said Mr Rezeda, laughing. 'You've most clever feet!'

'*The Lan-tern!*' said Sylvia, emphasizing each syllable as if she wanted to pay respect to every single letter. Then she took the paper and threw it on the top of the wardrobe.

Miss Horváth was mending some underwear. Above the shoulders of the editor, Sylvia cried out:

'Clara, put away the drawers!'

In her first fright, Clara pushed one or two white bits of clothing under her skirt, then she pulled them out again.

'You're a fool, Sylvia. Mr Rezeda isn't interested in our drawers, he's seen enough of 'em. Anyhow, these are just like those worn by the decent matrons of the middle class. Or the pupils of finishing schools... Not one of them is lace-trimmed for they are not intended to be seen by anyone when we wear them...'

Mr Rezeda, however, unlike his usual custom, advanced in a most lively fashion and picked up the pieces of feminine underwear with considerable interest.

'Excellent, I have long loathed lace-trimmed underwear. I longed for this kind—with little holes and tiny leaves embroidered in red and blue. And around the waist there has to be a ribbon tied in a bow.'

Whereupon Clara took them from his hand in spite of all.

Mr Rezeda rumpled his hair and threw his hat on the floor like a student on a May outing.

'Actresses at home! My God, how I loved to visit in the old days in the homes of actresses! When I was as enthusiastic about them as if they were all, without exception, ladies of days long past, pictures to be worn over one's heart, pastel miniatures covered in silk, songs played long ago on the virginal, copies of Madame Déry with her dreamy eyes... Where is the gilt-edged diary with flowers, letters, locks of hair pressed between its pages? Where are the books of poetry, the Tales of Kisfaludy, bound in red with a gold wreath on the cover and inside a name, the name of a long-dead countess? Silk slippers with thin soles, white stockings with satin ribbons swaying under the knee around the legs that were gradually swelling and arching; a skirt with a pattern of big flowers which—like a glass cloche over the rare plants of a garden—hides a precious treasure, fastened around the waist; a small hat tied with a pink ribbon under the chin with waving locks that look like snakes; sensuous, big eyes, a delicately painted face; a shabby travelling trunk and a few withered wreaths and faded old playbills; that's how I used to imagine actresses. I wonder how much is left of the old pastel?'

Clara bit on the thread. She pointed to the sewing machine.

'That's where I do my sewing.'

Sylvia lifted the lid of the piano. A shepherd and a shepherd-ess, both with powdered hair, gazed from a pink medallion. Her white, fleet fingers ran over the keys.

'That's where I do my dreaming.'

Mr Rezeda, however, wouldn't let himself be jolted from his mood—one which seemingly he had nurtured for a long time:

'An actress, my ladies, is a strange creature. Every actress can be a goddess or the heroine of a novel. Even old Dame Locsarek, the famous comic actress, appeared strange and magnificent when she spread her green shawl over her shoulders. And it was only a green shawl... The strange-coloured and strangely-cut dresses, cloaks, hats and feathers which seem to be expressly manufactured for actresses, aren't they designed to make the ladies of the theatre more interest-ing by their very garb than the "civilian" women? The faces marked with make-up and the various veils, tulles, bows which the actress places at strategic points—they are for one purpose only: to drive men crazy. Now then: you only need a little imagination to visualize all the religious adoration, the beloved roles, the long nights spent learning lines, the struggles and sufferings, the journeys and miseries, the love-affairs and the beautiful memories that occur in the life of every actress... Actresses are the most interesting women in the world. The orphan daughters of the Good Lord.'

'The woman from the dairy often refuses credit. And you have to make up to the grocer.'

But Sylvia turned her shining eyes, her blushing face enthusiastically towards Mr Rezeda.

She began to play and sang, full of emotion, the love song of Hoffmann.

While she performed, Clara asked softly:

'Well, what news of our friend? The Count of Monte-Cristo? Do I still have to wait for the good fortune of meeting him?'

'Do you really want to?' murmured Rezeda, his face darkening.

Clara caressed his head and said, maternally:

'My boy, don't you know me yet? Do you think I can be seduced if I do not want to? By His Lordship Monte-Cristo or anybody else? If I ever give myself to anybody, it will be you, Casimir.'

Casimir Rezeda was almost thirty; in these years he had worn shoes with holes and once when he had inherited a thousand crowns he had possessed twelve pairs of riding breeches. So he had tried more things in life than an average person. But still...

Far wiser men have already been drawn in the net of feminine wiles. The editor of *The Lantern* blushed under Clara's caress.

'Very well: tonight,' he said with a quick decision. 'Madame Louise is giving a party and I have permission to introduce you to her mansion...'

Miss Horváth got up and quickly kissed Mr Rezeda's forehead; but he stared sadly at the ground.

'It's exactly as if I sold you at the slave-market in Morocco...'

'No matter.'

'I'm throwing the firebrand of disaster, sorrow, discord into the quiet hearth of your soul. You'll go to the bad. Maybe up, maybe down, but that doesn't matter. Maybe you'll become a countess—or a street-walker...'

Miss Horváth did not reply to this any more. She was opening both doors of a wardrobe at the same time.

Perhaps neither of them noticed at this moment that the piano and the singing stopped suddenly. There are songs that are never sung to the end.

Sylvia had turned pale as she pressed her lips together.

'Put on your blue velvet suit—the one you wore in *Fedora*,' she said later, softly.

For a while Mr Rezeda watched Clara's nervous, joyful preparations, nodding his head sadly. There was an ironic smile on his face; then he began to giggle quietly as if some-one had tickled his leg with a hack-saw. He cried in a trembling voice but with a gay gesture:

'The old scarecrow—did she get bored with Pest?'

He had to repeat the question twice before he received an answer.

'Mrs Urbanovics has invited Kürtös to a hunting party along the Drave,' replied Sylvia formally.

'A wild-boar hunt!' shouted Clara.

IV

THE FRIENDLIEST HOUSE IN PEST

Madame Louise was an authoress. She wrote poems, short stories (we who frequented her drawing-room all remembered the volume called *Anemones*), she rivalled Madame de Sévigné in her splendid letters which she addressed to writers and artists (sometimes inditing no less than twelve pages and always with feminine grace and poetic verve). At other times she was the equal of George Sand, frequenting, in a man's hat and in riding boots, the masked ball of the Redoute; while at home she was Marquise de Pompadour—though, unfortunately, Louis the Well-Beloved was no longer alive in those days.

Madame Louise (or, to call her by her real name, Vilma Srottis) was the last romantic lady in Pest. She was born in a small Transdanubian village. Her grandfather was proud of his imperial knighthood and his telescope. Her mother—in the romantic fashion—ran away from home to become an actress, while her father served the Emperor of Austria in some distant Bohemian garrison. Grandpa always gazed at the stars or polished his coat of arms. Vilma scrapped with the peasant brats or read *Corinne* in the arbour and thus reached the age of sixteen; she studied French, the harp and singing; the old Hussar who used to be her father's batman before he was sent home, taught her to ride. In February a company of Uhlans was quartered in the village and in May

Vilma eloped through the window of her grandfather's house with a captain. And she became a flower-seller in Pest.

This was the fashion in which old novels were written; and let us believe their authors that there were actually such women, such men, harps, arbours, May nights, eloping misses. These days all of this sounds like the twang of the snapping string of an ancient spinet, standing in an attic, while outside there is a moonlit midnight. The shades of the magnificent women of long-faded days walk waveringly across the old garden and the tower of the castle shines in the night.

It is possible that the women of yore were different from those of today. Some of them are preserved in monstrances by our memories—as if men had done nothing but kneel to worship at their altar and as if neither their lips nor their hair had possessed an exciting scent. Others—and the magnificent Madame was one of them—followed and became responsible for these matters—and no was history. The women, sitting in golden monstrances (who were adored by their extensive families, loved passionately by husband and children) read the works of the writers and the history books and smiled gently at all this foolishness. The women of Madame Louise's sort, however, pondered one thing: how could they repeat the life-story of Marquise de Pompadour? Old ladies still talked copiously about the light-footed escapades of Fanny Elssler, the dancer of Vienna; the Lady of the Camellias made all the flighty creatures of the world weep. The fate of Alfred Musset and lame Lord Byron added to the romantic hoard; no wonder that women of such bent ran away light-heartedly from the paternal home. These days there are highly respectable old ladies warming themselves at their hearths whose great ambition once upon the time had been to emulate no one but the frail heroine of Dumas fils.

So Madame sold flowers in a small shop on the Square of the Servites; but in the evenings she wrote and read novels. In addition she exchanged long daily letters with Fritz, the captain of the Uhlans (a habit she kept to the very end). Madame was beautiful and young; as we may read in the collected works of poets, she was the loveliest woman in Pest. Her noble figure like a young doe's, her brown hair, reaching to her knees, covered her like a tent; her eyes were bright, clear and sentimental, her feet tiny and her waist could be clasped by a child's hands; her forehead bore melancholy sorrow which ennobled her face and made her look like the icon of the Virgin Mary of Kazan. In those days counts and dukes frequented flower shops in person because they were romantically inclined. Madame, when she was 'ruined' for the second time—how Gothic this sounded in those distant days!—became the mistress of a count, a gentleman of Roman character, fervent Catholic faith and the most high-minded way of thinking—a nobleman in whom both the Hungarian nation and the Vienna Court liked to see the most powerful statesman of the immediate future.

The noble count took everything in life most seriously.

First of all, he had a great respect for religion. St Louis and his knights could have learned a good deal from Count Ferdinand. The Holy Mother Church had no more loyal son. There was a sincere piety of medieval loftiness in his voice whenever he spoke of Heaven and its Saints.

'Louise, you must be religious,' he said with pious zeal. 'Religion is everything. Life cannot wound your heart so deeply that faith should not heal it. And you can always count on the forgiveness of your sins.'

Secondly, Ferdinand respected his father, a retired Imperial Cabinet Minister.

'As long as my father is alive, no one must know that we are acquainted. Be honest and faithful. I shall provide for your future.'

The third place in the heart of the high-minded magnate was occupied by the Emperor and the nation. But of these he talked but rarely to Louise, because he did not consider her mature enough to understand such difficult matters. Exhausted by politics and public duties, he would knock at the door of the little apartment he leased for Louise and put his head in her lap.

'Tell me of your childhood,' he said.

As for love, wild embraces or orgies which were supposed to take place behind the silk curtains of the love-nests of kept women—and which were accepted as the most natural things in the world—there was precious little of these. The count always faced Louise with as much noble dignity as a marble column on the Acropolis; his purity and lofty mind awakened in the Lady of the Camellias the piety of those holy women who frequent the places of pilgrimage without apparent reason and kneel in front of the altar-piece of St George.

This modern crusader was Madame's good fortune. It was this saintly man who prevented her from going to the bad in the whirlpool of the city and continue to cling to noble, almost lofty thoughts for many years to come—though she was only a kept woman, nothing else.

It is a pity that a love of spicy food and always-snuffling gossip did not permit Madame Louise to end her life as a holy woman. The noble count was far too involved in politics, taking ideals far more seriously than reality, and the little love-nest where an ancient crucifix hung on the wall and a rosary was under the pillow—like in the bedroom of a Catholic princess—saw less and less of him. In those days there were considerable difficulties for the true faith in the country. The knight of St Louis had to do battle for weeks and months in the arena as a champion of the Holy Roman Church. The Semitic race which had only recently discarded its yellow garb, demanded more substantial rights in addition to the right of money-lending. The ashes of John Huss and Hieronymus Savonarola, scattered in the wind, were resurrected and the *heyducks* of Gábor Bethlen hammered on the table in the Lower Chamber, fighting for the freedom of the sons of Sem. The count wore his symbolic armour day and night, fighting like Tancred against the enemies of the Church: at night he had terrible visions about Nation and Crown perishing miserably. 'Pray!' he wrote in every one of his letters to the deserted little Louise whom he soon sent abroad in the company of a highly educated but impoverished baroness. For the pen-pushers of Sem, the young warriors who used poisoned arrows, had almost penetrated into the little love-nest in order to launch a flank attack on the noble Tancred through this pink bastion.

In dreamy Munich, Louise met two Hungarian magnates at the table d'hôte of the Bayerischer Hof. The gentlemen were friends of the count and naturally took their friend's lady-friend under their wings.

One should never send one's mistress abroad alone, not even under feminine supervision—nor, maybe, even to the neighbouring street.

Wives are shining, dazzling decorations on the full dress of the diplomat; their disappearance is quickly noticeable. But mistresses are only delightful little charms on a watch-chain; we can travel a long way before we realize that we have lost them—and then we have no idea how and where.

The two good friends opened to Louise's dazzled eyes the whole great world, the brilliant evenings of the Opera, the fairy-like pomp of Parisian balls, the luxurious suites of the Grand Hotels and the bewitching atmosphere of the Monte Carlo Casino. The express trains rolled swiftly along the main routes of Europe, but Louise's mind and world of ideas opened up even faster. The great world which she had only known from novels turned the formerly stubborn, defiant but above all honest Transdanubian little girl into a lady longing for pleasure, determined to dazzle everybody, in silks and velvets and diamonds. Through her excellent connections she had the great good fortune of meeting His Majesty, King Milan, and at the Nice races she was able to give her visiting card to an honest-to-goodness American millionaire, a redoubtable beer baron. She told him that he would be very welcome if he ever came to Budapest. The visiting card read: 'Louise de Péczely.'

And during all this she still found time to keep her travel diary and to write voluminous letters every day to Fritz and Ferdinand.

The noble Ferdinand had to draw on certain savings so that he should be able to send to Madame Louise the sums required and requested. Yet he only had a single remark to make about the incident: 'Darling, in Paris you forgot to pray—that's why we lost our battle at home!'

True enough, during her foreign travels Louise did not pray. She left her rosary at home—though its beads had once passed through the fingers of a genuine Princess Metternich.

The gallant and amorous Alvinczi (who was then attaché in Paris) gave a luncheon in honour of Count Ferdinand's mistress which was a rare event even in the diplomats' club. At the Longchamps races poor Ferdinand's girl-friend was already surrounded by a whole crowd of Hungarian aristocrats—while the noble count fought at home with death-defying courage for Throne and Church...

'I swear that I've been faithful to you,' said Louise earnestly, her eyes dewy, when at last she returned to Budapest and the count.

Ferdinand kissed her forehead.

'I heard that you had a good time—and that is enough for me!'

...What was the rare quality in this extraordinary woman that made her the centre of society both in Paris and Budapest? Perhaps some ancestor of the Srottises had visited the court of Louis XIV; or was she simply lucky as those poor women used to say who finished their butterfly-careers in the same shabby petticoat in which they had started? Men admire women of magnificence and do not seek to discover the secret of their magic—the kind of magic which such ladies exercised even before Ninon de Lenclos.

The party to which Mr Rezeda took Clara was held in honour of actresses and authors. (On the whole Madame Louise only liked princes and poets; she did not consider other men as quite human.)

The lady of the house had discarded her stays and was wearing a very light silk dress with a pattern of tiny flower-wreaths; instead of a tiara she only put a red rose into her hair to mark the informal character of the party. In the course of the years she had grown more matronly and (since poor Ferdinand deserted her to marry at long last the princess, daughter of an ancient Catholic family, to whom he had been affianced by his parents since his cradle) there were a few tiny crow's feet at her temples. Only her forehead shone with the innocence and sadness of a little girl, sorrowing for her Christmas toys.

'Welcome to my shack,' she told Clara gaily as if she had known her a very long time. 'We have a village feast today, we drink peasant wine... Come on, Sylvester, let me introduce you.'

Rezeda touched Clara's shoulder.

'Alvinczi's private secretary!'

Sylvester had discarded the cloak of Sándor Balázs for the party; instead he wore a red, tasselled cap and held a short-stemmed wooden pipe between his teeth. He was just reading one of his poems to little Béla Bonifácz who was blinking behind his pince-nez as he listened to the ode addressed to an ancient piece of stone on János Hill:

> *And thus speaks the stone:*
> *Your tomb I shall mark.*
> *A wild rose-bush upon*
> *Your grave grows dank and dark.*

Sylvester rose, bowed to Miss Horváth and as he was always extremely courteous to women, kissed her hand.

'If I were younger, I'd write a poem about you. But I'm an old fellow now and Béla Bonifácz is my friend.'

Bonifácz was a little dark man, with unkempt hair and beard—the sort of man Russian girl-students imagine saintly Russian Nihilists to be. But his eyes were as soft and melancholy as a child's that thinks of nothing but its dead mother.

'Master Fugitive,' said Madame Louise to the little Nihilist, 'I'll leave the beautiful young lady in your care. At such village parties I superintend the kitchen myself. And someone has to receive the guests if anybody should stray this way.'

Her gay, full-throated laughter, her deep warm voice filled the little drawing-room where the gift of the Prince of Wales, a golden crane, supported on its back the tray for visiting cards. In her light dress, her slipper-like shoes she moved as agilely as if she had never left her village and her ancestral home.

'Make sure there's some scrambled eggs, too,' shouted Sylvester. 'My teeth are pretty bad.'

'Don't worry, my dear fellow. Scrambled eggs—that's what I always cooked for the Shah of Persia, too, whenever he honoured my house.'

Sylvester made a gesture of disdain.

'What? The Shah of Persia? What does he know about the proper way of making scrambled eggs? There was a Mistress Német who kept an inn at Máriabesnyő... I courted her quite a bit when I was a young law-clerk...'

An elderly maid, in a white cap, her face wreathed in smiles—the sort of girl who used to follow in her mother's steps, serving in old country mansions—put a long-necked bottle of red wine on the table. The golden-legged crane of the Prince of Wales was removed to a corner of the room.

'Transdanubian wine!' cried Sylvester.

'From our village. From Madame's village,' replied the maid.

'We'll drink some of that!' said Mr Sylvester and started gaily to fill the glasses. 'Lovely lady—your health!'

Clara wouldn't have been a professional actress if she hadn't immediately adjusted herself to the mood of the company. She laughed, touched her glass to Sylvester's, drank. Madame Louise hurried in, her face pink from the kitchen fire. She touched her lips to the rim of a glass.

'We're going to enjoy ourselves tonight. Dinner's ready in a moment. I can already hear the shuffle of Ivan Ilich, my household enemy.'

Sylvester fixed his eyes with evident delight upon the beautiful Louise—like an old uncle gazing at his niece.

'That's the spirit, my dear gossip! The devil take the Shahs of Persia and the English princes. The Hungarian poets, the Hungarian hussars lead the world. D'you remember how often we spent the night carousing with poor Sándor Balázs in that little Buda inn?'

'Once I even missed the visit of the German ambassador because of it!'

In the meantime Clara looked around in the little drawing-room which was frequented by kings and ambassadors. Neither here nor later, exploring the other rooms of the apartment, did she find any trace of cunningly refined, sense-tickling taste—though she had read about them in her novels. These were middle-class rooms, far from being furnished with a royal comfort. One of the *salons* was a eulogy of early Victorian taste, the other showed traces of rococo. The dining-room contained a wide walnut table and a sideboard—like some village mansions where the furniture bequeathed by the grandparents was treasured. The only difference was the mass of portraits—such numbers one would only find normally in a photographer's studio. All were males. The inscriptions—which must have been at the lower edge of the photographs—were discreetly hidden by the frames. But even so Clara recognized in one King Edward of Great Britain. Not far from him there was a cardinal's delicate face, with young and old peers dressed in the costumes of some masked ball. The place of honour was occupied by a wreath in the national red-white-green colours of Hungary. This was a gift from the youth of suburban Kőbánya where Madame Louise had appeared with an amateur dramatic society.

Elsewhere photographs of the lady of the house occupied the walls. Louise on horseback, Louise in riding coats with a pert little top-hat; then, looking girlish, in a simple little dress, with a small bouquet in her hand; still another, where she was dropping her opera cloak from her rounded shoulders. Louise in mourning clothes, Louise as a Spanish dancer; then in a splendid evening dress with a long train, a precious fan between her fingers. Here she was depicted as a bourgeois matron dressed in the fashion of the Eighties; next, reading a book; then again, leaning on her writing-desk which had pointed legs, working no doubt on her *Anemones*.

It is in old provincial drawing-rooms where the ladies of the house do the cleaning themselves in the mornings and where the doors are locked during the day, that daguerrotypes are preserved with such anxious care, the likenesses of fathers, grandfathers, kinfolk, showing to later generations the ladies and gentlemen in Hungarian national dress. And the photographs are marked with the name of Jeney, the fashionable master of light and shadow. Our grandmother gazes back at us across forty years, in a pearly bonnet and wide, flowery skirts.

Above the wide bed of Madame Louise there was only a single small picture. The portrait of a pale old gentleman in an oval gilt frame; upon his head a pertly-tilted forage cap as worn by the *honvéds*, the soldiers of Kossuth.

On the bedside table, next to the rosary of Princess Metternich, the photographs of a young gentleman and a lady.

'You're looking at my son!' exclaimed Madame Louise as she returned to the room. 'That's my son and his fiancée. My second son who's getting married. They leave me, they go away, as soon as I've raised them. Menfolk are all ungrateful.'

'They aren't her real sons!' old Sylvester interposed an explanation.

'That doesn't matter. I love them as if they were my own flesh and blood. This Marci was especially close to my heart. He wasn't even three when his father, Captain Szentléleki, fell from his horse. In his will he bequeathed the boy to me— for he was a good friend of mine. It took me about half a year before I found the child and its mother in a Galician music-hall. Then I took him away and brought him up. His mother saw him only once in twenty years. She's married a leather manufacturer in Moscow. She has other worries than the son that Szentléleki sired. But since then I've a new son, Sylvester. I got him by mail. Sent to me by a poor girl-friend of mine from Paris; she's doing badly. But I have him raised in the country. I want somebody to run my little farm when I've grown too old for it. But now let's have dinner. Ivan Ilich is hungry.'

In the dining-room they actually found him waiting. Ivan Ilich had a crooked nose, slyly narrow eyes and greying hair. He was sharpening the table-knife with a pocket one.

'How dull your knives are, Louise!' he said reproachfully.

'I wouldn't dream keeping sharp knives—one day when you get angry with me, you might stab me with them!' replied Louise, laughing. 'You'd, too, s'help me God, you would. Ivan Ilich's a most dangerous man,' she added, for Clara's benefit.

Ivan Ilich sat at the end of the table, his head hanging sadly, resembling an ailing bird.

'Mr Ilich is a romantic figure,' continued Madame Louise who obviously was fond of this subject. 'I chose his name from a Russian novel. For twenty years he has been my table companion at dinner—and at cards in the afternoon. Heaven help me if I ever won a redoubled bid! He'd immediately stab me with his knife! Ilich, you old pig! Were you drinking again last night?'

Ivan Ilich twisted his face in a childish grimace.

'Fury! You're again all Furies in one!' he said, then he cleared his throat as he filled his glass. 'Phooey! Homegrown wine! I'll have a sour taste again for a week!'

But he poured down the wine without even swallowing. Then he looked most unhappy again as if he had bitten into something exceedingly sharp.

He leant both elbows on the table and gazed with a sneering and challenging smile towards the door, as if waiting for dishes not at all to his liking being served in a row.

'That's how it goes, if you please, for twenty years!' continued Madame Louise, spinning her thread about the little man who resembled a marmot. 'Every day at noon he's likely to beat me because of our cooking. My servants believe that he's my fiancé—or maybe, my secretly wedded husband. Yet if I ever choose a husband he must be like the Archangel Gabriel. Tell me, dear gossip, couldn't you recommend someone? I'm getting bored. I need a man in the house.'

Ivan Ilich gave a mocking laugh.

'As if any man would dare to marry you! You'd start henpecking him the very first day.'

'If he were your kind of coward, certainly I would.'

Béla Bonifácz had drunk three glasses of wine. After the chicken soup he stopped eating.

'I know where I ruined my life,' he said, his voice unusually loud. 'I should've blown up that hateful Hentzi statue. Everything would be different today. Maybe my newspaper would be still alive...'

'What ails you, Master Wanderer?' cried the hostess. 'It's you about whom Eötvös wrote his novel: *The Eternal Exile*...'

Bonifácz jumped to his feet with a violent gesture. He adjusted his spectacles.

'But what else can I do? Three times I was put in prison for *lèse-majesté*. Six times I was gaoled for criminal libel, if you please. I was accused innumerable times of incitement to revolt. And yet I was always dodged by ill luck! Why didn't I succeed in blowing up that blasted statue!'

His face was burning, his hair was tousled, his eyes shone with missionary zeal.

'This country will never get anywhere until it becomes a republic.'

A new guest arrived, interrupting the lecture of the Nihilist poet. It was an aged and retired actress, Lenke Bártfai, who made her entrance; she was the recipient of Madame Louise's cast-off clothes and shoes. She was still sporting the bustle that had gone out of fashion decades ago. She greeted the company ceremoniously and kissed Madame Louise's face and hand.

'Forgive me, darling, I didn't want to compromise your house... A gentleman in a top-hat started to chase me in Váci Street! I didn't wish all-and-sundry to see me turn in here. What would be their opinion of you, then?' she fluted. Her face was tinted brick-red by grease-paint; with her strange curls, bows, buttons and ribbons she seemed to have come from the fair of provincial actors that used to be held half a century before in front of the Hotel Pannonia, to hire the repertory companies. She continued with lively indignation: 'I beg you... I wouldn't mind another time... But just today, when I'm due at an evening reception?... No. It was impossible. Forgive me, darling.'

Ivan Ilich was giggling at the far end of the table. Lenke Bártfai lifted her eyebrows to her hairline.

'My friend, the court jester! Or should I say court chamberlain? Take due notice of the fact that a Bártfai never lies.'

Ivan Ilich had a fit of stormy coughing as he swallowed a glass of wine.

'Which was your company, my dear?' the newcomer turned to Clara. 'Komjáthy's? I know him. He was a better actor than manager. No? Krecsányi's? Old Náci is very old-fashioned. Shakespeare, always Shakespeare. Or Verdi. He simply ruined his artistes.'

Béla Bonifácz, as he was unable to address the whole company, turned to Mr Rezeda, sitting next to him and began to explain in a rhetorical manner but quietly enough, his sufferings—about which he was usually most uncommunicative, except when in his cups. Bonifácz was a strange anomaly of Hungarian life. He took things seriously. He started as a poet. His dramatic poem 'Jesus' would one day be unearthed from the dusty archives; but then came Istóczy and Verhovay, and poor Bonifácz forgot about Jesus. He became a fanatic journalist of the radical Left. His modest fortune was lost in various journalistic ventures. Where did he live? Where did he roam? For ten or fifteen years he honoured his old friends by borrowing sometimes fifty, sometimes twenty coppers from them—tramping from one end of the city to the other to raise these loans.

The company's mood grew gay. The dishes, cooked according to peasant recipes, were received with enthusiasm as most of the guests came from the provinces themselves.

'I'll act the *Gil Blas* sketch for you!' cried Madame Louise suddenly. 'Lenke, help me dress.'

'Bravo!' said Sylvester resolutely. 'And you, Béla, shut up now with your Hentzi statue!'

Madame swiftly disappeared in the next room; she returned soon dressed as a Parisian grisette. She had only pinned up her skirts, threw a small shawl around her shoulders and was carrying a hat-box.

But before the performance could have started, the grey-haired maid entered. She looked startled.

101

'Old Szentpéteri has died again,' she said with sincere sympathy and handed her mistress a letter.

Sylvester, author of the *Gil Blas* sketch who had already for some time taken up the position which authors liked to occupy when their work was being performed, grumbled angrily:

'The old poet dies at the worst possible time. He always sends me his obituary notice when I haven't got a penny.'

Madame Louise read the letter with a sad face. (She was more beautiful in sadness than in gaiety.)

'They're collecting for wreaths, for the coffin... I've seen the old man laid out three times already. I tickled his nose. He didn't move. How could he have moved? There were six small children in the house. Send in the messenger, Julis!'

She went to the cupboard and took out some money.

A janitor, smelling of wine, came into the room.

'Oh, so it's you old Krecsák?' Madame Louise said jovially. 'Here are ten forints—but don't spend them on drink on the way back. My best regards to the old poet.'

'Are we going to start?' Sylvester demanded impatiently.

Madame Louise began to walk up and down in the room, in true grisette fashion, swaying her hips as if she walked the streets of Paris. She was waiting for an omnibus. The vehicle was almost at the stop...

'Notre-Dame?' asked the little grisette.

Suddenly the sounds of a violin could be heard from some distant room in the house. Someone seemed to be tuning it.

'It's Gyokó!' said Ivan Ilich at the bottom of the table. He was squinting with tipsiness. 'You forgot to give him dinner!'

'Be quiet!' cried Madame Louise and, blushing crimson, hurried from the room.

Sylvester sighed.

'She can never finish the sketch, poor woman... They won't give her any peace...'

Mr Rezeda filled Ivan Ilich's glass.

'Who's Gyokó?' he asked slyly.

Louise's court chamberlain put his hand over his lips but when he had emptied the glass, he began practically to brag.

'It's nobody's business at all! Our Lady of Fury is a rich and independent woman who can do as she pleases. She has stocks and shares, she has an annuity from the Count. Why shouldn't she keep a Gyokó for herself? Gyokó is the rebel in hiding who must stay in his room whenever there are guests in the house.'

Miss Horváth smiled sadly as she whispered into Mr Rezeda's ear:

'I think we might as well have stayed home. For *this* company it was hardly worth-while putting on my blue velvet gown. I sit here like a knight's lady, bent on hawking, from the court of Marguerite of Navarre. And I wait in vain for Alvinczi.'

'He's standing right behind you—like Satan,' replied Mr Rezeda softly, with a grimace of irony.

Alvinczi stood in the doorway of the adjoining room, wearing his winter overcoat, hat in hand, a bored and wry expression on his face. His skin looked perhaps even more yellow than usual and every hair in his beard seemed to bristle separately. He could have removed himself as a scarecrow to the Asian wastes where the north wind is known by the name of Jal. He looked as if he were cold or had just made a long journey in stormy weather while the icy rain whipped from the back and sides the woven mats of the carriage... The collar of his overcoat was turned up, covering his ears, as if hiding the cardinal's habit in which he used to roam downtown in the evening like an old prince of the Church. He gave an indifferent bow, taking great care that the mossy, cobweb-covered wine bottle should not slip from under his arm. He was strangely embarrassed as if he had found himself unexpectedly faced with company in the house where at other times he was received like a king in incognito.

103

Mr Sylvester almost hid under the table in his fright. But little Bonifácz lifted his glass and cried out in his gay, childish voice:

'Welcome, Your Excellency! Long live the Prince of Asia! Please to take a place at our festive board!'

The short little Nihilist grabbed the arm of the yellow-skinned Khan and led him to the table. Because of his hat and the bottle of wine, Alvinczi couldn't very well parry the attack. He sat down about two paces from the table and as there was only one lady present (Madame and Lenke had left the room), he turned at once to Miss Horváth.

'I'm sorry to have disturbed this gay company... Please, go on, enjoy yourself.'

He bowed modestly, almost with reverence, to Clara—as if he were addressing a Princess Esterházy. His voice was so soft and formal like a saintly knight's and his glance was truly pious. (Being a bachelor, he always saw something strange in women and respected them sincerely like the men who had greatly loved their mothers.)

In the meantime Sylvester had recovered and came immediately to the Prince's aid. He would have liked to free him of his hat most of all but Alvinczi only responded with a cold look, as if Sylvester were to blame that he had become mixed up with this unexpected company.

Madame Louise rushed into the room, quite breathless. One could hear her using very harsh words to reprove the clumsy chambermaid.

'Sire,' she said, 'forgive me. Truly, if I had known...'

But by now Alvinczi's smile was jovial. He cast a superior look at Louise.

'I intruded without being properly presented. Please, Madame, assist me!'

'Mr Monte-Cristo, Miss Németh, Mr Tulipán... Really, my gossip, where were your wits?' Madame Louise was speaking very fast. 'And the Nihilist gentleman, but Your

Excellency already knows him. He sent from the Asian wastes the grass called Hun's Heart for Your Excellency's racing horses. It was on this grass that the horses of the Magyars setting out to win our country were raised and the fodder they brought from home lasted in their saddle-bags as far as the mountains of Ung...' the lady continued with true oratorical flourish; being a good actress she knew how certain words should be pronounced.

But the Count of Monte-Cristo only nodded wearily and cast a fleeting glance at Miss Horváth's blushing face. (It seemed as if the young lady were showing enthusiasm about the Hun's Heart.)

'As I see, your convivial company is after dinner,' Alvinczi said very earnestly at long last and took the cobwebby bottle from under his arm. 'I shall provide the wine. It is a very good wine, from the cellar of an old French abbey. I think it was grown on the hills of Avignon where once upon the time the wine of the Popes, the Châteauneuf du Pape, was growing... Here, the signature of the abbot himself provides proof of the genuine vintage. And the seal is unbroken. Drink it to the health of beautiful women.'

At this he rose, bowed quietly and walked with soft, lazy steps from the room. Madame Louise accompanied him to the ante-room. A delicate smell of Havana cigars remained in the room. Miss Horváth spent a long time staring silently at the sanctified blood of the Avignon hills in the crystal glass... Mr Rezeda giggled softly.

'My God,' Madame said later to Sylvester, 'I'm tired of shooting myself for the sake of every lover of mine. A small bullet has already swished past my heart and Death, drawing its pointed cap down to his nose like some Venetian mask, sat for weeks in his ample cloak at my bedside. Because I dared to love. And I was abandoned.'

With a light, natural gesture she opened the silk dress on her bosom. It was true: the lead ball had left its souvenir in

105

her white flesh, in the shape of a small indentation. Though the miniature hole, hidden by the plump sphere, was no horrifying sight. Death would be a most pleasant, noble cavalier if he worked always with gloved hands like the notable surgeon, Dr Paulikovics, who picks bullets out of the bodies of men—men who shoot at each other or at themselves for the sake of women.

'It was a fine shot,' said Mr Rezeda expertly as if pistol bullets were his personal friends.

A stealthy tear appeared in Madame's brown eyes—as if she were moved by some fine, sentimental song.

'Ten years ago. It was a winter evening. I was alone at home. And suddenly my heart began to ache very badly for Elemér. I think it was Elemér I loved the most, the truest in my life—though for two years while Elemér studied in Paris at the Sorbonne, we only exchanged long, sentimental letters. Every day. No wonder that I took the little gun from my bedside chest, stretched myself on the bed, pressed it to my heart... I felt nothing—I only became very happy all of a sudden. I didn't hear the explosion, nor did I smell the smoke of gunpowder. It was as if a sudden sleep had fallen upon me and I was looking through some window, seeing in a single picture Hatvani Street, Hat Street, Sebastian Square, the whole Inner Town. And I also caught a glimpse of the clownish Sándor Grosz, though I only danced one or two valses with him in all my life—I saw him suddenly jumping to his feet in the gambling den of the Korona café which was called The Nest. He jumped up: "Children, Louise has shot herself!" he cried. And the news passed from one café, from one street to another: "Louise Péczely has shot herself!" The news flew down the twisting, narrow streets on the wings of the wind, the room filled with doctors, good friends, kind acquaintances, only *he* wasn't here, he was far away, in Paris... And I smiled happily at the throng around my bed. Behold, this was the true last act of the Lady of the Camellias and not the one Dumas fils wrote… My servants cried through the night around me. I always kept servants for a long time. My own nurse, her daughter and her granddaughter lived in my house. My maid Milka was with me twenty years; I brought the janitor from my former home, the apartment house where I was a tenant. They kept on wailing and crying and I couldn't speak to them because blood was bubbling from my mouth. But my old nurse understood my look. She put Elemér's photograph into my right hand—while on my left she placed that old skull which had once rolled in front of my horse's hooves one night when I rode past a small village graveyard on the highway… Thus I lay all night. In the morning, it was scarcely light, they brought me the papers: the Lady of the White Camellias, the famous Louise Péczely, had committed suicide… And a great writer wrote a piece about me in the *Magyar Hírlap*…'

Ivan Ilich who stayed until now in the dining-room to keep the bottles of wine company, called stammering through the open door:

'You left me out of the story completely! Who wrote the article in the little illustrated paper about the reason why you shot yourself? Who was the only one in town who knew the truth?'

'Be quiet, you old wineskin! You wrote about me that I shot myself for purely financial reasons, because I had lost all I possessed on the stock exchange… And yet—I was in love…'

Mr Sylvester kept shaking his head, deeply moved. Romantic Madame Louise was the only person whom nobody could accuse of trying suicide because of financial troubles. She was much too noble a creature for that!

Miss Horváth's eyes shone like two stars. My God, maybe she'd also attempt suicide once in her life…

Lenke Bártfai was sobbing softly, not unmixed with giggles, in the background—but no tears resulted.

'Madame, you are a magnificent woman,' she kept on repeating. 'I adore you, Madame...'

Madame Louise smiled limply, placing two fingers against her lips as if she were thinking about long-past matters and would seek to find a mistake in the story.

'The gun I had bought in England. In a medical book I looked up the exact location of the heart, my hand didn't tremble; still, I survived. Yet if I'd died then, how much suffering I'd have escaped! I wouldn't have been disappointed in anybody any more. The Devil could have taken Ivan Ilich... I wonder where he would grumble now over his dinner?'

'And for whom would the musician play his violin?' Ivan Ilich called from the next room in his sneering voice.

Madame Louise suddenly became seriously angry:

'You wretch! You know best of all that I'm bringing up the son of a dead girl-friend of mine, he has a small back room in my house and I pay for his musical training at the Academy. The boy is sometimes nervous, because he isn't allowed to come in when I have guests... Tell me, Mr Sylvester, what need has a boy of sixteen to see all kinds of things here that would only confuse him?'

Instead of replying, Mr Sylvester rose as if he were about to chastise Ivan Ilich, who was bellowing with laughter. But Madame Louise held him back:

'Let him be, my dear gossip; around midnight he no longer knows what he's saying. If I ever marry in the end, it will be only to get a man into the house who can deal with Ivan Ilich. I can't, not any more. He'd grown too big for his britches. Every day I expect him to box my ears or beat up my servants! A terrible man.'

Her eyes were bright with genuine tears.

The men—Sylvester, Mr Rezeda and the Nihilist poet—looked angrily at the short, hirsute man who was feasting in the next room. (Ivan Ilich always fed at midnight. Whether he was in a café or at Madame's: at midnight he became hungry.)

He filled a glass to the brim with wine. He adjusted the napkin around his neck and bowed solemnly to the company in the drawing-room:

'Long live our Fury's bridegrooms! All thirty of them!'

Madame Louise couldn't help laughing at the little comic figure.

'Be quiet, you old malefactor!'

Then she added, sadly, confidentially, turning to old Mr Sylvester:

'Ivan Ilich is some use after all. I had at least thirty fiancés in the last ten years. Ivan Ilich spied out all their secrets, he's a brilliant agent—he found out all about them and proved that they wanted to marry me for my money. My God, I don't deserve it after all, when princes and kings kissed my hand, that some village notary should take his bell to me in my old age!'

Miss Horváth, who had made several attempts to leave in the course of the evening, got up now to make a definite move.

'It's getting late!'

Madame Louise stepped close to her as if she wanted to adjust the neck of her dress and whispered into her ear:

'Before I forget... Monte-Cristo asked me who was the miss with the beautiful eyes?'

Then she turned away as if she had said nothing.

Mr Rezeda walked with long strides beside Miss Horváth along the dark streets of the Inner Town. The editor was very bitter because he felt that Clara was dreaming.

'Well, was the party worth the trouble?' he asked ironically. 'Wouldn't it have been better if Sylvia and the two of us had gone to some little inn in Buda to eat fish or some lonely café in Joseph Town to read illustrated magazines? I must say I felt very ill in that house...'

'You don't understand this, Mr Rezeda,' replied Miss Horváth. 'After all, this is the gate of the great world... Madame's palace in my life is like a frontier station. My train leaves behind it boredom, poverty, cares and the dull passage of the days. I think what follows now is nothing but gaiety, light and luxury. The hotel in Cairo, a trip to Bombay, the Grand Opera in Paris and Paquin's dresses... Maybe I'll have jewels, too. And I promise, I shall always wear classic pieces. My God!' said Miss Horváth and continued after a short pause: 'That's just so wonderful about Madame, that she's so simple and unaffected like some village matron. And yet I'm sure she can speak King Milan's language, too. And she could converse with the Archbishop. Lordy, I wonder what she said to the Prince of Wales when she received him in her drawing-room? That's what I'd like to learn from her.'

Mr Rezeda gave a shrill laugh as if someone had been turning a sharp knife in his heart.

'Ah, so you became envious of the Lady of the Camellias, milady? Yet she said nothing for which she could be envied...'

'That's just it! She kept silent about the delights of her life, the days that had the glitter of golden pheasants... Maybe I'd have also come to loathe her if she had mentioned even a single adventure, say, with the British Ambassador!' Miss Horváth replied most energetically and pulled the lion's head of the bell to summon the janitor of the old house in Bombardier Street.

V

THE CRIMSON COACH APPEARS

Miss Horváth, in a melancholy mood, was darning some old underwear—she always did this when she felt sad—as Mr Rezeda appeared in the actresses' little apartment and presented both Clara and Sylvia with bunches of violets with a contemptuous gesture as if he had found them in the street.

'What's the news?' he asked and painfully bit his lip when he noticed the well-worn undergarments. (He knew that this was the sign of trouble in the house.)

Sylvia put her hand on his shoulder.

'We were in the theatre yesterday. We saw the puppets. The Eyetee made his marionettes jump gaily and in the background of the stage the toy-size houses had beautifully illuminated windows. As if snowy fur had framed them... It was a very amusing evening,' said Sylvia in an earnest and well-considered tone as Mr Rezeda had still not put her feet in *The Lantern*.

For a while Clara plied the needle silently as if her thoughts were very far away. (On the whole only the Good Lord could tell what women were thinking about while sewing. When they darn children's clothes or their husbands' shirts or when they repair the holes in their grandchildren's stockings, they must always be thinking of different things. Once they have reached fifty, women, using the excuse of darning and sewing, may be doing the same thing as men do when they sit alone at night in the coffee-houses and scribble all kinds of figures on the marble tops of the tables.) Then she lifted her eyes which were now as huge as if she were a cardiac case.

'I would like to drink once again from the wine of the Popes of Avignon, Mr Rezeda!' she said quietly.

The dreamy journalist understood the gentle hint. He began to laugh as if Clara had said something very amusing.

'The old popes are all dead and perhaps there was never any wine grown in Avignon—the lie was invented purely in your honour. As if someone would have betrayed the fact that your ladyship is a great admirer of the high-ranking princes of the Church, of white-habited popes whose faces are gently pink and of cardinals in their red robes...'

'Indeed, the colour of that wine was just like that of the cardinals' robes. And its taste! They must have dissolved old episcopal rings in it... Mr Rezeda, I would like to see again the magnificent Count of Monte-Cristo!'

The journalist held a short cigarette butt in his mouth which was already burning his lips. With a strange grimace he caught the fiery cigarette end in his palm.

'As you wish,' he said, rubbing his scorched lips. 'It would give me the greatest happiness if Mr Alvinczi at last noticed your flattering admiration for him. Being a most refined gentleman, maybe he would deign to give you an hour or so. He is the first and foremost cavalier of Hungary, he always likes to grant the wishes of women; he even bestows gifts upon Princess Esterházy. And in aristocratic quarters he is the only one left who sends flowers to old countesses. He is attentive, kind, obliging to everybody like a medieval prince. I think he supports our friend Lenke Bártfai, too, with a monthly stipend, though it was only one of his late friends, poor Richard W., who had any relations with the no-longer-springlike actress.'

'Wonderful,' said Miss Horváth, most seriously. 'I respect him more and more every day—though I haven't yet exchanged a single word with him. And the other day when he drove in his carriage in Hatvani Street, he didn't even notice me!'

'So you've already spied on him!' cried Mr Rezeda and clapped his hands like a clown. 'Upon my faith, princess, the old proverb is right: a man only has to be a trifle less ugly than the devil. Alvinczi isn't exactly handsome.'

'You don't understand that, Mr Rezeda. I think, Miklós Zrínyi must have been the same...'

'You're an apt pupil of Mrs Urbanovics, ma'am. But that makes no difference now. Get dressed— for, to confess my secret, I've come here with the idea of taking you to a place where you can see your adored Alvinczi again. I'm like a medieval fool. I don't feel well without scourging myself with scorpions. Let's go.'

Sylvia who had been using some orange pips to form different patterns on a plate, spoke now in a resigned voice:

'And I have to stay at home again?'

'Why? You can come with us!' said Clara dryly, half turning away and cast a stealthy glance at Mr Rezeda.

Sylvia was still grouping the orange pips for a while, then she rose from the table.

'I know you're not pleased about it, Clara, but I'll still come with you. I don't want you to commit some folly in the end. Mr Rezeda, turn to the window, we're going to get dressed.'

This took a long time because, unlike their usual custom, the ladies did not assist each other.

'I'll advise you to put on some galoshes,' Mr Rezeda said suddenly. 'It's still thawing out in the fields...'

'But where are we going?' the two girls cried in unison.

'To the place where Edward Alvinczi is to be found now. At Budazár.'

The two women assaulted him from both sides; he defended himself laughingly. (And only one eye winked slyly.)

'You needn't be frightened too much. Budazár is a small hamlet in the hills. That's where Mr Alvinczi has a summer home. Every year he spends a single day there—this day. From morning to evening. The date is always March the third. The weather is quite sunny. I think it will be pleasant, if only for your health's sake, to take a little walk in the Buda hills.'

'It's not my habit to take walks, Mr Rezeda,' Clara murmured with a pout.

Mr Rezeda had such a strange face that sometimes one half was laughing while the other cried. Now he turned his laughing profile to Clara.

'You'll enjoy yourself, milady. You know that all my life I have been intent on making you contented.'

Beyond the bridge they got on a horse-tram.

In those days the long cars, smelling of fresh giant rolls and beer, were still in service in the Buda hills. The driver sounded his horn but rarely and at the stop called Helen the Fairy they always had a long stop. Because of the single track they had to wait for the car coming from the opposite direction; the passengers all crowded into the inn. The conductor tried a few throws at the bowling alley which was being repaired; the driver drank, chalking up his bill to the summer account. There was sunshine and spring serenity everywhere. The trees with their sparse foliage were almost ashen-blue and a small spotted dog ran gaily along the forest road.

'It's spring!' said Sylvia and dug a number of small holes into the soft soil, using the tip of her umbrella.

Miss Horváth watched Mr Rezeda's Janus face with a certain amount of suspicion.

'Is it still far to the castle of Count Monte-Cristo?'

'We'll be there shortly,' replied the mysterious young man.

The horse-tram arrived from the top of the mountain. The long car seemed to be weary as it stopped outside Helen the Fairy.

'How much love, happiness, sorrow, joy these little horses carry every summer,' opined Mr Rezeda, 'when they take the loving couples into the Buda hills! To stretch yourself in the June grass on Sunday afternoons, while the sound of the barrel organ comes from afar and to tell a lie, for the first time, about lifelong passion to a little girl whom one has lured from the paternal home on such an excursion! To drink beer at the Green Hunter and take home all kinds of wild flowers! Those who haven't tried this don't know what it means to live! When I was a student in Pest, I lured all my girl-friends to the Buda hills!'

'That's enough of that!' said Miss Horváth. 'A well-brought up girl would never lie down in the forest!'

Mr Rezeda laughed.

'Of course she would. On summer days and Sunday afternoons many things are possible of which one doesn't even think in winter. Love is only beautiful in the open air. Do you remember Mrs Börcsi, the comic actress? Even in winter with the snow waist-high, she would take walks in the cemetery of Debrecen with the young men of the chorus!'

Beyond the terminus of the horse-tram the small company walked about fifteen minutes—when Mr Rezeda suddenly placed his hand over his lips.

'Let us be quiet, ladies. The French romance begins.'

A stone's throw from the forest path there was an old, small summer cottage; for a stretch the trees hid it, only its mossy tiled roof rose, as pointed and dreamy as in some ancient steel engraving. The roadside ditch was filled with last year's faded leaves, and the rose trees still stood in their brown straw overcoats in the garden. The tall trees rose with melancholy silence around the house as if they were waiting stealthily for evening to escape from the place. The garden was surrounded by a high lattice fence and the summer cottage hid mysteriously, almost abandoned, at the bottom of it. On summer mornings when small bells of dew announced

115

the approach of the day it must have been magnificent to awaken here. But the nights—what ineffable anxiety must have filled them! Wind, rain, storm must be roaming like unearthly mysteries around the forsaken house. Maybe wild beasts emerged from the mountains and lurked around the cottage in the darkness of the night. Secretive men, bent on evil, tested the handles of the doors, the bolts of the windows. Rain walked with ghostly steps upon the roof and the twigs of the trees might well be shaken by the hand of Death when they knocked on the carefully closed shutters. What reassurance one could find on such long nights in a brave and faithful dog and some reliable arms! Though what could they do against the nocturnal mysteries?

But now the sun was still moving beyond the forest and sent a golden strip stealthily between the blue trees into the deserted garden.

Suddenly the swishing of grass, the crackling of small twigs could be heard along the garden path—their hearts almost quaked from these sounds suddenly replacing the silence. Perhaps something extraordinary was about to take place. A murder, wild beasts or mysterious sylvan spirits... Miss Horváth pressed her hand to her heart...

Along the garden path, in the light, the figure of a man, tail-coated, top-hatted, white-tied, emerged suddenly. His face in the daylight was as pale as parchment—a very old parchment guarded by a lame librarian in some ancient collection. His black beard and his weary, almost sad gaze seemed to wonder dreamily among the bushes of the garden.

On his right, dressed in white bridal finery, orange blossoms upon her golden hair, with a long white veil and holding a small prayer book in her long-gloved hands, a slim female figure walked along.

Wordlessly they walked side by side on the garden path, between the violet-coloured bushes and the shivery rose trees as if they were corpses freshly risen from the ancient

116

crypt under the little mansion, to take their wonted afternoon walk.

The white bridal veil soon disappeared at the turn of the path.

Mr Rezeda gently took the arm of Miss Horváth who was trembling violently.

He said nothing, he just forced her to leave the summer cottage's environs.

Sylvia followed her friend though now and then she glanced back toward the mysterious habitation.

For a good while they walked in silence.

'My God—what was that?' asked Miss Horváth, wiping her forehead.

Mr Rezeda did not answer. Sylvia stabbed the ground absent-mindedly with her parasol.

At Helen the Fairy's they took a table near the window. Mr Rezeda ordered mulled wine, for the afternoon was already growing chilly and the ladies had begun to feel the penetrating cold during the forest walk.

While they sipped the wine, they suddenly heard the loud cracking of a whip in front of Helen the Fairy.

Four long-tailed bays pulled a huge, crimson-painted carriage which resembled in many ways the stage-coaches once used for travel in Hungary. The curtains of the coach-window were half-lowered and the old coachman, wearing an old-fashioned hat, flicked his horses with his whip as he passed the inn. The huge wheels carried the crimson coach away and it disappeared in the spring evening.

'Alvinczi!' said Clara, almost fearful.

Mr Rezeda smiled ironically.

'Ah, so you didn't recognize him in a tail-coat? Perhaps you didn't see Mademoiselle Montmorency either, under her veil?'

'Yes, that was she. The dancer of the Grand Opera,' Sylvia said now, seriously, and stirred her wine. 'As the young lady

117

essayed in vain drama and singing, now she has devoted herself to dancing. Maybe she will have better luck with it.'

'But my God, what does this strange promenade here in the forest mean? In a tail-coat, in a bridal gown? Are our acquaintances lunatics?' cried Miss Horváth.

'It's all very simple. During the summer the old Montmorencys—that is Papa Stümmer and Mama Stümmer—live in the villa which Alvinczi bought them as a gift. In the spring, that is in March, Alvinczi celebrates the anniversary of his engagement to the young lady. She can be very happy even with this celebration. There can be hardly any question of a marriage,' replied Mr Rezeda and wished he could produce a most superior smile.

Miss Horváth stared for a long time through the window of Helen the Fairy towards the bluish mountain highway as if she expected the crimson coach to return—for her.

'Let's go,' Mr Rezeda said sulkily. 'The festivities are over.'

Miss Horváth started quietly to button her gloves.

'Lordy, if someone would make me walk in bridal finery on the paths of an old garden… The walls of the castle must be decorated with the portraits of ancestors. Does Mademoiselle de Montmorency stop in front of the long-dead ancestors and ancestresses in her white dress? Does she kiss the old crucifix that used to belong to her bridegroom's mother? Can she converse with the old pieces of furniture, does she play on the old piano, standing in the corner, the Wedding March from *Lohengrin* on each anniversary of her engagement? Does she pray in front of an old icon which has been the cynosure of the eyes of the long-dead women in the family; does she wind up the old musical clock which used to provide the accompaniment to the lonely drinking bouts of an old gentleman, now passed away?… No, Lottie does not wind the clock. But I wouldn't forget to do it.'

Thus spoke Miss Horváth and left the inn of Helen the Fairy with the sorrowful steps of ancient ladies. And as she took her place in the horse-tram, she glanced with a self-assured, proud smile over Mr Rezeda's shoulder.

'I would have wound the old clock,' she said and smiled sadly.

Mr Rezeda shrugged and replied in a tearful tone:

'Madam, you talk like a hysterical Jewess of Pest who becomes heated with love after the romantic opera performances...'

VI

THE LAST NIHILIST

Béla Bonifácz, journalist and the delegate of Danton and Robespierre for the administration of the Danubian Province, one day encountered the greatest possible difficulty in crossing from Buda to Pest.

In those days he lived in the hills, amidst melting snows and biting March winds. Then the weather not only covers the corpses of little birds that perished in the winter woods, shielding them from the eyes of a young lady—the very image of spring—with her white feet and scent of violets, but tries, with the greatest passion, to create order and cleanliness in the ranks of human beings as well. The long-suffering invalids who had become asthmatic during the winter and whom the nocturnal snowstorms have kept restlessly awake, the decayed lungs, tired-out hearts, cancerous stomachs and blood, sick with the fever of love, start their work at the burgeoning spring breezes with a great effort—as the fungi start to consume the beam lying beside the old mill-dam. The coffins are carried to the cemetery, rooms are aired and the living survey the old coats, torn pants and faded hats left behind in order to sell them to the old clothes man. Out at the distant end of the city sometimes the poor beggar prays to all-powerful Nature to remove the tormented invalid from the way so that he can inherit at last a pair of boots. But the old man, dying of cancer, who has only an abstract interest left in his shapely nurse, is just as little inclined to say farewell to his bed, wet with the sweat of pain, as a young lady-in-waiting who has only recently been lucky enough to attract the attention of His Grace. In the spring Death makes a long promenade in his domain to use human corpses for manuring the meadows and fields for the fine flowers of the approaching summer.

Under the graveyards, deep in the earth, there must be sewers and canals and the pretty eyes of princesses, the breasts of street-walkers, the brains of scholars and the hearts of poets are spread far and wide across the distant meadows and gardens to turn into fine blooms, sunflowers or rose-bushes. Today you still muzzle with your lips the nape of your mistress and your hand reaches, trembling with excitement, towards her warm underclothes; tomorrow these heart-racing treasures live on in the kitchen garden of a suburban farmer in the shape of lamb's lettuce, and the bull-necked Budapest innkeeper serves it in salad according to Brillat-Savarin's directions. You, with a gourmet's appetite, delighting in the excellent meat-dish, eat the salad while your eyes already roam over the living shape of new women, seek under different crisp dresses new, intimate feminine flesh— and only the bitter brandy reminds you of your dead and devoured lady-love.

Though these thoughts could occur to anybody, Béla Bonifácz, Nihilist and newspaperman, still tried to use the excuse of meditating deeply over such matters when he attempted to slip past the toll-gate of the Buda tunnel without payment. He was wrapped in a small brown cloak which even a scarecrow of southern Hungary would have been ashamed to wear.

But the tollkeeper was alert and demanded harshly that Béla Bonifácz should pay the toll.

The poet shrugged and turned back. How foolish people were! If he had money he would not have left the field-guard's hut on János Hill. It was exactly the lack of money that sent him from Buda to Pest in order to visit his friend Sylvester and borrow from him one or two forints or maybe twenty-three *krajcárs* or pennies. (For he had figured out that this was the exact sum he needed to survive the present day.)

The tollkeepers looked as angrily at Béla Bonifácz as their ancestors had once looked upon Michael Kohlhaas, the horse-dealer of Kohl–Haasenbrück upon the Elbe River— thereby provoking devastating wars, many deaths, misfortunes and princely sorrows as one could read all about it in Heinrich von Kleist's book. Tollkeepers have always been severe people and on this occasion acted with similar rashness when they insisted on the grim and inhuman law in connection with Mr Béla Bonifácz. Isn't it strange that someone, a thinker, perhaps not the least talented in the capital, should not be able to walk through a tunnel simply because he forgot to put two coppers in his pocket? The children of the rich roll in their carriages without being stopped under Gellért Hill toward Christina Boulevard; then, around the Town Farm, the attentive coachman slows down the horses, the windows of the carriage are lowered and the soft, fresh spring air caresses the offspring of people trading in cheese and liquor. Old women and obese old gentlemen in whose intestinal canals the terrible cancer moves stealthily, to punish them for their youthful crimes, incest and all those beautifully served luncheons where the French chef had produced the offal of animals, of swallows or the insides of songbirds with a piquant sauce—such people take a deep breath of the air of the Buda hills as soon as they pass through the tunnel with its damp walls. 'Nature! Romance! Love!' cry the girls of Mrs Oesterreicher when they drive on spring afternoons among the strange Buda houses, across the meadow of Martinovics, so that they can offer not only rouge but the pinkness of the spring sun to the poor men, the foreign salesmen and Budapest dandies who look for love in the Magyar Street harem. Surely the sewers under the Inner Town must be the most despised among all the sewers of Pest. The shaggy, tousled village *komondor* may be lifting his back leg towards the men of Pest. The love of the Swabian dog does not outrage the noble laws of Nature.

So Béla Bonifácz was driven away from the toll-gate and the blood became as hot around the Nihilist's heart as the Gulf Stream in the cold oceans. 'I'm right! I'm always right! If I throw the bomb, I'm right!' the waves of his blood were saying and he started to climb Castle Hill with the happiness of martyrs so that, lacking two coppers, he could cross from Buda to Pest without having to pay.

For two days he had not eaten anything…

Béla Bonifácz's journey to Pest did not achieve the slightest success. Mr Sylvester, his friend and patron, had accompanied his prince to the race track. Mr Alvinczi, wearing his old silver-gold necktie and blue hat, drank beer on this spring afternoon while the yearlings, restless and wild stallions and dreamy-eyed, nobly-shaped mares, galloped down the green field. By the sixth glass of beer Mr Sylvester impatiently rebuked the spirits of Lord Derby and Count Elemér Batthyány—for he had not won a penny on this playful spectacle of the racers. In the meantime Béla Bonifácz in his fluttering cloak—the sort of garment poor wandering minstrels might have worn while calling at the towns of northern Hungary, Eperjes, Löcse and the others (not to mention the Polish gentry whose red boots always itched to try some dance-steps when a wandering student walked into their homes straight from the highway, reciting three poems and having nothing else to live on)—as we were saying, Béla Bonifácz zigzagged his hurried way through Pest. It was getting dark and he had met no one who might have offered him at least a glass of wine. He inspected the spot where he would place his dynamite bomb in Váci Street—or should it be picric acid?—and planned to light the sulphur trail at six o'clock in the afternoon. Then he set out for the main railway bridge so that he could cross the Danube without having to pay toll. By the time the houses of the city were left behind, the unhappy little man who had walked ten miles on the chance that poor Sylvester would offer some of his wine to him, was no longer defying with his shaggy beard and long-unbarbered locks the whole of society, his bomb-throwing fever had vanished and his eyes behind his pince-nez were wearily at rest. He thought of Christ as the poor did when they were forsaken by everyone.

The man of Nazareth helped Béla Bonifácz to cross the railway bridge and gave him enough strength to climb János Hill where he spent the winter in an abandoned field-guard's hut without paying rent.

Down in the city night had fallen; only the towers shone. But up on the mountain it was still light.

In front of the field-guard's hut there was a tree-stump and a lady in a black veil sat on it, waiting for Béla Bonifácz.

It was Dideri-Dir, the poetess, the divorced wife of a lawyer from Transylvania; Béla Bonifácz met her during his wanderings in the provinces. He had instructed the lady in poetics, read poems to her, treated her to long and dreamlike stories about hearts, love, verses; two days later when he was again caught by the *wanderlust,* he moved on, but before he did he prescribed poets for the rather morbid matron: the sad Reviczky with his golden cobwebs, Tompa whose voice was like the evening bells, and Ivan Turgenev's *Waves of Spring...*

'But don't forget Punin and Baburin either, dear madam. And I'm sure your psyche will be healed,' Béla had said and fastened the clasp of his cloak at his neck as if a storm raged outside.

'And afterwards?' asked the woman whose hair was greying and whose eyes looked as if she suffered from heart trouble.

124

'I'll write and tell you the rest!'

Thus Béla Bonifácz and Dideri-Dir exchanged a few letters. (In those days poetesses chose pennames of this kind for they considered Violetta or Dawn no longer fashionable. Catholic women put aside the old prayer-books, too, when Baroness Orczy wrote a new one. That's how ladies keep up with the modern times!) Dideri-Dir sent her poems which she had written since the poet's visit. Bonifácz always had money for postage when he had to reply to ladies' letters.

'How did you get here?' asked Béla Bonifácz sternly. 'Didn't I tell you to beware of Pest? This is a most depraved place. Women are seduced here.'

The mountain bushes and trees were asleep now, the great stones and mossy trunks dozed off, too; so there was no laughter in answer to Béla Bonifácz's words.

The woman took hold of the Nihilist's hand.

'I'm not angry because you do not live in the palace on Andrássy Avenue as you said you did when you visited me.'

Béla shrugged.

'I moved to the mountain for reasons of health.'

'It took me three days' wandering before I found you.'

'I wish you'd stayed at home, madam. The city of Pest dyes all the blackest, as the adage goes. There are no poets here. If there are any, they woo the strumpets of the night in the Beliczay café. I hope you do not wish to go to such a place?'

'Oh yes, I do,' replied the cardiac lady. 'I would like to see young Endre Ady as close as possible. Oh, I have learned a great deal since you deserted me. I corresponded with someone, a woman, and she told me everything about the poets who proclaim in their verses the revolution of life, promise great, sacred rebirths in love to their lady readers, while at night they drink beer and patronize the little orphan girls of the Lady Yolanda in the musical café... My God, if I were only younger!'

'Maybe you'd join Yolanda's as an orphan girl?'

'Please, Mr Bonifácz, guide me to those places where the poets spend their nights. I'm burning with the desire to see them at close quarters.'

The Nihilist shook his head.

'Madam, you're knocking on the wrong door! I'm no longer familiar with the young writers and poets. My time is past. Aladár Benedek who has a lion's head is the last lyric poet whom I have the honour to know. His slightly greying beard has still some successes among the ladies of Joseph Town though he is sixty. Or if you command me, I'll introduce you to Imre Gáspár who rests in the afternoons in the bowling alley somewhere in the Joseph Town, too, after he has spent the whole day writing letters to diocesan bishops and Jewish wholesalers, with his glasses shining with a marvellously high intellect. His pen demands all his strength and imagination; the tiny letters pour out with biblical plenitude and more than once original lines of *Manfred* or *Onegin* appear... The old messenger, Stecz, never carries less than ten letters which Gáspár dispatches to various points of the city. By the time dusk comes, enveloping Joseph Town, the old messenger in his red cap returns mysteriously to the bowling alley. Or you may learn to know Gyula Erdélyi with his white hair and red waistcoat, the novelist of long-gone time who was paid twenty gulden by the daily *Pesti Napló* for his novel *Poor Desider* and these days only writes odes to the racing horses of Miklós Szemere because he thinks human beings are no longer worthy of having poems written about them, if you please... Or I can introduce you to László Seffer or Adorján Szeles. These are all excellent and serious men. True Spartan characters; they always have some slow-match ready in their pockets in case there is a need to set the country afire... I can even present you to the editor of the *Restaurant-Keepers Journal* who smells of mineral water and wax candles; he carried the torch at the funeral of Kossuth and he still carries the bit of wax he had saved. Lajos Csete, who begot the famous comic figure of Ádám Pokrócz, the rudest man in the comic pantheon of Hungary, drinks his thousandth wine-and-sodawater in the bar of fat Ligeti; while Béla Jaskula Virág edits the *Municipal Magazine* in Práter Street, gazing with his blue eyes dreamily from his top-floor window at all those whom he suspects to be prospective patrons. These are the half-saintly, half-mad men of long-gone times, sometimes poor sinners who never dare to emerge from the little wineshops of Joseph Town—though they had long done penance for their crimes. Their ideals are sometimes Chatterton, the young English poet who died of starvation, or Reviczky, the Hungarian poet who perished on a hospital bed... At other times their admiration is directed at Robespierre and Danton. They follow the law passed in the great Calvinist Church of Debrecen, the law that dethroned the Hapsburgs in 1849 and proclaimed Hungary a republic... I consider as the best company in the world my friend Béla Pongrátz, the poor little poet, forsaken by God and man, who remained so noble and pure in his holy enthusiasm, in the years of the greatest misery and poverty, like the ancient gold coins found in the depths of ancient castle wells, bearing the image of a young emperor wreathed in laurel leaves... The younger Görgey, the son of the general, in his grim lonely wanderings often finds himself in the place where the poor poets seek refuge, in attics, old cellars, miserable furnished rooms where the principal tenant himself is in arrears with the monthly rent. The younger Görgey is constantly on the move, roaming restlessly from Pest to Buda as once upon a time he used to tramp the English roads leading south from London to the cherry trees and hop-gardens of Kent. He only calms down when now and then he is settled in the quiet asylum of Lipótmező. There he is given every week a day off when he can visit the theatre in the company of the Countess O. B.; usually they choose some classic play which Görgey junior had seen in his youth in Paris or London, and after the performance he dines with the countess. The cunning doctors have plotted this well. In the company of ladies Mr Görgey does not touch alcohol; he tries to prove himself a young, witty and well-educated gentleman. He talks to Countess O. B. about the royal treasures of England, the marvels of the British Museum and of Haydn's music which has so many devotees in the pious English households. He returns well before midnight, accompanying the countess to the quiet distant asylum—for the Countess O. B. is also a patient there... These are my friends, madam. I'll be glad to take you to their circle.'

The poetess Dideri-Dir (like women in general) preferred the moon approaching from the height of spires to the fading stars of the Western horizon.

'You must get new friends, Béla,' she said, rising from the tree-stump outside the field-guard's hut. 'The people of whom you talked must be ice-grey, grim, lonely, cranky, misogynistic old men. I had enough of old men at my husband's side... I long for the friendship of young men with starry eyes whose stars are rising, to whose cart I can hitch my horse. I want to get ahead for I feel I have talent. Among all those whom you mentioned not one has a review to edit or publish...'

'Alas, the magazine *Read It!* has ceased publication,' replied Béla Bonifácz sadly.

The lady with the greying hair gazed devoutly at the firmament over János Hill where the evening stars had already appeared.

'I'd like to fall in love... to be in love once more, for I won't live very long. In love with Endre Ady or Béla Révész, Viktor Cholnoky or Károly Lovik... with some writer who is young, at the start of his career, as George Sand was in love with Alfred Musset... I'd love to be another Marie Bashkirchev. Oh, what perfume rising from royal gardens it could be: to rise with someone upon the ladder of fame! One day it is

poems of Dideri-Dir that are published in the papers; the
next day the song of my handsome lover, my dear Alfred.
And sometimes our names would appear side by side
in the columns of *The Week*. No, my dear Béla Bonifácz,
I didn't leave the snowy mountains of Transylvania to
drink beer with old Imre Gáspár in a Joseph Town bowling
alley...'

'You are a climber, madam!'

'Maybe... I want to sit in a box at the National Theatre
with the writers, dressed in tails, visiting me in the intervals.
Maybe I shall keep a salon, have at-homes and the editors
shall kiss my hand... I do not mind if you visit me sometimes
when I have no other guests...'

After this Dideri-Dir kissed Béla Bonifácz on the forehead
and departed with most dramatic steps from the neighbourhood of the János Hill hut. Bonifácz stared after her a long
time and murmured into his greying beard·

'You'll come back one of these days to me, my poor
daughter!'

A week later two daughters of Dideri-Dir called on
Mr Bonifácz. They were about sixteen or seventeen, neither
beautiful nor ugly. Olga was an enthusiast of literature, Gizi
of art.

'Uncle Béla, our mother has gone crazy. She spends all her
nights in the coffee-houses with long-haired budding poets
and phoney journalists... We are so ashamed. We don't want
to stay in Budapest.'

'Go home to your father.'

'Our father lives with a servant-girl. We decided to leave
Hungary. We know how to dance. Olga sings French songs,
accompanying herself on the harp. We are pretty and young.
We arranged everything with an agent yesterday. We're going
to Russia as artistes. We'd like you to come with us. As our
father or our dear old friend...'

'My poor little ones,' exclaimed Béla Bonifácz in distress.

'You'll perish, burn to cinders, die. You'll become *vengerkas* and end in a hospital, rotting away...'

'Come with us and don't let us perish!' replied the daughters of Dideri-Dir. 'You've nothing to keep you here. You're just guarding this field-guard's hut...'

Béla Bonifácz began to ponder.

'I have *something* to do here... I have to write a weekly article for the *Restaurant-Keepers Journal*. Literature is a terrible poison. If men and women of the middle class taste it, they become syphilitic. Writers are all impostors. They proclaim their toil a royal profession, the most glorious of all. Yet strictly speaking no one needs literature. People would be far happier without it. They would go on getting born and dying. Life, great and glorious, has nothing in common with small, serried rows of letters. Writers, like some secret conspiracy, have been poisoning the souls of people for centuries —so that they could make a living themselves. Their tales and songs are only fit to cause uneasiness and confusion in the human souls. And if the sweet poison of literature has invaded a family, unhappiness is sure to follow. The wives of writers are all unhappy women. The sixteen-year-old daughter of my friend Sylvester hanged herself. And you are deserted by your mother because she listens to poems at night in the cafés...'

'Are you coming with us?' asked the girl.

'I am, my poor little ones. I won't let you be sacrificed to the madness called literature. The lunacy labelled literature can dwell in green alcohol, or in the unnatural longing of the nerves or in the flaming fire of the blood. We'll leave this country where a half-crazy lawyer's wife is let loose—with the excuse of literature...'

Gizi who was the more practical of the two, inspected Mr Bonifácz's apparel.

'First of all let's go to the tailor, Uncle Béla,' she said and took the shaggy old man's arm.

...For two years Béla Bonifácz travelled over Russia with the daughters of Dideri-Dir. The girls earned beautiful clothes and quite a bit of money dancing from Moscow and St Petersburg, all along the great Trans-Siberian Railway where the Cossack officers of the garrisons received the first music-hall company of Warsaw almost ecstatically.

Then, at a railway station, in distant Asia, they were robbed of everything—their money, their trunks, their jewels. Many thousand versts from the Hungarian frontier, in a Siberian station-building half hidden under snow, between Mongolian horse-thieves and half-savage Muscovite officers, in a place where there was only one train a week, Dideri-Dir's dancing daughters and Béla Bonifácz, the poet, were left without a penny, without clothes and without food...

VII

VIENNESE WOMEN IN BUDAPEST

It was May then in Pest.

The Vienna express which enters the station of Pest along the best-built track with its low top-hatted engine, produces such a self-important panting sound as if it were desirous of imitating at least its distinguished distant relative, the St Petersburg–Nice express, pretending that the long Pullman cars are about to stop and from their silk-lined, gold-decorated, electrically lit compartments Russian grand dukes, Polish princes and millionaire Czech manufacturers will soon emerge. In May the Vienna express arrived in Budapest fully laden, bringing the scum of the Vienna cafés, with all their dubious characters — especially the women of easy virtue. It was the racing season in Pest.

From the luxurious carriages the regular types of the Police Gazette alighted. Sporting gentlemen dressed with striking elegance who in the winter months seek their living in the stalls of the Ronacher Music Hall, find refuge at dawn in some gambling café and are perhaps lodging with some old flower-seller; money-lenders and pimps with determined expressions, reddish faces and peculiar moustaches, hairdos and neckties cultivated by the Viennese mashers, with white spats and immense binoculars in large yellow cases. The slip-on patent leather shoes or the orange-coloured, high-heeled lace-up boots step with full self-assurance on the Pest pavements.

Rings flash on the little fingers and the Lerchenfeld dialect is decorated with thieves' slang. These characters acquired sagacity and intellectual superiority in the Vienna cafés and they look down with impudent sneers Kerepesi Road.

The women are even more peculiar: they are addicted to white blouses and simple skirts. The round Girardi hats or the so-called Rembrandt hats with their large feathers fit their heads extremely well. Their brown hair which has blond tints is combed tight and their colour is reddish as if they had just sprinkled cold water on their faces. They have blue eyes and pink lips. Their teeth are white and they grow plump early. They are well-tempered and sure of themselves. The sporting ladies receive the courtship of any well-dressed man without ceremony, their lover may be a billiard scorer in the Café Hapsburg and they come to Pest only to win.

While the Blue Cat and the Flora Rooms were the most distinguished night-clubs in Budapest (later Károly Somossy built one of the most beautiful music-halls of the world) it was the Viennese type of women that represented true artistes. The plump ladies whose bosom was milky white and whose pink-skinned faces resembled that of piglets, drank beer or French champagne and plundered men heartlessly and coldly. While they made love, they thought of Max, the cabdriver. Then, suddenly they left Budapest. In the *cafés chantants* of Király Street (where Edward VII while Prince of Wales learned to dance the *csárdás*) one could still find a few survivors, mature but still smartly dressed—those who had not succeeded in making their fortunes in Budapest. At night Cecilia Carola appeared at the Beliczay café which counts and barons visited in full evening dress; while old Mr Blau played billiards in shirtsleeves with young Lazarovics, the millionaire. Lazarovics was followed day and night, every step of the way, by Hartman and Lefkovics, his faithful money-lenders, who drank the young nabob's champagne as if they were true alcoholics. The night of Pest echoed the valse of Kmoch and

133

Reiner's *Battalion of Women* to which eighty beautiful young ladies in tights danced on the stage of the music-hall. Cecilia Carola (among whose admirers there were old Jewish stock-brokers and young counts alike) commanded this splendid battalion in the uniform of a captain of the Hussars. A special train took the troupe to Nagyvárad in order to appear at the Black Eagle and the houses of Várad had perhaps already been decorated with flags when the telegram arrived from Turin: Kossuth, the great champion of Hungarian liberty, had died... Cecilia, whose long, thick hair was so rich that it covered her from head to heel, wasn't given the chance to drive the people of Várad absolutely frantic, the performance was cancelled. Mesdames Küry and Fedák might have been great prima donnas, but they never aroused the immense enthusiasm of theatre-goers which little Cecilia (who still looked rather naive) stirred into flame in Pest. Ask the old gentlemen, the loan-sharks who have emigrated to America, broken-down dandies and Ferenc Rajna, the critic, who was Cecilia Carola—when she unfurled the national flag in the *Battalion of Women!* Pest was still a half-German city and yet the applause was never-ending, continuing outside the music-hall when the performance had long ended, even the cab-drivers cheered and the music echoed down the boulevards... What was finer? The *Battalion of Women* or the current hit *Falling Leaves?* Oh, the old conductors were extremely mod-est. Whoever writes the history of Budapest, ought to devote a good deal of space to the figures of Károly Somossy, the Hungarian C. B. Cochran, and Cecilia Carola. These two taught the town how to paint itself red. I am sure that French champagne is still drunk in Budapest—for champagne will always be sold as long as there are rich gourmets and ladies of easy virtue in the world. But those were the days! It was May, the racing season; Carola put her legs covered in black silk stockings upon the marble table of the Beliczay café and Diogenes Blau drank champagne, with the utter

134

devotion of a romantic knight, from the divine lady's patent leather shoe. Elemér Batthyány and Miklós Szemere were still young men; grey-bearded Munczy played French songs and Mr Somossy joined in the jollifications of his guests. Lantos, witty and inventive, opened in Pest the first truly elegant restaurant where the kitchen fire was kept burning all night and all day and where entertainment was cheap—only to go bust at once though he used Brillat-Savarin's recipe in preparing his chicken-broth. Astute restaurateurs set up pubs which only opened after midnight; in the 'Graveyard' somewhat aged gilded youths caroused at ten o'clock in the morning, applauding the songs an artiste named Strasser performed in the manner of a young horseherd and the members of Krauser's circle had a barrel of beer placed on the table. It was the fashion to drive in May at noon to a garden restaurant in the City Park, using Móni's fast trotting team—while driver, horses and harness alike, dreamed of Vienna. It was fashionable to rout the pianist out of his bed; the red-headed Friedmann wore a star-studded belt and, together with Szekula, declared Budapest to be a world metropolis. Music-halls and variety theatres were built at the pace of San Francisco; Negro dancers and other international artistes were brought to the city in hordes. 'The Ancient Castle of Buda!' people murmured in awe while all the pomp and circumstance of East and West appeared in their imagination at the name of Budapest's Luna Park. The *demi-monde* that had been hidden until now, women who loved in secret suddenly spread like spring flowers and squeezed out the old-fashioned, wide-eyed courtesans. (Captain Kapy, the admiring friend, patron and expert consumer of these ladies, who was a kinsman of the King of England, filled many a notebook with the names and addresses of these beauties, writing with a gold pencil in a diary bound in finest morocco; in his library one would certainly find the address of sweet Mitzi Schwarz of twenty years ago.) Deaf Papa Fritz cooked wonderful broad bean

135

soup in Vasvári Pál Street and in his drive cabdrivers, club-
men and street-walkers danced together in the morning
around the piano of consumptive Master Breitner. Breitner
had an eerie talent to stud the lyrics of his songs with obscene
and frivolous words, while the black cavern of his half-open
mouth gaped like the darkness of a re-opened old grave and
during the feverish merry-making he often spat blood—while
his sick wife and sick child waited for him at home. In this
age of thoroughbred wastrels and passionate drinkers, the
age of gentlemen seeking life in intoxication and of Viennese
girls who had almost sunk to the level of animals, when Fifi
replaced her knocked-out eye-tooth with a piece of a wax
candle, when crazy Grete cut her clothes to ribbons in a fit,
while Mitzi wanted to commit suicide every morning—in this
age Messrs Roeder and Pommery in distant France must
have been fully aware that it was May and the racing season
in Pest. Flora Freystaedtler, the red-headed millionairess,
made her actor and cabdriver lovers bathe in the liquid gold
of the hills of Champagne before she accepted their wooing.
In the heroic age of Budapest orgies when in a single night
whole fortunes were wasted on champagne, flowers and
music, the drunken voices of Viennese women sounded like
screaming sirens.

The Halls!

What a warm, musical, almost intoxicating sound these
words had in our salad days! We saw dancers and princesses,
the white shirt-front of the gentlemen was dazzling, the
auditorium, bathed in pink electric light, was filled with the
scent of flowers, the Grand Duke Vladimir sat in his regular
box; a French *soubrette* in short skirts trilled on the stage;
the bald-headed waiters whose faces were like those of old
roués, carried the wine of the French hills in the silver coolers
with the solemnity of funeral directors and the swinging-
singing music-hall tunes rose enchantingly from the orchestra
pit. The great world, Paris, Nice, came to visit us for an

evening. Then Cecilia left and they all went away. One or the other had a tobacconist's or a hat shop on the Vienna Ring; it was only in May that their memories took them back to Pest, to the races that were called festivals in the old days.

That was the time the newspapers reported that high society had arrived in Budapest.

*

Miss Horváth had never been to the races. As a little girl she watched on the boulevard the huge hunting-carriage of Count Géza Andrássy, the red-wheeled, light fiacre of Mr Wahrmann, the banker, which he had imported from Vienna, while Mr Blaskovics drove a four-in-hand. For ten or fifteen minutes all the aristocracy of Hungary rushed past the gaping crowds. Neszmélyi, the lame journalist, with his huge sideburns in his capacity as chief stage-manager of life, bent forward eagerly and greeted all his acquaintances by raising his crutch. The cabbies drove their short-tailed horses with as much enjoyment as if everyone had won a packet at the races. The veils of the ladies waved freshly and the men pulled up their checkered trousers over their knees. The lovely, glittering great world!

Mrs Urbanovics provided new succour for the ladies of Bombardier Street and luckless Rezeda's eloquence was all in vain. The actresses, having acquired new spring outfits (Miss Horváth bespoke a tailored suit with checks, the jacket swallow-tailed, while Sylvia chose a girlish creation of blue-and-white spotted pongee), ordered one afternoon a cab to take them to the races.

'My ladies, only cashiers from low dives and the butterflies of the *demi-monde* go to the races on weekdays,' declared Mr Rezeda.

But the actresses laughed and waved to him.

'If you're ashamed to come with us, don't,' said Clara sharply.

The sad young man resigned himself to his fate.

"pon my honour,' he grumbled, 'I already feel like a pimp. Taking my lady-friends to the market...'

The ladies were naturally most curious about the countesses. Mr Rezeda pointed out some aristocratic celebrities whom he knew by sight. The young countesses, sitting in their armchairs, looked like pastel pictures. Their delicate, amazingly fine skin, their dresses, gloves, shoes made them look like hot-house flowers as they sat in the enclosure marked off by a red cord. Where did countesses get their hats whose style and shape differ so much from the hats of middle-class women? Do glove-makers devise special patterns for a Countess Andrássy? And are the ladies, growing up in the atmosphere of carefully guarded palaces, in the midst of works of art, paintings, Asian carpets and carefree years, truly different from the other women of creation? Where did they get the pink lace of their lingerie and the ribbons on their shoes, the fresh wave in their hair and the brightness of their eyes—so that not even the cleverest, richest Jewess can imitate these?

The suppleness of their bodies, even with the older ladies, seems to be the result of a refined admixture of blood that has taken centuries to achieve. Blue blood! the old novelists used to say. And the middle-class dreamer sighs—because he feels he will never be able to know these blue-blooded ladies intimately.

As they turned (for the young ladies kept constantly on the move so that they shouldn't miss anything) Alvinczi's black-bearded, white-hatted head appeared in the field. He approached at a leisurely, almost bored gait and swung his field glasses impassively on his arm.

'Let's go!' said Mr Rezeda nervously.

But Miss Horváth stopped, she looked into Alvinczi's eyes

with a smile that only highly expert courtesans or completely innocent girls could produce in order to cover up their excitement.

Alvinczi gave the lady a confused look—as if he were searching among his memories.

'Good day, Alvinczi!' said Miss Horváth with a sly wink. 'You don't remember me, do you? But I haven't forgotten you!'

(Mr Rezeda felt that the earth was about to swallow him in his shame.)

The Tartar khan doffed his hat with his white-gloved hand.

'Delighted to meet you...' he said without a trace of conviction and cast a fleeting, questioning look at Rezeda.

Mr Rezeda shrugged and murmured nonchalantly between his teeth:

'At Madame Louise's... the party...'

Alvinczi smiled wrily He produced his handkerchief and gave a small, bitter, dyspeptic cough.

'Oh yes... Let me give you a good tip...' he continued quickly, in a tone of utmost cordiality. 'I'm sure the ladies want to win—though if you listen to me, you won't bet. No one can win on the races. But in order to have some share in the amusement of the game, let me offer you a few tickets... If you permit me... *Au revoir*. I must hurry—they're about to start...'

He quickly lifted his hat, touched Miss Horváth's hand lightly and disappeared down the stairs leading to the tote. The crowd yielded to him everywhere respectfully. He was the biggest punter. In the City of Racing Alvinczi was king.

Mr Rezeda's face was dark red as he took Miss Horváth's arm.

'Dear soul,' he began, his voice heavy with suppressed passion, 'you behave like some village miss. Do you think you're in Kisvárda where the *ingénue* of the company is

139

known to every cobbler's apprentice? We are in Pest, dear soul, where it is not the custom to accost men.'

'Alvinczi was certainly very rude,' replied Clara, growing serious. 'I was stupid, I admit it. In my thoughts I was so much occupied with this strange man that I thought it quite natural he would recognize me at once when we met... Forgive me, Mr Rezeda.'

But Mr Rezeda did not forgive her.

'Look around,' he continued severely. 'Can you see all those women in their striking hats, their strange clothes, with their determined faces? These are all here in order to get acquainted with Alvinczi or some men whose wallet is equally well-stuffed. But even they wouldn't dare to accost anybody!'

'What an ass I was!' murmured Clara with tearful bitterness.

There was a sharp ringing.

An old gentleman, wearing a pert hat, a red waistcoat and sporting a white beard, tried to make his way towards the trio. He wore a brown cloak and he waved his ramshackle walking-stick.

'My dear little girl!'

It was Mr Sylvester, Alvinczi's secretary.

He pressed a few brown stiff cardboard tickets into Miss Horváth's hand, selecting them from a large number.

'The Prince is sending you these,' he said, out of breath in his hurry.

'How are you, Uncle Sylvester?' asked Clara, relenting.

'I'm in a hurry. I'm in a hurry. I must give some tickets to Countess X, old Baroness B. and the widow Ábrándi. And the race is already under way...'

'Why did you accept them?' asked Mr Rezeda darkly.

'Ten forints. Three times ten forints. On Number Six. Look it up quickly, Mr Rezeda, which is Number Six?'

'It's Ignatius, Alvinczi's horse.'

Miss Horváth stared excitedly at the pieces of cardboard. Suddenly wild shouting filled the course. It seemed that thousands of people had gone mad all at once. They jumped on chairs and benches. They shouted the names of horses. Eyes bulged. Women screamed hysterically.

'You won't see anything of the race from here,' said Mr Rezeda. 'Turn around, ladies. Mr Alvinczi's sitting on the grandstand. We can judge by his face whether Ignatius is likely to win or not...'

Mr Alvinczi was sitting in the place reserved for the members of the Jockey Club and he certainly held one of the best binoculars in the world as he watched the race.

He leant back rigidly in his seat as he stared tensely.

Suddenly he bent forward as if this energetic move would contribute to the result of the contest.

The binoculars seemed to tighten in his hand as he followed the course of the thoroughbreds during the last few yards to the finish.

Then he dropped them.

A happy, childishly blissful, triumphant smile appeared on the dark, sad face—as if Santa Claus had rung his bell over the racecourse... His neighbours offered their hands in congratulation.

'Ignatius!' roared a thousand throats.

'We've won!' cried Miss Horváth, carried away, her eyes brimming with tears. 'Ignatius! Dear Ignatius!'

'The devil!' grunted Mr Rezeda.

Miss Horváth rushed to the white railing when the winner was led past. She clapped happily with her white-gloved hands at the small bay.

'Ignatius!' she said softly, amorously.

...However much Miss Horváth would have liked to meet Mr Alvinczi again that afternoon, she failed to do so.

'Why did Alvinczi avoid me?' asked Miss Horváth when, tired and dusty, they started for home.

Mr Rezeda shook his head morosely:

'Miss, you'd better learn about this: someone pouring out gratitude is the most uncomfortable company. One doesn't know what to do about it. In any case, Alvinczi has an old superstition—whenever he backs some horse with a substantial sum, he arranges for the distribution of betting tickets among his poor acquaintances and friends. And for some people he bets at the same time on other horses than the ones he backs himself. You ought to be glad to be counted among his lucky acquaintances...'

'He's a wonderful man!'

'The more wonderful, because while he helped you to make two hundred forints—so that you should pray for his win, like the old aristocratic ladies whom he helps and who go on the mornings of the race to the Franciscan Church to pray for his good luck—he himself, as a well-informed friend of mine told me, collected almost a hundred thousand forints with the triumph of Ignatius. This is the source of Alvinczi's wealth which is believed to be inexhaustible. That's why he's called Count Monte-Cristo.'

Clara clapped her hands.

'I adore him,' she said.

VIII

THE DREAMS AND THE CARDS

It was spring and every afternoon Mr Rezeda read poems and novels to the ladies of Bombardier Street.

It was an old method the young editor used in the wooing of women, calling poets to his aid. He owed his loves to poetry (the bareback rider who graced Henry's company; the waitress in the old provincial pastry-shop where the windows were covered with softly-swinging purple curtains and the liqueur bottles bore vignettes with flower patterns; then the merchant's widow who suffered from heart trouble and whose large eyes sometimes mirrored, in a wonderful fashion, the longing for oblivion)—he won them mostly with the poems of Byron or Pushkin. Like a youth of the early Victorian, *Biedermeier* age, he carried a delicately-bound volume of poetry in his pocket; and whenever he caught the ladies alone, he read the appropriate strophes wildly and quickly or softly and dreamily, bending close to their ears. Sometimes they permitted him to kiss their hands; at other times they caressed lightly his forehead, called him dear Rezeda, and pressed a flower between the pages of the book of poems; then they dismissed the journalist who walked along, his head bowed and invoking Heinrich von Kleist who had died a suicide. Thus Mr Rezeda lived for his loves—and did not even get as far as the bedroom of the merchant's widow. And yet she had thick blond hair, long eyelashes, eyebrows that had grown together and she was as plump as an oriental dream. He only recalled the ribbon, tied in a bow, that replaced the garters on her lovely legs; it was of a pale lilac colour. She gave him, as a souvenir, a small handkerchief which he hid at home under his pillow. Examining Mr Rezeda's private life, we must think that in the last act women somehow became alienated from this dreamy and melancholy youth. He never succeeded in placing a kiss on the particular spot of a feminine nape—a kiss that can drive even a saintly nun wild. His fingers only reached their hands—and he was almost ashamed walking behind the ladies when they displayed their ankles on rainy days. The merchant's widow—to mention once again and for the last time that plump little woman—came into the flower garden wearing only a thin *peignoir* and in the shady spots the sun showed pretty clearly the shapely curves under the transparent, gossamer fabric. His heart racing, Rezeda asked about the names of the flowers and wouldn't have dared to open his eyes wide for anything in the world. The little woman visited the sunny spots two or three times, let the wind puff up her dressing-gown, she often lifted her arms (barely covered by the short sleeves) to her hair while the *peignoir* slipped almost down to her shoulder... 'And that blue one which looks like a poem by Richepin—what's it called, ma'am?'

At night, in his bed, Mr Rezeda was the most determined bluebeard who stripped every female he knew to the skin and kissed even their throats with small biting kisses. No wonder that on the spring afternoons in the little apartment in Bombardier Street where the perfume of two young women mingled with the scent of the potted flowers, where the embroidered sofa-cushion smelled of feminine hair, where female dreams emerged almost stealthily from under the bedcovers and from the mouths of the little red slippers used in the morning, from the folds of the towels, the combs and the soft, thick shawls poured the happy odour of two young

144

women destined for love—no wonder that Mr Rezeda read the poems of the limping Lord and a whole May afternoon, destined to celebrate life, was spent in commemorating Lermontov's *Hero of Our Age*.

'Tomorrow I'll bring Boccaccio,' Mr Rezeda threatened every evening with a sad smile. 'The Florentine friars and naughty matrons may perhaps have some effect upon my ladies...'

'Bring Boccaccio, my dear,' replied Sylvia dreamily.

But Mr Rezeda didn't dare to produce the loveliest book of the world. Perhaps he was worried about the morals of the actresses...

At other times, in the narrow hall, he moved so close to Sylvia that he felt under the light dress the gently swelling, warm touch of the girl's body. Sylvia's dewy brown eyes, half-Jewish, half-Gipsy, gazed calmly at the sentimental young man.

'Excuse me,' stammered Mr Rezeda. 'I didn't mean to...'

But that night (in his solitude) he even took off Sylvia's stockings and made an exact estimate of the delicate details of the girl's body from the thickness and softness of her hair.

It was afternoon again and the potted flowers in the windows stretched their leaves towards the sun; the lilac's white clusters quivered gently like the prayer of a virgin rising all a-tremble under the incense-laden arches of a cathedral on its way to heaven. The sun sent fiery little arrows into Sylvia's thick black hair which curled naturally like the hair of Spanish *señoritas*; the arrows gave her hair a sly halo as she sat at the piano near the window. There were tender tendrils on her bare neck and the light blue down on her upper lip seemed to carry jokingly-sad thoughts as she whistled, quite audibly, a sorrowful Hungarian song. Mr Rezeda read Turgenev's *A Sportsman's Sketches* and articulated the melancholy tale of the Hamlet of the District of Shchigri; turning the page, he lifted his eyes from Sylvia to Clara, as if he were himself that particular nocturnal guest who is glad that he has reached the utmost degree of unhappiness.

Sylvia stopped whistling.

'How long is this going to last?' she asked, but she looked neither at Mr Rezeda nor at Clara.

Clara (who was once again darning some underclothes), shrugged, without looking up, while Rezeda continued to the end of the sentence, then closed the book.

'Did you ask something, Sylvia?' he enquired, bending forward politely.

Sylvia heaved a sigh.

'Oh no, nothing at all. I couldn't anyhow, for no one among those present could provide an answer... I'd like to know why I am here in Bombardier Street and what prevents me from taking an engagement with a provincial company? When we came to Pest, we thought that this was the start of the wonderful, amusing, society life. I, at least, always believed in secret that something extraordinary was going to happen if I, a creature of unusual beauty, talent, sagacity and kindness, settled in Budapest. But nothing happens at all. One day passes after another. In the morning the sun shines into my bed but I remain prone... I'm afraid to get up, because I know that once again, the boring long day is to commence. While I am in bed I believe at least that something is going to happen after I rise, something unexpected, extraordinary... Someone will arrive... Or I'll receive a letter that will make me glad. Or that Mr Rezeda will bring in the afternoon a book of poetry in which I can at last find the poem for which I longed all my life but of which I cannot remember a single line. A boy called Teddy-bear recited it to me in Calvary Square and I was fifteen. I never saw Teddy-bear again and however I torture my brains, I cannot remember the poem. Sometimes I think I'm under a spell from which I can only free myself when I recall the poem heard so long ago and I say again in my heart whatever I said on Calvary Square that day...'

'What sort of poem could it have been?' asked Rezeda, growing serious.

Sylvia shook her head sorrowfully.

'I don't know. I can't remember it even in my dreams—though sometimes at night, half-asleep, I remember things of my childhood which I thought I had forgotten. Only suddenly, like an image or a song, its outline appears in my soul. The other night I remembered the checkered coat of the gangly barrel-organist who used to visit our courtyard when I was a child. It was about that time we came to Pest—I no longer remember my mother, only my father who always bisected his short cigars carefully so that he should have an extra smoke left. But I'll never remember the poem which Teddy-bear recited to me.'

'Who was this Teddy-bear?' the courteous Mr Rezeda continued his inquisition.

'I don't know that either,' murmured Sylvia, embittered. 'A little pastry-shop where we drank coffee with whipped cream, a blackbird in a cage, a French magazine called *Frou Frou* hanging from a nail in the wall, and Teddy-bear...This is how much I remember definitely... I can't even recall his eyes. As if he had gone away from me—as far away as the happiness of my life. I think if I'd remember the poem and would find Teddy-bear again I'd be as happy once more as I was at fifteen...'

'Poor little girl,' said Mr Rezeda with sympathy. 'I'll look for your Teddy-bear.'

Sylvia's delicate, blue-veined nose grew a little pink in anger.

'Mr Rezeda, you're such a good boy—it's almost scandalous.'

Miss Horváth laughed softly.

'I think Teddy-bear didn't exist at all. You only dreamt him once. In my young days I dreamt so much about a lieutenant that sometimes I thought I was no longer innocent. And I never saw the lieutenant outside my dreams when he visited me every night in his blue tunic and patent leather top boots. You've never dreamt of girls, Rezeda?'

The delicate young man softly flapped his white hand.

'Of you!' he said with bitter irony. 'I have two wives every night. You, my ladies!'

Sylvia supported her chin in her palm. She, too, looked embittered.

'Every woman was once happy. One because she became unhappy, another guards a portrait in her heart and believes that its original will turn up, the third waits to be married… I'm waiting for nothing, I believe in nothing. The other day a Slovak linen-peddlar came into the courtyard. I thought I would be much happier if I married him. He had such beautiful white trousers.'

Mr Rezeda laughed softly, Miss Horváth loudly.

'Don't you laugh, Clara,' Sylvia continued reproachfully, 'because there was no woman happier than you. To fall in love with an impossibility—with Edward Alvinczi! All it lacks is that you should pray for him every night.'

Miss Horváth's forehead grew pink with blushes.

'You don't know for whom I'm praying.'

'You don't even pray at all.'

Miss Horváth put down her darning.

'Always… At night, in bed, I clasp my hands in prayer over my heart and close my eyes lest I should see anything in the light of the street gaslamp. And I always whisper in my heart: My God, my Lord Christ, my Mary! Let me be always as happy in my life as I am now. Let me never be more in love. Let me never have any other love than the one whom I hardly ever see. Let me never be his, let him never even touch my hand… He must not see me, he must not think of me... Let me only be allowed to love him always and never be disappointed—just as the nuns are never cured of their love for the knightly St George. Isn't this better, isn't this finer than if I were to have a fight every day with my drunken husband or lover?'

Sylvia shook her head stubbornly.

'Mrs Péteri, our prompter's wife, was the happiest woman I ever saw—though her husband got drunk every day and went to the brothel to smoke his pipe in the afternoons—that was where he copied out the plays. They were always fighting, starving, miserable!... And yet she was happy, for when Péteri was asleep, she could sit at his bedside and watch his breathing. So it really makes no difference whether a woman loves a count or a Slovak linen-peddlar!'

'Because the prompter made the kind, foolish woman believe that he didn't go to the whores—it was only the strange atmosphere of the stews which his organism required—as if it were opium. He could only copy the parts for the actors where drunken men danced at night and the piano was pounded to pieces. Sometimes he took his ten-year-old son along—and he read his fairy-tale books there, lying on the carpet. Péteri deserved to be beaten to death!' said Clara severely. 'No one would talk to him in the company. I wonder whether he still visits every afternoon that place in Jerusalem Street?'

'I am sure he does,' replied Mr Rezeda gaily, for he had liked the story. 'At home his head, his eyes, his back start to ache, as it happens with such scoundrels. He groans, complains, until his wife tells him on her own: go on, my dear... but come home early!'

Sylvia muttered bitterly:

'So there's no difference between Alvinczi and Péteri, the prompter. Clara's beloved is also chasing strange women...'

At first Miss Horváth laughed — but then she grew serious.

'My dear,' she said in a poignant tone, 'leave my heart alone! I'm really very happy that at last I could fall in love with someone in my own fashion. I am like the women who knit stockings all their lives and knit into the purls and knits all their thoughts, longings, dreams. And they never stop knitting to go next door where the beloved man is smoking a pipe or drinking wine...'

The little argument died down quietly like the rings on the surface of a lake. Mr Rezeda picked up the book to read about the magnificent Chertophanov and his friend when a carriage stopped in front of the house and Mrs Urbanovics's martial tones could be heard in the corridor.

The Croatian widow was more blooming than ever; the folds of her grey raw silk cloak followed her billowing. There were three golden pheasant feathers fastened to her hat.

'I only came for a day, for one little hour to Pest, my children. They are building sawmills at home, along the Drave, I must be there from morning till night otherwise they'll steal me blind. Not long ago they even stole the nails... But I must visit Mrs Tórics.'

The actresses caressed flatteringly the rich lady's cloak.

'How lovely you are, Auntie!'

'Don't be silly. My hat, my dress—all last season's. Such village matrons as myself are not obliged to know about the latest fashions. I only differ from the wives of the little clerks of Budapest in buying always the best and the most expensive. So a pair of my gloves remains serviceable for years. Because I buy a dozen pairs at once. But let's go to Mrs Tórics—I want to take the night train home.'

'Who's Mrs Tórics?'

'Don't ask me, I have been told everything about her by my neighbour, my Miklós Zrínyi, with whom I talk every evening by telephone across the River Drave. My neighbour was in big trouble last spring. The timber business was in the doldrums, the banks cancelled their loan, the lawyers talked of compulsory sales and my neighbour faced the future in total despair—though otherwise he was as correct a man as a Swiss watch. In our district merchants sometimes go bankrupt without any proper cause. Business stops like a piece of rock in the River Sava. It needs much water to move it again. The gold-digging peasants sometimes spend months sloshing around the mud of the Sava in their sieves without a single grain of gold glinting in the wet sand. At other times the river goes crazy and carries the gold by the handful from the mountains. Our merchants know already that they can do nothing about this. One must wait for the bad times to pass like the ague... Or go quietly bankrupt if that is the order of fate. My neighbour, I don't know how and why, turned in his great trouble to a witch in Buda, to Mrs Tórics. Being a Catholic, he couldn't write to the wonder rabbi of Sadagoria for advice, he had to be content with this witch or herbhealer. They exchanged a letter or two, then he came up to Pest and visited the woman. I don't know what happened or how it happened—but my neighbour's sadly hanging head started to lift, a bank gave him money, he turned back to his neglected affairs and by May everything was all right. Since then he has had no troubles at all. He doesn't even complain about his liver though he used to be taken bad with it...'

Mrs Urbanovics talked so violently that she didn't even notice: the young ladies had got dressed and stood ready to leave.

'I took a large carriage, a four-seater, we all have place,' said the widow and planted Mr Rezeda's hat on his head.

The witch lived in a part of Buda that could not be reached in a carriage, in a steep little hillside street, in a house with a mysteriously locked gate; a house that may have been built in the days of the Turkish occupation. Mrs Tórics sat in a curtained room, at the end of a twisting corridor. Her hair was swept back, her eyes were calm, her face smooth and a lively pink—once she could have been even beautiful. Before she spoke, she wetted her lips with her tongue.

'Madam, you want my advice in a business matter?' she asked, after a brief momentary glance of her black, intelligent eyes. 'Please sit down here beside me—the others needn't hear what I'm going to say.'

Mrs Urbanovics settled down expectantly, a little tensely, beside Mrs Tórics. The white witch looked calmly and seriously at her face.

'Well, what's the matter?' she asked in a lowered voice as if she had known her for a very long time. 'Are you in love?'

'That, too,' replied the widow, confused. 'But the business is more important. I don't know how it's going to turn out, what's going to happen. I invested an immense amount of money in a venture and now I can't sleep at nights...'

The wise woman shook her head indifferently.

'You're in love. That happens, if you please. Don't be ashamed—I've had white-haired countesses here, bringing their troubles to me. The other day a grandmother came to me. She fell in love with a schoolmate of her grandson. No need to feel sad over it. We're all human. And love doesn't ask how old you are. Love slips even into the church, following you, surprises you while you pray, in your sleep or while you're doing something that has nothing in common with being amorous... Don't be ashamed. I had here very great ladies from Pest. Many have already found their happiness in this house.'

The wise witch spoke calmly, without raising her voice or pausing; her black eyes were already fixed searchingly on the actresses and Mr Rezeda.

'Well, tell me how it's going to be?' asked Mrs Urbanovics.

'Don't ask me that, please, I am not a fortune-teller. The fortune-tellers all lie and make their living from the belief of

152

people in their stupidities. I can only tell you whatever I experienced during a long life. No magic, no pretense! You, madam, listen always to your heart alone and then you'll be lucky in all your business. You're a wealthy woman, don't deny yourself the one thing the heart and the body need like your daily bread. You're an industrious, hard-working, good woman. You're a healthy woman, with good hot blood. Only: don't deny yourself the one thing you need, then you'll be lucky in all your dealings. More I can't tell you. Well, young ladies! You, blonde missy, will you please come closer!'

Mrs Urbanovics would have liked to pose a question or two, but Mrs Tórics had already turned away her eyes. So she rose and yielded her place to Clara who sat down with a certain embarrassment. Mrs Tórics cast a quick glance at the girl.

'You came to me so I can tell you whether you'll ever belong to the one you love?'

'No,' replied Clara. 'I know that I can never belong to him.'

'Don't argue, little miss. You can't deceive Mrs Tórics. I had such saintly girls here who don't even dare to go into the street alone—yet the devil dwells in their hearts. Don't worry, you are no better than the rest. You'd be glad to give yourself to that man and you'd never pause to think what would happen tomorrow or the day after... But don't even think of it. You'll never belong to the man you love. Better if you get it out of your head. You're still young, a beautiful girl; you're not so far from him who loves you truly, who has no thought but for you. Love him and you'll be very happy in your love... Now then, pretty black miss. For you I'll look at the cards...'

She took from the drawer a pack of cards, their edges worn to roundness, their faces barely discernible—they looked as if Lenormand himself would have used them for fortune-telling. She made Sylvia cut the pack, then looked at the spread-out array thoughtfully. Next she gathered them up, made Sylvia shuffle again and cut and then laid out the dimmed figures from left to right.

Sylvia smiled at the strange images with Hour-glass, Dancer, Death and Old Man following one another—this was a truly magic pack.

'Here it stands,' murmured Mrs Tórics pensively, 'here the whole matter stands, quite close. Strange—as if this very day, before sunset, you'd be destined to meet him in whose hands your future, your happiness is placed. Miss, I can only tell you what the cards show. You'll be very happy within a very short time—someone thinks much about you and is already on his way... He's on a journey, he's coming, soon he'll be here...'

She quickly gathered up the cards, as if the mysterious figures had already betrayed too many secrets. She wrapped a long thread slowly and silently around the pack. She closed the drawer and then lifted her eyes, surprised that her visitors were still in the room.

After Mrs Urbanovics placed a banknote on the table, they left without a word. Mrs Tórics didn't touch the money, didn't thank for it, she nodded and remained unmoving in her place.

The company walked silently down the narrow little Buda street whose houses were as old as those in a fairy-tale, as if they were all pondering the words of the white witch. Only Mr Rezeda appeared to be laughing silently.

There was a little square which was barely large enough to accommodate an old ramshackle well and an old little pastry-shop. They had some coffee with whipped cream and slices of coffee cake. Sylvia looked around absent-mindedly.

'I've been here before,' she said, 'but I can't remember when. These yellow silk chairs were less shabby then and the coffee was better.'

'This was a famous pastry-cook of Buda. The lovers of Pest used to come here for rendezvous,' murmured Mr Rezeda. 'Love dwelled here constantly, happy faces looked into the old mirrors. How wrinkled and tired of life those once gay faces must be now, how cobwebby the once bright eyes! This little pastry-shop has also grown shabby—like a keepsake book whose pages have been filled. It has become dusk, after all the sweet nothings and lustful promises that were, spoken on this yellow silk chairs, the lights have gone out here. That's how it is in life.'

'It's the cage with the blackbird I can't see anywhere!' wailed Sylvia. 'And the copy of *Frou Frou* with its overdressed Parisian ladies and gentlemen in tails!'

Until now a quiet young man, dressed in black, was sitting in a corner hidden behind a newspaper. Now his curly head and his smooth-shaven face became visible. He wore flashing glasses; he turned his pale, passionate forehead attentively towards the group.

For a moment Sylvia stared at the pale young man silently, stricken, her eyes almost full of tears. Then she laughed, softly, mysteriously and waved happily to him.

'Teddy-bear!' she cried. 'Where have you been, Teddy-bear?'

The young man blushed, then rose from the table.

'I've been looking at you for a long time but didn't dare to accost you!' Teddy-bear said in a soft, timid voice. 'You've become very beautiful since I saw you last.'

'And you—how you've changed! But not for the worse!'

When the introductions were performed, it turned out that this was Mr Ursus, the conductor.

He was a very serious, taciturn young man. But Sylvia chattered gaily, at a great pace.

'We talked about you this afternoon. Do you remember, we once went to a pastry-shop... How's your life? what are you doing? where have you been since I saw you last?'

Teddy-bear barely replied to all this because he was a very quiet young man. He only stared with wide-open eyes and now and then stroked his hair.

'Teddy-bear, dear Teddy-bear!' said Sylvia.

About nightfall, when they went home, Mr Rezeda demanded of Sylvia sarcastically:

'Well, my lady, did you remember the poem, the old poem?'

The actress gave a soft, cooing laugh.

'Yes, I did. But I won't tell anybody.'

ONEGIN

Mr Rezeda lived in Buda, on Castle Hill, and at night when he walked home he often met old kings who emerged from the stone wall. Rezeda doffed his hat, well-mannered, to Matthias in his student's cloak or the grim, black-bearded Sigismund and stood, his head bowed, near the bastion until the ghostly figures of the ancient kings, the shadows woven from the mist of autumn night, the silver of the pale moon and the dully echoing bell-strokes of the historic towers disappeared somewhere along the castle wall. At other times he stopped, listening, in one or the other of the deeply slumbering streets; as if he heard from underground, the cellars or arched tunnels under the Castle, the sound of revelry. From deep down it sounded: the voice of the fifes, the clinking of the metal winecups, the wine-sodden singing of the revellers. It was the same sound as the singing of soldiers at night as the rushing train carries them across the plains to the wars. Who knows what old king's stalwarts had remained behind, making merry in the cellar under the Castle; the doors had been locked from the outside, the archway of the entrance had collapsed, blocking the exit for ever... Then maids-in-waiting, wrapped in hooded cloaks, slipped past him in the silent night and their steps were as soundless as the graveyard breeze. One or the other had golden heels to her slipper. The cloak touched Mr Rezeda's shoulder, but he never permitted himself the unchivalrous act of spying on the ladies of olden times, haunting the night. The golden-heeled slippers carried their mistresses secretly along the twisting streets of Castle Hill to some ancient house where the knight of past centuries must have been certainly waiting.

Perhaps our melancholy hero took lodgings on Castle Hill so that his midnight walks should differ from those of the young men of Pest. Mr Rezeda loved mysteries and the night.

In former times he was a gay and life-loving young man in the towns of the Great Plain and Upper Hungary where he spent his quickly-passed youth. In Késmárk he sang in the Méze Garden the student song together with the others, hoisting his beermug; he wore a white English tropical helmet, high-heeled, pointed shoes and a thick walking-stick (the end of which he pushed into his coat-pocket). He was in love with Miss Hermina Stolcz, for all Késmárk students were in love with Miss Hermina Stolcz, and he fought his first duel for this dear lady and no one else in the empty dancing pavilion of the People's Park where the two young men, bare to the waist, faced each other with curved, deadly sabres, dating from the seventeenth century. The god of youth watched over the sabres that swung with such menacing swishes and only a thimbleful of blood was spilled on the floor of the pavilion where, not long before, Miss Hermina Stolcz's white, bow-tied slippers danced to the music of a Polish polka. But the duel became known and before our conquering hero could receive his reward from Hermina (a provocative smile, a warm handclasp or a flower she had kissed), the severe staff expelled the duellists from the school. Hermina's blue eyes and bubbling laugh accompanied Mr Rezeda in the rattling train—though until then he had hardly read any estimable poets apart from Horace.

The secondary school of the town on the Great Plains stood among green trees. Its pointed, arched windows, its open arcades made it look more like a rococo hunting lodge than the halls of learning. The younger professors and the older students joined forces when they went carousing to the nearby spa. Any student would have gladly sacrificed his life for Steve Gró, the art master. Mr Rezeda took part in the orgies, raced his two-wheeler and drank brotherhood with the gipsies—but never gave any serenades under a girl's window. He moved sadly, with a mysterious *Weltschmerz* in the little town of the Plains; like an incognito prince of the Land of Sorrows. Though he never told of his heroic duel in Késmárk, letters soon arrived from Upper Hungary which disclosed his transgression. And the deed which, according to the conception of that part of the country, almost ruined the career of a young man who deserved better, raised our hero on the Great Plains, near the River Tisza, to the status of a most celebrated youth. The professor of Hungarian history, Pál Porubszky, when he finished his brilliant discourse about the Jagiello Dynasty (the way only the old, provincial professors could lecture who educated the tough Magyars), hinted that heroes existed not only in history but also in actual life around us... (Later it was also Pál Porubszky, professor of Hungarian literature, who added to the beautiful life story of Bessenyei, the guards officer and poet, that there were poets today as well, their talent developing with us, at our side and in front of our eyes... And the poet was again Mr Rezeda, for he had decided to choose poetry as his career after being crossed in love. That was how professors in those days educated youth!)

The brooding, moody youth who was handsome and prepossessing loved to roam alone in the copses, at the bottom of gardens, and his face only brightened when he espied by accident a couple of lovers in the deserted Morgó cemetery or under the hazelnut bushes of the Bujdos Woods. In this town ladies and gentlemen were just as amorous as in other towns—they even had a greater inclination to sacrifice to Eros, for it was the custom to forgive girls if they got into trouble.

It was a strange town. Between the sandy hills the population was one descended from the embraces of Magyars and Slavs. Proud Tirpaks, dressed up to the nines, drove their beautiful four-in-hand teams, their women wore their silks with such magnificence as the ladies-in-waiting of King Svatopluk; the men were brave, sober, thrifty and self-assured, of truly noble temperament, as if they, too, had come from the land of the Don. There was a Russian church on the hill where the Greek Catholics, descended from the mountain counties of Ung and Bereg, sang and their daughters were as blond and dreamy as their songs. The Tirpaks were born and died in the faith of Martin Luther, the Hungarians in that of the Virgin Mary. Under the onion-shaped towers of the Jews the young men already wore top boots and carried fox-hunting whips, they pasted hundred-crown bank-notes on the forehead of Benczi, the gipsy bandleader; but their women were still as if they had just come from the Lemberg ghetto, they seldom ventured to go into the street and if one of them did appear, men went crazy at her sight. Oh, those lovely Jewesses! In the eyes of the tobacconist's wife you see the starry sky of Andalusia, while the apothecary's lady is as dreamy and soft as if she had stepped straight from the *Arabian Nights*. The doctor's wife is blonde and curly-haired, her thick eyebrows, the down on her neck and the scarf she throws over her shoulders when she goes to call next door, remind you of the clock of the Jagiello Tower in Cracow, sending its sonorous strokes over the Jewish houses.

One day the roaming Mr Rezeda met Bertha, the young wife of the veterinary, who was as beautiful as Esther and as virtuous as Susannah. The melancholy young man's lonely, uncomplaining life moved Bertha who spent a year in a Budapest finishing school before she married. Perhaps she was a little intrigued by the sixteen-year-old, precocious youth who battled with a sword, once used to batter Turks, for the sake of a Késmárk miss! In the town of the Tirpaks, Bertha was a lady of the great world, she ordered the material of her dresses from the Parisian Bon Marché, the French heels of her shoes were fashioned by a Budapest shoemaker and her pale, delicate face was so pensive as if her thoughts roamed somewhere far away and she wouldn't even notice the shop window of the newly opened emporium which the Ruzsonyi Brothers had launched. She knew a good many French words which she mixed skilfully in her speech and Maupassant was her favourite writer. And this when the local circulating library, managed by the freckled and stoop-shouldered Misses Rosenfeld, purveyed Rocambole and similar blood-and-thunder trash and it was necessary to reserve such pulp stuff weeks ahead. She subscribed to the magazine *Parisian Fashions* and to the literary review *The Week*. When she spent some time in Budapest before her marriage she met Jenő Heltai and other literary celebrities. So she was well-educated and the Christian and Jewish ladies turned up their noses when she walked at noon alone on the promenade of the town. She played Tchaikovsky's *Romance* faultlessly on the piano and in the evenings she remembered the Opera in Pest where she had once seen the ballet *Viennese Waltz*. Her nails were as shining and clean as those of a French princess and perhaps she even kept a diary—but maybe she did this only for the gentle annoyance of the ladies of the place. For exercise she took long walks on the outskirts of the town when she hid a small, pearl-handled pistol in her long cloak and always carried a yellow-covered French novel in her hand.

Mr Rezeda accompanied the lady on her long walks and usually trudged silently at the side of the severe little lady whose shoes left tiny traces on the footpath. Those who knew Mr Rezeda closely in those days, can state with almost full certainty that during these walks on the outskirts and in the copses, at the side of the delicate lady, the prematuraly aged young man invoked romantically his first love, Hermina

Stolcz, though apart from the poets he studied at school not a single rhyme had yet sounded in his heart.

One evening, when they had walked to the distant windmill and had listened to an itinerant singer on the way, Bertha told the student:

'My boy, you are too uneducated. Soon your moustache will grow and the time will come to get married. By then Miss Hermina will be married, too, and will bathe her dirty brats. You must plot the conquest of new women. Tell me, what can you tell a woman if you want to please her?'

Rezeda shrugged. 'I do not want to please.'

'My boy, you're talking nonsense,' said Bertha very seriously. 'Women and men are in the world in order to want to please each other. That's the only reason why women stick birds' feathers on their hats. I'll give you a book from my library. You'll learn a little of life from it. But promise me that you'll read it!'

'I'll promise,' said the brave boy after a brief resistance.

In the evening Bertha (who was smoking a thin gold-tipped cigarette) handed Mr Rezeda a small morocco-bound volume through the window. Its title was *Eugen Onegin*. For days the student didn't open it, for he was occupied in writing his last will and testament. He was disposing of his maternal inheritance—which did not exist. He left his favourite hounds, horses, estates all to the girl of Késmárk. A pity that he had no reliable old retainer at hand whom he could send on horseback to her with the document. It was unsafe to entrust such an important matter to the post.

On the third day, stretched on his bed, he opened the book and after he had read the first pages and discovered in the poet's biography that Pushkin had been shot dead in a duel by a handsome guards officer, he settled down with appreciative interest to reading the rather long poem.

Onegin! Perhaps the only reason why it would be good to be once again a young student is the chance to read on the bench of a lonely park, leaning against feminine hearts and initials carved into the wood—to read *Eugen Onegin* for the first time! To travel to Moscow and applaud the ballet! To receive Tatiana's letter and walk along the Neva! In our youth we are all Eugen Onegins. And who has not shed tears upon the sad grave of Lensky?

Bertha had chosen well. The reading of *Onegin* opened all at once the wonders of a new world to Mr Rezeda: he decided to choose a goal in life, to become a poet, a journalist, to become Alexander Pushkin—and all this in a single night while, with his forehead burning and his heart brimming over, he read the singing lines of the Russian poet. Next day, walking towards the old cemetery, Mr Rezeda courageously and with tears in his eyes took hold of Bertha's hand, clad in yellow gloves.

'Tatiana!' he said.

The lady caressed his moist eyes,

'I'm glad I awakened you, my boy. "But do not hurry to live, do not drive too hard your feelings..." Wait quietly. Tonight you will find the book of a new poet in my window and you will get acquainted with a new world of marvels.'

'I love you.'

'So *Onegin* has already taught you to love, to conquer, to be brave, my dear?' replied the lady with a smile. 'Oh, you're a magnificent pupil. I hope that once you'll want to die for me, too, like Alfred Musset. So the book will be in its place tonight and now let us no longer talk about it.'

The second book which Mr Rezeda read thanks to Bertha was *Dombey and Son* by the great English story-teller. No one had ever written more finely, with deeper insight, about England, London, the young and the old in Britain and the fleecy clouds drifting in the hearts of English women. Mr Rezeda almost bathed in his tears the hand of the beloved Bertha and, walking towards the vineyards of Oros, they discussed in full detail the life and death of little Dombey.

'You're Miss Florentine, my lady,' whispered Mr Rezeda, moved.

'Thank you for considering me the heroine of a novel,' replied Bertha gaily, 'while in town I am derided as a lady of fashion.'

The third book which Rezeda read was written by Andersen and contained fairy-tales. And from that day onwards they passed with special awe the old windmill at the outskirts of the town and inspected closely the old lead gutters which they hadn't even noticed before.

The fourth book was Boccaccio's short stories... And it was the Florentine's fault that the beautiful romance was suddenly interrupted.

One night in May Mr Rezeda opened from the street the window of Bertha's bedroom—just as Boccaccio would have suggested. He moved on tiptoes, feeling his way through the room in which he could hear quiet breathing in the darkness. He knew well where Bertha was sleeping and he already felt the feminine scent rising from the bed; the lady's soft breathing seemed to settle like a wreath of tea roses upon his head.

And now a deep voice thundered in the dark:

'Who's that?'

Mr Rezeda made a flying jump at the window; upsetting chairs, tables on his way; the flashing electric light showed him the way—but it also provided illumination to the veterinary who fired his revolver at the flying would-be lover. The bullet whistled past Mr Rezeda's ear, sounding as if Death had drawn a long sound from an endless string. The same night he packed his few belongings and fled from the town... Oxford, a diplomatic career, all that which Mr Rezeda's well-to-do parents planned for him, all these faded like a dream. This was the tale of Mr Rezeda's youth. After that night he became a wandering and more or less unemployed poet, a provincial journalist and later an inhabitant of Buda. Only his awakened love for the night, his sympathy for mysterious matters remained fresh and unjaded, though he had read every book already that was worth reading.

With Bertha, the veterinary's wife, Mr Rezeda corresponded for about a year. His days generally passed in writing letters to women in a cool, vaulted and dim room rented by the month which could have been once a prison or a monk's cell. The desk had rococo legs, he mixed the ink with gold dust and he signed his name like an abbot, while he pressed the coat of arms of an ancient pope into the violet sealing wax at the back of the envelope. Sometimes when he used the name of Bessenyei, the poet-guardsman, to conduct his correspondence with the ladies he wrote with a quill; at other times he drew red initials upon the parchment, writing in the name of the knightly Frankenstein to a provincial miss; he wrote as Onegin wrote to Tatiana; he wrote as Sindbad, the sailor of the *Arabian Nights*; he was Henri III, King of France, and wrote to 'Marguerite of Navarre', *poste restante*, to the Water Town post office in Buda. Sometimes he had no money for lunch, but he spent his time trying to think up new, fine pseudonyms he could use to sign his letters to the ladies. He was especially successful in imitating the signature of György Zápolya, the sixteenth-century magnate, which he found in an old document. He exchanged long, long letters with the romantic ladies of the Tabán and Castle Hill— without meeting any of the darling creatures personally. In the evening or at night he slipped these letters through the windows left open by hazard, under doors and gates; then he entrusted his secrets to the post and the ladies were never angry, if he used the name of some old lover to interpret his amorous feelings. He only had trouble with Isaura, a little chambermaid, for she couldn't read.

Bertha had long ago forgiven the nocturnal intrusion—was there any woman in the world who wouldn't forgive such a thing? She asked him to write to her *poste restante*, addressing it to Susannah Bornemissza; and she often told Mr Rezeda in her letters that she felt towards him more or less like a mother or an elder sister who keeps house in some old Transylvanian castle, while her brother serves at the court of the Queen. She sent books and marked the passages in them which she herself had once read with special pleasure; sometimes a single hair, sometimes a pencilmark showed where the lovely eyes rested dreamily in the distant provincial town. Thus Mr Rezeda became familiar with Thackeray and Dostoevski. Of the French, Bertha adored Maupassant; while among the Spaniards she was best entertained by Cervantes and Alarcon. E. T. A. Hoffmann and the wonderful Chekhov arrived simultaneously in Buda and the *Idylls of the Kings* by Tennyson supplied material for several letters. Thus Bertha educated and instructed from the distance Mr Rezeda, until one day she wrote that she was coming to Pest with her husband and would visit her knightly brother Whitmonday afternoon at the Queen's court. Mr Rezeda fled from home, roamed the Buda hills until late evening, lay in the grass, cried, composed poetry, felt most miserable, considered suicide and at midnight entered his rented room on tiptoes. He had always described it in his letters as a wonderful knight's hall where he promenaded in a cloak of golden silk and a purple cap; where a large clock in the corner played Haydn's church music at midnight, and a medieval crucifix hung above the ancient praying stool upon which he used to pray for Bertha... (Maybe it was because of shame that Mr Rezeda fled from home—or because he was such a peculiar man that he did not dare to meet the one whom he believed he loved best?) He found a single yellow rose on his table. It was Bertha's message. After that they never corresponded again.

It was summer and Mr Rezeda moved from Castle Hill to Pest, to Joseph Town where leafy trees stood in the courtyard and the windows were open at night in the one-storeyed houses. Our hero used to stop and listen to the breathing of sleeping women. He made friends with little sempstresses and spent his afternoons in cafés where he hid himself—a lonely, unrecognized being—behind the newspapers and called the waiter *garçon*. His correspondence stopped completely, he no longer thought of fine pseudonyms, no longer set a rendezvous with unknown women under the Castle Bastion and no longer menaced the Buda misses that he would kidnap them from their tranquil homes. He longed for the knowledge of living, actual women. He took the phthisic little sempstress and her friend, the little *midinette*, to the pastry-shop Sunday afternoons, but alas, he by no means felt any longer happy in the company of simple girls. In his dreams demonic vamps, music-hall stars, night-club singers, French *soubrettes* whirled around. He thought of dancers who came to Budapest from Canada and he saw a bareback rider smiling at him from the saddle while her stallion stepped daintily to the rhythm of the music of the orchestra above the ring. The great world tempted him and he paused for a long time in front of the music-hall posters. Miss Florence, the somnambulist, or Señora Frasquita, the Spanish dancer, entertained Mr Rezeda in the evening—though he never saw them. He set Miss Florence against the background of the hall of an old Scottish hunting lodge, between ladies of reddish-blond hair, very delicate features and shining eyes; her slim hips were certainly covered with a red riding habit and she held a circus whip; while the *señora* sent the intoxicating grace of Seville women and the fire of Xeres wine into the heart of our lonely dreamer. And soon he managed to become acquainted with a flower-seller called Hortense for whose sake he spent his nights in the Music Hall Café; at dawn he accompanied the Jewish girl home and in the less frequented streets he took her basket from her. Among the marvellous artistes after whom gallant gardeners named roses, apples and pears, it was Hortense who told Mr Rezeda tales about the *haut monde*, Russian grand dukes, pimps and spendthrift embezzlers when at dawn they settled down in a small deserted café. She ordered coffee and he asked for plum brandy...

'And what's news in the ballet, my dear?' asked Mr Rezeda Hortense who was a little past her first bloom.

Months flew past again, we find Mr Rezeda in the little office of an illustrated paper where at dawn in the hot, lead-smelling cage he proofread the damp galleys; he called himself a journalist and being able sometimes to obtain free passes to the theatre, he fell in love with an elf in green who sang in the first row of the chorus. He frequented the New York Café and consulted Messrs Hirsch, the owners, whether he should become a critic or a poet? In those days Messrs Hirsch were still addicts of literature—that is what my grand-father once told me.

Thus Mr Rezeda lived in Pest until his provincial acquaint-ances, the actresses, arrived and he read aloud to them in Bombardier Street the fine novels and poems which were the gifts of Bertha to him. He lived in the Inner Town, but at night he stopped under the open windows—what if a woman decided to gaze at the stars, the nocturnal sky's clouds or the moon?—but no one ever looked through the window when Mr Rezeda trudged homewards. He alone stood at the open window on Easter morning in the entire city to greet the rising sun in the fashion of Faust, while he told himself poems and would have been glad to sell his soul to the devil if he could have found a buyer.

One of the consequences of the encounter in the Buda pastry-shop was that Mr Rezeda could never give a reading of the magnificent story of Chertaphonov and his friend; the tranquil and pure afternoons came to an end—those after-noons when the clocks of the Inner Town church towers struck almost romantically, echoing in the little apartment, and in the spring sun the room was filled simultaneously with the scent of the potted flowers and the young ladies. Sylvia now got dressed in the early afternoon and as an independent lady left home alone, buttoning her gloves on the staircase. For a day or two Miss Horváth grieved over the faithlessness of her friend.

'I wonder where she is going?' she asked Mr Rezeda, who walked about with his head hanging sadly as if there had been a death in the house.

Mr Rezeda did not answer, he only shrugged his shoulders, indignantly, painfully. He walked up and down in the room and sometimes gave a laugh as if someone kept on stabbing him through the heart with a sharp dagger.

'Where?' Miss Horváth repeated.

Mr Rezeda laughed ironically.

'You are asking me, madam? Madam ought to know better the secrets of your girl-friend; on the other hand, madam also belongs to the feminine sex and women must understand each other! Strindberg was right: women are strange little animals, one must not take them for humans. A single beckoning, a sole signal is enough for them to stumble and forsake the path of decency. Men ought to punish women—in order to reduce them to slavery again. If it depended on me, I would have every second woman in Pest burned on the stake...'

'Because of Sylvia?' asked Clara and gave Mr Rezeda a sly look.

'Because of Sylvia and because of the others, too,' replied Mr Rezeda violently. 'Isn't your girl-friend strange and ridiculous, my dear? She meets a stupid conductor who may not even know that he is alive or what living means. Thereupon Sylvia immediately upsets her peaceful, tranquil life... She goes to Buda, to the pastry-shop, like the little women of Pest who lust for adultery, waiting for an officer or a long-haired musician, rolling in curtained cabs along the quiet, deserted streets under Castle Hill. Love is a very fine thing—if only it did not involve so many ridiculous, clumsy posturings! The thick veils which the ladies making the excursion

169

to Buda wrap around their heads, the completely fresh, scented underclothes and the new gloves—they are all instruments of sin. One ought to pass a law that if some Pest matron crosses the bridges wearing new stockings, she must be burned under Gellért Hill. I know, by God, the ladies would lose their penchant for Buda pastry-shops, adventurous cabdrives, stupid officers, half-mad musicians... Before now Sylvia never put pink ribbons in her slip!'

Miss Horváth shook her head, amazed.

'How do you know that, sir?'

'Because there were no pink ribbons in the house. Why does she do it? She wants to please that idiotic conductor? Who's that Mr Ursus, what is he? A good-for-nothing, ne'er-do-well, a skirt-chaser. I am sure he was waiting then for some hysterical miss at the pastry-shop whom he was dazzling with music, art and other things used for bewitching silly women. Dear Clara, we must do something, we can't let Sylvia become the victim of a foolish whim, the sentimental mood of a Buda pastry-shop where the clocks play oversweet Mozart music and rococo cavaliers and ladies walk arm-in-arm on the yellow wallpaper—all this to make little women slip on the parquet floor of life!'

Clara laughed, full-throated and loud.

'You're a most amusing person, Mr Rezeda,' she cried. 'Once an acquaintance of yours told me that when you wanted to turn from the faith of Martin Luther to Roman Catholicism, you went to the Jesuits in Maria Street and asked their lame gardener to become your godfather. Well, you're once again appealing to the lame gardener... What have I to do with the Buda pastry-shop and Sylvia's outings? I am sure she is far happier than we both together. Can there be greater bliss than to walk, loving and beloved, arm-in-arm on a fine spring afternoon in Buda where one does not meet any acquaintances? The old houses, the twisting streets all beckon to you like accomplices and in the Tabán the church is open even in the afternoon; the flowers of May bloom on the altar in the Virgin's honour, their scent mingles with the incense and in the last pew, in the silent church, one can pledge eternal troth. Perhaps you have never been in a deserted, quiet church, with your mistress on your arm, and so you could not see that all images of Mary turn gently forgiving and encouraging and the saints with their big moustaches almost bend forward from the darkened canvases when the young man and his lady kneel side by side in the last pew... Have you ever been to church, Mr Rezeda?'

'I have,' replied Mr Rezeda angrily. 'I was in the chapel of St Roch on a dark dawn in the early spring when the nave is filled with sad, coughing nuns who may be just coming from the bedside of a dying man and are praying for his soul. I frequented the chapel for a while, because I was dying too and I wanted the nuns to close my eyes. Why doesn't Sylvia become a nun, I wonder?'

Miss Horváth got up quietly and put her hand on Mr Rezeda's shoulder. She looked into his face for a long time:

'Let me tell you something, Mr Rezeda. No use wailing at each other. Outside the sun's shining and it's spring. You go downstairs, I'll get dressed, then we'll go for a walk—to Buda, if you please. Where no one sees us, I'll take your arm.'

Mr Rezeda kissed Clara's hand. The actress caressed both his cheeks whereupon Mr Rezeda gave an ironic laugh.

'I owe you a certain confession, my boy,' said Clara, a little moved. 'I am a sinner. I was brought up in Calvin's faith, I cannot go to the Jesuits for confession as the happy Catholic women do. I'll confess everything to you.'

Mr Rezeda grew pale.

'What's happened?'

'Don't be afraid. Nothing's happened. Do you like red? I'll put on a red hat.'

X

ESTELLA

Mr Rezeda sometimes felt during these days like Henry Esmond, colonel of Her Majesty Queen Anne, for he happened to read the novel of the one-time London journalist, sitting in a tower where before him a crazy old gentleman had lived. Now he was walking silently beside Miss Horváth as they set out in the spring afternoon towards Buda. It was only when they crossed the Chain Bridge that he murmured in a paternal tone:

'Clara, the wind's blowing, watch your hat!'

In general, Mr Rezeda behaved as if some misfortune had befallen his family. His foster-father, friend of the great Oliver Cromwell, had been stabbed through the heart in a duel in the flower garden of England; his foster-mother, the most unforgottably beautiful feminine character of the world in the presentation of the London newspapermen, gazed with melancholy eyes in the distance from the Welsh castle and the loveliest eyes of the island kingdom were lightly clouded... Or maybe it was Miss Horváth who had deceived her faithful knight, indeed or in thought, no matter; and now they were bound for the Meadow of Blood, where The Very Reverend Martinovics and his company had been executed. They were bound for the tragic spot in order to bury the precious corpse that might be called love or friendship, an Easter morning, sunshine dripping through the leaves of poplars, the dream of winter nights. (Outside the snowstorm whirled around the ancient roofs of churches, the punch burned with a blue light upon the writing desk laden with fine old novels and books of poetry; someone sat at the fire, stared into the flames and thought of a woman.)

'That's the way Mihály Táncsics was escorted when he was freed from prison,' said Rezeda, his teeth almost chattering, yet his smile still superior—as if this little remark were his most important concern—and not the desperate fear, the burning anxiety about what Miss Horváth was going to tell him as soon as they had left the Chain Bridge and reached the foot of the hill named after the saintly Bishop Gellért. My God, what awful things she would confess! In the French novels, fashionable in the middle of the nineteenth century, deceived husbands clamped their teeth together in dull despair when Madame broke down at last under the load of proof and said: 'Monsieur, I'll tell you everything.' Oh Lord, if only she did not say anything! If only she would lie shamelessly, denying the undeniable, calling the white black and produced sufficient falsehoods... But they were still on the bridge, Mr Rezeda stared into the great river rolling beneath them into which so many had descended in resignation. Nor were they all fished out in the riverside communities, some got as far as the Black Sea where the little Pest slavey whom her mistress had beaten was flouting in the company of strange big-headed sea-spiders and peculiar snails. Mr Rezeda spoke slowly and dreamily:

'The Danube fish must have a fine time below Pest. The river that performs such shining twists under Visegrád as if the Angevin kings and queens would still examine themselves in its mirror, by the time it passes our city, is filled with corpses, filth, sin, dirt, and probably loathes itself. In the middle of the stream cholera swims wrapped in a ragged black shawl; scarlet fever has applied for a place amidst the moulds of a rotting piece of lath and finds pleasure in stopping

173

over near the small villages, under the willow trees, with children playing in the nearby meadow. And travelling with the waves are typical citizens of Pest who never even crossed to Buda while alive and yet now set out in the direction where the steamer for Mohács passes. A cashier in a café wanted to get to her lover, an infantry lieutenant garrisoned in Komárom, and jumped into the Danube. Poor girl, she had never been to school. She did not know which way the Danube was flowing. Maybe she wouldn't have died if she had known that she couldn't float upstream to Komárom…

At this moment they left the Chain Bridge.

'That's enough now of your useless chatter, Mr Rezeda,' said Miss Horváth with a sad severity as if she had to deal with a naughty child that had lost its mother. 'Let me think for a moment where I am to start, what shall I deny and shall I tell a lie or two?'

'Queen of my heart,' murmured Mr Rezeda, 'there is no sense in trying to thin up some lies. You can tell me the truth without fear: where and when and how often you have deceived me and with whom. I'm a sick man, tired of life, it is only in my thoughts that I take my pleasure of women, an unhealthy fear restrains me from touching their dress, though in my nocturnal thoughts I'm wrestling with you every afternoon in that small apartment, like a peasant lad in the barn with the harvesting wench. In my dreams you pant in my face, bite my chin, your waist strains away, "no, no, no!" you cry with your teeth clenched—but in my youth I was a famous wrestler… I am the invalid gentleman who finds delight in his malady, for he acquired it when he was hopelessly in love in his childhood…'

Miss Horváth's eyes brightened.

'We had a musician, a pale flautist who—whenever the score permitted it—quite often behaved most shamelessly down in the pit whence he could peep under the skirts of the actresses. It was in vain that kind-hearted ladies playing mother roles undertook to improve his morals; our kindly manager was finally forced to dismiss him. And since he no longer plays in a theatre orchestra, he's become a decent citizen. But let us not dwell upon these strange juvenile vices! My girl-friends at school used to look at various pictures and were very happy, they cut letters from the newspapers and combined them into all kinds of words and wore poems hidden in their stockings or their corsets. Several of them have turned into happy mothers of families by now. Don't worry, Mr Rezeda, you can still become a happy and tranquil man in time.'

'I'm not worried, dear mistress, I seldom worry about myself... But what has happened to you, what caused this change I've been noticing for some time?'

By then they were sitting on a stone bench under the statue of the saintly Bishop Gellért. Mr Rezeda stared at the ground. Miss Horváth gazed pensively at the panorama of the Pest side.

'Estella is a town in Navarre and that's the name of one of my early girl-friends who had the loveliest hats at the drama school,' Miss Horváth started in a dreamy voice as if she were not about to tell her own story. 'Estella was a blue-eyed, red-haired and very depraved creature; she bit old Újházi's hand, called Emma Márkus a princess and enquired impudently where she bought her hay-scented perfume. Nor did she stay long at school, life soon extracted her from between those four walls and for a while her pretty hats, her delicate stockings and her very good shoes disappeared from my sight.

'A few weeks ago I met Estella in the spring noontime on the Promenade. My God, how common she'd become! I thought to myself when I saw her first. Yet Estella hadn't changed, she was the same as at school, a *femme fatale;* only perhaps my point of view had become different from that of the earlier days; just as the houses and trees we believe to be

175

huge in our childhood appear to have shrunk into the ground when we see them again adults. Estella still fancied green dresses and striped stocking. She wore low shoes with wide soles—the kind Englishwomen wear on round-the-world tours, a rusty-red veil covered her face and the wing of a blue jackdaw decorated her little postilion's hat. She shook my hand in a masculine gesture and called me milady. We entered a café on the Danube quay for her sake; she gave a few old gentlemen, engrossed in newspapers, a lingering look, then we sat down in a corner, my friend ordered a cold fowl, then she suddenly looked at me and laughed: "I'm an English lady now, my dear, that's what pleases the men in Pest!"

'I've become used to my colleagues' professing more liberal views than myself. Their morals are often far from blameless, after all, I was a provincial actress, sir, and our old manager loved to bite the shoulder of the new female members of his company. I knew that Estella hadn't stuck to the path of virtue; I can't really describe my own mood as I sat down beside her in the café on the Danube quay.

' "I'm taking lessons from an English teacher and I know at least three hundred words by now," continued Estella, eating delicately. "The British sovereign is the loveliest money in the world, the best underwear is made in England and whenever English gentlemen arrive in Pest, Madame Stein sends the janitor's wife for me. I only consort with foreign gentlemen, the men of Pest are corrupt, stupid, by no means discreet and they openly point out on the Promenade or in Váci Street the women with whom they had luck. It's enough to make the acquaintance of a single one in Pest; next day the whole town knows the colour of your garters. I like the Germans, too, though they're clumsy, they torment you for hours, try to bargain, luckily Madame Stein is an energetic woman who won't stand for any hanky-panky about money. As for the French who stray to Budapest, it isn't worth talking about them. They're bigger rascals than the local variety

176

and you'd better take good care of your necklace if someone accosts you in French in the street. As long as old Uncle Baranyai was alive, the gentlemen from the Casino often visited Madame Stein's, Baranyai brought counts and barons along so that fat Madame Stein would permit him a caress or two. These, too, were gentlemen and for their sake I learned a couple of songs, accompanying myself on the piano while the champagne was put on the ice. The silk wallets of the tail-coats held big bank-notes and Prince T., when he had had a lot of champagne, gave me his handkerchief with the ducal monogram. (Later, of course, I had great success displaying it to my Hebrew gentlemen.) But Baranyai had a stroke and of the former aristocrats it's only Edward Alvinczi who sometimes turns up at Madame Stein's, smokes a good cigar and, humming a little, listens to her tales taken from life. She doesn't even think of offering her wares any more. There are no women in Pest, sigh the once gay gentlemen..." '

'Estella had been a chatterbox at school, too, but since then she had learned the art of prattling even. This constant gabble was part of her professional equipment to amuse men. She must have a few stories which she used to tell at night, in a *peignoir*, some jokes and anecdotes... You know, my dear friend, that as soon as Estella spoke that certain name, my heart gave three definite beats, like the bell of the signalbox in the midst of silent woods on the border, at night, in winter and in darkness, striking three times when the telegraph announces the approaching train. I felt my throat constrict with unhappiness, envy, pain and fury. This strumpet may have succeeded in filling one of Alvinczi's hours of boredom...I'd have liked to drive my fist into her face.

' "Well and Alvinczi doesn't like you either?" I asked in a choking voice.

' "Everybody likes me," she replied gaily and I saw a strange, lying light gleam in her eyes; I knew at once that she was lying. My heart no longer ached.

'Estella ordered some dried fruit, then took one or two drags at a cork-tipped cigarette.

' "Are you happy?" I asked.

' "What's happiness?"

'She looked at me, shrugged her shoulders; then, growing a little sad, she turned away her head.

' "Sometimes I think I'm very sick," she murmured. "Yet once my bones were like steel, you could have cracked nuts upon my bosom. I ought to take a cure. I plan to go to Dresden, they say there's a famous doctor there who... But I only have seven thousand forints in the savings bank. As soon as I have ten thousand, I'll go at once to rest, to be healed... maybe I'll even marry some German... To tell the truth, I am nauseated by men..."

' "You aren't in love, ever?"

' "Sometimes... I mustn't listen to my heart. It was enough once... at thirteen I took poison because of some wretch. I'm not scraping and saving so that some scoundrel should take my money, lose it on cards or spend on women all I earned with such bitter toil. I could find one of those crooks any day... They see that I'm well-dressed, that I'm respectable, for it's four years since I told Madame Stein not to introduce me to any local gentlemen—as soon as I had saved up my first thousand forints. That's all I need—to play the whore for these Budapest ne'er-do-wells! I wouldn't let any of them tie the laces of my boots—not even those who wear the most gleaming top-hats. I won't have them point after me in cafés or in the street: that's old Estella, I laid her at such and such a time, in such and such a place, for so much... I wish God would strike down all those rotten, loud-mouthed men!"

'And the distinguished English lady threw her cigarette on the floor with such violence that the waiters all looked at us. At that she pulled the veil over her face and lowered her voice:

' "Very well: I'm no longer young, I admit that there are prettier, younger around than me. These days every village maid-of-all-work turns *cocotte*. The milliner's apprentice gets tired of carrying hat-boxes and goes to Madame Stein to be licked into shape and dressed. The typist-girl needs new clothes—so after office she runs to Madame Stein. The engineer's, the lawyer's wife, the Buda matron with a golden cross on her bosom, waits around in Madame Stein's kitchen at dusk—her only fear is that the man who drops in might be an acquaintance whose wooing she used to enjoy at balls or concerts while she lisps behind her fan: 'Tchaikovsky? Oh, I do love music...' But most of them are ready for anything, for spring has come and they need new dresses. All the men work, steal, make crooked deals, rob, play cards in this city only to provide the doxies with new spring hats. They jump into the Danube, put a bullet through their heads, go to gaol for women in this city and poor fellows, they have no idea that the adored lady watches in Madame Stein's kitchen at dusk from behind the curtain to see whether a drunken German manages to climb the stairs—or a cabbie with a goitre who just won some money at the Alag races or the croupiers of the gambling dens who could pay enough to buy some silk stockings... The whole of Pest is one big brothel. The janitress of Madame Stein perhaps goes even to church and invites to the newly-wed young bride her mistress for the same evening... Let me be old, let me be sick, but I won't sell my honour for any money. No drunken gipsy band-leader or pickpocket was ever allowed to touch me at Madame Stein's... *Garçon*, a glass of V.S.O.P. cognac. Two, please..."

' "Thank you," I replied, "I don't drink."

' "It's easy for you, you're healthy—I only feel well when I've had a few drinks. Naturally, I take good care that anything I take shall be the best, impeccably exclusive and in good taste. The German patrons can't save money with me, Hungarian champagne is for the coachmen, *my* vintage

is Pommery and Greno. And only the dry one. Madame
Stein knows that when I'm in her drawing-room, she mustn't
pour cheap wine into an expensive bottle, I'd throw it at her
fringed forehead—for when I've been drinking, I sometimes
get wild..."

' "Terrible," I said.

' "I'm very unhappy," said Estella quietly and fell silent.

'That's how Estella talked and perhaps she said other
things, too, which I no longer remember or don't want to
tell you.

'Later she spoke of her childhood; they'd lived in the
country, in a one-storey house but the big trees grew higher
than the roof and at night faithful dogs barked in the yard.
In those days she became always sad at dusk when the
landscape grew quiet and the dimness walked sorrowfully
between the trees. Those who do not grow melancholy at
dusk, have no heart, really. Then she went to Pest and in the
late autumn afternoon the black smoke of a factory chimney
covered the city as if the houses spread underneath were
inhabited only by sad people. In the distance mountains of
fog and dusk rose, the lamps were already lit at the station
and Estella was still a virgin.

'We went for a walk in Buda and Estella kept on telling
me how miserable she was! Maybe because she felt that I
liked her for it and that it gave me a good feeling. She did
not talk any more about men, Madame Stein and the
depraved women...

' "There used to be a royal forester in the neighbourhood
who often declared that he would marry me. His face was as
red as the landscape pinched by hoarfrost and he himself
drove the fiery horses of his sleigh," said Estella.

'She spoke of her prayer-book, her diary and her bespectacled governess.

' "The cause of all my trouble was that my mother didn't
love my father."

'Then she recalled doing the laundry, a grape harvest and a wedding feast where she was a bridesmaid and wore a garland of tiny wild roses in her hair.

'We passed a small café where an old couple were sunning themselves in the terrace garden. Behind them the hill slope, an ancient, quiet square. The coffeehouse-keeper stood in the door in a worn velvet cap. Estella jogged my elbow.

' "Watch the venerable old!"

'The old lady sat there in a mantilla, an old-fashioned hat, crocheted gloves on her hands, holding an illustrated Viennese magazine. The old man, like some retired civil servant, studied the evening paper through his round glasses with close attention. Both were dressed in black, only the old gentleman's fingers were covered with more rings than it was usual to wear, with the strong glint of a ruby's deep fire and the little old lady's shoes were of better quality than the general fashion in Buda. The shoes had high French heels and the ribbon was tied cleverly across the grey stockings.

' "Well?" I asked Estella as we walked on.

' My friend lowered her eyes. The silken pansy trembled on her breast.

' "They kept the place which I used to frequent first, when I was still a student at the drama school. They used to live in Pest, in the Street of the Golden Hand, and Uncle Rókási used to be quite fleet-footed with his old legs when he ran for the girls whenever guests arrived. There was a small piano in the drawing-room and the old gentleman's hand trembled when he played the old valses... His wife spent later two years in gaol—in such a business these things can happen—and after that they retired..."

'We walked on and I remembered how tenderly the old man glanced over the top of his spectacles at the ancient little lady. My God, would someone look at me with so much love when I'd grown old and ugly and sit in a Buda café in a little mantilla?

'We sat down on a bench in a deserted garden and for a long time we remained silent. Estella suddenly began to cry; she leant her head on my shoulder and I also shed tears, though it isn't my custom to cry even if my teeth ache.

'In the evening when we parted we agreed that Estella would fetch me when Edward Alvinczi called on Madame Stein again and she heard him sigh in the drawing-room: there are no women left in Pest.

'All that night I dreamt about Estella, the old couple in Buda, the old lady in patent leather shoes; a sleigh with bells travelled across the snowy landscape and Estella's forester came to fetch me in a red jerkin and with hoarfrost on his moustache.

'At dusk an old street porter—maybe the oldest in Pest whose white beard was like Abraham's—called me mysteriously to the corridor and pressed a slip of paper into my hand. "*8 p.m. Golden Pheasant Street 3, First Floor.*" By the time I looked around, the old man had already disappeared as if he had been an apparition. I quickly started to dress, putting on my best stockings, taking a long time polishing my nails and putting a ribbon into my shift, a violet ribbon.

'What did I think of while I did all this? Nothing.

'I wanted to please Edward Alvinczi so that he shouldn't be able to say ever again: "There are no women left in Pest!" What would happen until and after that, I cared as little about as if all these things were long past. I was like Estella myself, strolling at noon on the Promenade, to pick up men and then crying softly alone in the deserted Buda garden. What would happen tomorrow? ...The most important thing was that my shoes should be well-shined.

'I arrived in a grey Pest house which, at other times, I would probably have hurried past, without noticing. Under the doorway the strange board with the tenants—whenever I took shelter during sudden showers, I used to read these with great amusement. But now my heart was racing when

I saw among the others the name of Mrs O. Stein. I was a little dizzy as I mounted to the first floor and pressed the bell. I had to wait for a minute—it sounded as if half-dressed women were running past the curtain of the hall, on tiptoes, wearing slippers. A voice called: "Mamma!" The door half-opened, a plump woman in a red négligé measured me from head to foot with her cold grey eyes.

'"Is it you, miss?" she asked in an unfriendly and severe tone.

'I nodded.

'"Please to enter," she said indifferently. "You've to wait... But here's Estella..."

'Estella stepped forward from some corner of the dim ante-room. She clasped my hand with both her hands and there were tears in her eyes.

'"My God, you've come!" she said, almost choking.

'Madame Stein spoke in a cold, commanding voice:

'"Ladies, you mustn't remain in the hall. It is unnecessary for you to meet everybody who's coming and going."

'Estella took my arm.

'"Let's go into the kitchen."

'There was only an oil lamp in the kitchen while the rest of the apartment was well lit with brilliant electric lights. Instead of the red carpet and green wallpaper of the hall here the wall was bare and the floor naked stone. The air was thick with the smell of food and onions; in a corner an old slavey washed dishes and swore in Slovak. On a low three-legged stool a lady, dressed in a cartwheel hat and a silk gown, sat under the window. She held her delicate parasol in her gloved hand and after she had inspected me coldly, she turned her head away again and stared under the pink curtain into the dim corridor outside.

'We settled down on a large travelling trunk, close to each other, for my heart raced so wildly that I was afraid to faint. Estella pressed my hand and as I gave her a sidelong glance,

183

I noticed that her blouse was unbuttoned at the neck and her hair was suspiciously tousled. My God, why was this girl so dishevelled? I felt a cold shiver down my back and I quietly withdrew my hand from Estella's grasp.

'Now and then the lady in the large hat gave me hostile glances. Evidently she disliked my shoes most—they had a checkered inlay, few women wore it yet in Pest. She watched Estella with a pitying, sneering smile—as it is the wont of respectable women when they see garishly dressed street-walkers. She had fair hair and blue eyes; her face was like that of the cats drawn by English artists and her black silk dress exuded a delicate violet perfume. She took a small mirror from her handbag and as she did so, a rosary with small white beads clinked against it.

'Now there were sudden steps on the corridor, the lady quickly turned on the stool and lifted the curtain on the kitchen window. There was a short ring on the front door.

'The lady got up in evident excitement. She straightened her skirt, her coat, adjusted her veil, took her parasol grace-fully under her arm and stood there, watching the closed door, as we actresses stand in the wings, waiting for our cue.

'Then suddenly she cast a glance at my shoes. Who knows whether we would ever meet again, so she asked in an icy tone: "Miss, where do you buy your shoes?"

'I was far too depressed to answer such a question. For a while she stared at me fixedly, then the door opened quietly and a voice said softly: "Blonde lady!"

'The lady immediately started to "act": she smiled mysteriously, timidly, shakenly, like the little woman slip-ping into the Buda hotel when, after lengthy pleading by her lover, she agrees at long last to go to the assignation. She even gave a little cough, the wretch! And, stepping lightly, she slipped from the kitchen in her silk skirt.

' "You did well not to answer the 'blonde lady'," Estella said in a purring voice beside me. "This woman is the biggest whore in Budapest, but because she is legally married she despises us all. Rosie the Cabbie's Delight has already threatened her once to throw some acid at her. Madame Stein is terribly greedy for women and the 'blonde lady' usually walks with a small boy in the street…"

' "Where's the boy now?" I asked, startled.

' "He's down at the porter's lodge. He and the porter's son are good friends."

'The Slovak slavey was throwing the cutlery into a basket, swearing loudly.

'We fell silent and I clearly heard the beating of Estella's heart. Or maybe it was mine.

' "Ladies, you can play cards in the kitchen, too, don't occupy my room!" I heard Madame Stein's voice. Laughing, slapping the plumper girl on the bottom, she pushed two tousled girls through the door and suddenly the small, half-lit kitchen was filled with the mood of maize-stripping village barns.

'Madame Stein, with a cigarette in her mouth, stood in the middle of the kitchen, her arms akimbo, her gaiety infectious. She scolded the old servant laughingly:

' "Why, you old strumpet, damn your eyes, haven't you finished washing up the lunch dishes yet? I'll have to do it myself, I think. I'll show you how to wash up! Of course, you still know how to run after the scoundrels…!"

'The old woman swore in a deep voice, the tousled girls laughed. Madame Stein lowered her immense body into the three-legged stool and inhaled her cigarette deeply.

' "I thought the chair would collapse under me."

'She shuffled the cards and the girls huddled beside her on the floor.

' "We'll play *marriage*… five bits the stake. Have you five bits, you cow?" she asked the plumper girl.

' "You'll lend me some, Mom."

' "Wouldn't dream of it."

'In the end the fat girl produced her purse from under her red silk blouse.

'For a while they played seriously and devotedly. I don't think any of them dared to cheat or Madame Stein would have killed her.

'Suddenly Madame Stein put down the cards.

' "Just remembered—the old Excellency must be waked. He can only sleep on my sofa—that's why he comes here..."

'She rose, stretched, yawned, threw her cigarette into the corner. "My God, how I loathe my life!"

'A cloud of serious sorrow passed across her face that once must have been beautiful—like the reflection of a brown rain-cloud across the mirror of a pool. Her deep, large brown eyes were still fiery; they held some dreamy, melancholy, truly Magyar feeling—which the great Lujza Blaha, our lovely actress, used to produce on the stage.

'She hummed an old Hungarian song as she left the kitchen; we could still hear her in the hall: "Heavenly apparition, toying with mortals..." As if she wanted to rouse the old Excellency with this song...

'After a few minutes she returned with a brass cage. There was a small bird in the cage, a siskin or a goldfinch, perched quietly in a corner. Madame Stein crouched on the floor and started to whistle. The little bird fluffed her feathers and soon started to answer her. Madame Stein lifted her index finger.

' "D'you hear? Like the little bells on the eve of Easter Saturday. My darling bird!"

'The door swung open, pushed by a bumptious and fast-moving dog. It was a ratter with a black patch on its head and with the shining gaiety in its eyes that is characteristic of faithful and good dogs. It leapt several times over the cage, then vaulted over Madame Stein, crazily, almost drunkenly carried away by its joyful exuberance as it danced around its mistress. Finally Madame Stein stretched out her hand, the dog kissed it and lay down on the floor.

' "His lordship!" Madame Stein pointed at it. "I've paid two hundred forints in fines because of him—he keeps on tearing the skirts off women in the street…"

'She went on playing for a little while with her pets; obviously she had no other real interest in the world.

'Steps sounded on the corridor, then a brief ring. Madame Stein hurried into the ante-room and returned with her face flushed.

' "Ladies, hurry, into the blue room. Baron Eugene's here… he wants scrambled eggs… He suddenly became hungry and came up to me for a bite…"

'Estella took my arm and led me through a side-door into the apartment proper. We still heard the grunt of the visitor as he settled down with a heavy sigh on the trunk in the kitchen.

' "You'll see how many crazy men there are in the world," said Estella as we settled down in the blue room, "Almost all gentlemen are a little mad. Some like fine stockings, others adore shoes, the third has to be slapped in the face because he enjoys that, the fourth has his hands and feet tied up with thin string by Mom, the fifth cries for his wife and you've got to ask him for money to buy shoes for his children… A very rich and very handsome young man—he's almost as beautiful as Prince Rohan—can only make love to women if their feet are muddy; while the dark, hysterical poet must be addressed as Prince Bourbon, because one of his ancestresses used to be the mistress of the King of France in Madrid… Sad young men turn up here who first cry on Madame Stein's shoulders, bewailing their amorous griefs and ask Mom for advice against insomnia and heartache; old gentlemen with waxed moustaches must be called Johnny and Stevie and made to stand in the corner like naughty little boys. Serious gentlemen escape from their lovely, pure wives to us and demand news from Mom about some whore in a ragged skirt. Journalists call who read to us their next-day leaders in the kitchen and demand Madame Stein's opinion about them. This is a crazy world here—all night there is a coming and going of miserable, unhappy men who all trust good-hearted Mom to console them with a few words, some advice, or a girl. My God, how many handsome, unhappy gentlemen there are in Pest! A thousand sorrows, wails, plagues of the metropolis are given tongue every night in Madame Stein's kitchen... Men who in the daytime walk proudly, with heads erect in the streets, display their deep wounds here in confidence. Bridegrooms ask for directives and old married men seek a panacea to revive their powers of love-making. Secrets are spoken which usually one only whispers into the ear of the Jesuit confessor or kneeling in front of the Miraculous Mother of God at Máriapócs, touching one's lips against the flagstones of the church. It is Life itself that pays a visit here every day; there is nothing to read in this house except a Jewish prayer-book and the Adventures of the Chevalier de Faublas. At night, in the silence and waiting, the ladies turn the pages of the prayer-book first and then of the saucy exploits of the amorous French youth... Madame Stein has a nubile daughter being educated in a Viennese convent, while her husband keeps a saloon in Canada. That's how we live here, my dear."

'I nodded, I felt sad, the blue room was terribly silent as if I had passed very far from life and Budapest, sitting in some fairy-tale house where nothing surrounding me was true.

'Estella was only a strange figure in the puppet theatre and soon the ballerina cut out of silk-paper would start to dance on the wall. The room smelled of cigarettes in which the tobacco was mixed with opium; there was a deck of solitaire cards on a small gilt table with rococo legs, old racing tickets and dance cards were hanging from the chandelier. The ashtray was decorated with a woman's head, her face covered with a black mask, her glass eyes shining and there were two other pictures on the wall. Rococo gallants in red coats and with powdered hair amused themselves with slim ladies in an ancient drawing-room and the valet in kneebreeches served coffee. Then there was the portrait of an old man in a cap who looked like an old-fashioned village innkeeper.

' "Madame Stein's papa!" said Estella.

'And beside the old innkeeper the steel engraving of Jókai's, the great story-teller's portrait.

'Madame Stein entered, her arms naked to the elbow. Her face was flushed with the flames of the cooker, her eyes shone gaily.

' "One of these days, when I get tired of you, girls, I can go to Baron Gene's estate and become his housekeeper. He's already engaged me. To raise little sucking pigs, hatch yellow goslings and waddling little ducklings, to drive in the spring across the fresh green meadows in an unsprung cart... and in winter the snow is waist-high in the yard... That's what I need, I'm a country girl after all. My father used to sell wine on the banks of the Sajó river, in an isolated inn, and in the winter evenings the foxes barked, the wolves howled in the reeds across the river. Miss, you still have to wait! Estella, show the lady our photograph album."

'The matron in her red *peignoir,* looking truly house-wifely, turned on her high-heeled slippers and quickly left the room.

'Estella took from a drawer an album bound in red velvet. It contained only male photographs. Young ones, old ones, civilians, prelates and soldiers. Here were actors, here the great writer with a lock of hair falling into his forehead as if he were the hero of a novel; then the Archduke in a colonel's uniform, a small boy on a wooden rocking horse, a poet, leaning on his elbow; a journalist taken by some photographer in the City Park; here a priest with a golden cross, then the famous Pest dandies: the noted tailor with his huge beard and another two or three who pleased women; the manager of a circus and a popular singer, another poet with a leonine head and a very old newspaperman (who was only put among the collection of Adonises because at night he used to smoke his Virginia cigar among the ladies of the music-hall, Mr Rezeda thought); then some pleasant faces, dear to women: a handsome playwright and several actors, editors, lawyers and what-have-you whose pictures were exhibited in the shop window of Calderoni, the optician; the girls bought them as souvenirs. Then there were innumerable women, in old and new fashioned clothes; some had a piece of black *crêpe* placed next to them, these must have been dead. Then Estella turned the page again and there was Edward Alvinczi, dressed in the colourful trappings of a Hungarian magnate, standing on a balcony. The bell rang in the little signalman's hut.

' "Pssh!" said Estella suddenly.

'In the next room a woman was screaming and laughing, cooing like a pigeon, wailing hysterically and shouting words that were drowned in tears, sobs, ecstasy.

' "That's Pepita, the strumpet," said Estella, full of hate. "She simulates madness to excite men. The other night a friend of mine, an English racing trainer, slept here, waiting for a morning train. Pepita raged all night next door, the Englishman kept waking up and at the same time woke me, too. That crazy Englishman, he woke up at least ten times. My God, how long it seemed until dawn!"

'I jumped up. Blindly, dizzily, beside myself, I rushed at the door. I don't know how I got out. It was already dark in the street, a cold rain was falling, my face was tearsodden and I pushed a tipsy young man out of my way...'

While she told the story, Mr Rezeda was holding both hands of Miss Horváth.

His eyes brimming with tears, he looked into the overcast eyes of the girl.

'Is this how it really happened?' he asked quietly.

'Upon my honour!'

Thereupon Mr Rezeda kissed the lady's hand.

XI

MOMENTARY MENTAL ABERRATION

My Mistress, I kneel down and commend my soul to God.
The old Werndl rifle lies loaded on my sofa; I'm only sorry
that it will be an ugly pose when I pull the trigger with my
big toe. According to my old favourite writers and my own
conviction: six ounces of powder and three and a half
ounces of lead are bound to help me.

I'm going away though I long to live—as the tenor warbles
so movingly in *Tosca*. (Though the one I heard had two left
feet, alas!) Do you remember Jacques Mannheit in the role
of Count Almaviva? You and I sat together in the theatre—
but *Tosca* I had heard all alone in a corner of the stalls and
I decided that once, if God decreed thusly, I would have
this aria played into my ear by a sad-faced cellist—it is
almost dawn in the Castel d'Angelo—and by morning
I'll be dead.

I raise the curtain and upon my window, desolate in its
nocturnal rest (for no one has ever sighed under it at night;
the moon stood like some fairy-tale symbol above the ancient
roof of the house, no one has whispered: "I love you, I love
you, I long to be with you, my own, my all!" and my balcony
was silent as in novels about Seville)—yes, on that window
the sun was glinting playfully, rising from Rákos, carriages
rolled, people stirred down below, four storeys down; maybe
I'm thinking of an early morning journey when I took an

express train north or south and all night I was entertained by the clatter of the chains under the carriages, as they clashed together and separated again; like a gentleman fleeing from an illness, I hid in my berth—though the desirably tousled Rumanian lady passed in front of my compartment, milk-white, dressed only in her petticoats... I should have talked French to her, introduced myself as the Comte de Navarre, talk about my saintly younger sister who was passing her novitiate in the convent of Avignon, because she could not find a husband of suitable rank; talk about my ancestors, Philip the Mad and the bandit chiefs of Széchény; refer to the club-footed lord, the mansion in Orléans, point out the mysterious mountains and melancholy plains, the strange valleys of the Hernád river or the iron forge glowing red in the dawn dimness; going half crazy with the drug of poems and love—and seduce the lovely Rumanian lady who was, by the way, looking for the sleeping-car attendant with his Henri Quatre beard. I remained unmoving in my narrow bed and I only thought of you, the unknown and only one, the queen of my heart, all the time...

Other women paraded, in yellow silk gowns, Jewesses whose gestures, eyes, peculiar necks, lustful noses, thick lips (sweetened by their red tongues) and arching, swaying, love-expectant backs passed seductively in front of the young poet...

I'm sorry, My Lady, that I put this on paper. (I hope *The Sun* will print this, my last letter!)

No one approached me: this is the truth. I stared at the lovely women who walked past me in the street, in cafés or theatres, half-dead with desire. They walked on with paunchy and unprepossessing men who in the daytime floorwalk in ill-smelling shops on Andrássy Avenue or Király Street, write briefs or are doctors to the poor—while I watched in vain the number over the front door through which they disappeared.

Sometimes I was happiest at night. I inserted the knife into the left eye as deep as I could. I sent the pistol bullet between the two eyes. My hard fist struck a blow, aimed at the stomach and the nose. Or I had sabre duels with the unknown men of the unknown women; on such occasions I recalled with full confidence my childhood friend, the Polish Prince and dancing master Casimir A., who taught young men only cuts between the ribs, tricky ripostes aimed at the belly or the knee, hamstringing and spitting the opponents. Once upon a time the slim foil moved as lightly in my hand as a delicate cigarette and I got used to aiming the frontsight of the pistol at my enemy's foot.

Murder, death, to kill somebody, perhaps to land in prison, be sentenced to hang, to draw the Browning with a single gesture, to wrestle, to bite off noses, tear off ears, shatter front teeth—once upon a time all this seemed to me the normal order of things. I loved to stop run-away horses, to face officers' wielding sabres with bare hands, my ten strong fingers would have perhaps strangled a bull—and now, My Mistress, I write to you and the melodies of *Tosca* roll through my wild heart, telling me I'll be dead in the morning.

I forgive everybody, including My Lady. In humble adoration, my head bowed low, freed of wild passions, wearied and trusting only the lead, I confess to you, my dearest: I can no longer love.

Once I was a romantic hero; now I am a bored, bad-tempered, tired gentleman. Perhaps there might have been women for me to embrace?...

No, you were the only one whom I ever loved. A little while ago I shed some tears for you. Strange, isn't it, that I'm trying to justify myself to you. What have you got to do with this whole business?

It is morning.

The sun, the greatness of life and similar idiocies...

I'll read some parts of *Onegin*—about the ballet, or the spring.

Good-bye, my queen...

*

Miss Horváth received the letter in the evening. She took a cab and drove to Mr Rezeda's place. By then the journalist had been taken away in an ambulance. The army rifle had cut a brave wound just above his heart. He was still alive; an old nun sat beside his bed in the hospital and the screen was in readiness for the night in case he got worse.

XII

AUTUMN IN THE PAST

It was autumn in the Tabán quarter of Buda, in an ancient house, where once upon a time royal mistresses must have dwelled—for the underground passage, half blocked, could only have served royalty to pay nocturnal visits. Some of the doors bore the Corvinus coat of arms; the remnants of the broken balcony still showed the raven, erect. The old stones peeded from the walls as if curious about the life around them; in the underground corridor a lonely otter promenaded; of the weathercock only the tail was left, turning strangely, with a fairy-tale grotesqueness as if it wished to replace the deserter cock.

Mr Rezeda took a flat of two small rooms in this house. Into one he moved Miss Horváth with her hat-boxes; into the other his books, his blue tail-coat and lace-fronted dress shirts which he preferred to all others, being a romantic gentleman. (Miss Horváth was a wizard at pressing such shirts!) Mr Rezeda slept in the narrow bed, while Clara made herself an improvised one on the floor; they burned an ancient nightlight under the crucifix in the wall recess and had long conversations nightly.

Sometimes they had a visitor too; little Béla Bonifácz who, after endless wanderings, on foot, by train and by raft on the Dnieper, accompanied by the daughters of Dideri-Dir, had made his way back from Siberia. He brought tuberculosis and a veneration of Buddha from the far corners of the earth. For a year he had travelled by freight train, with sheep, shaggy ponies and Buddhist priests; his excursion took him to somewhere on the Chinese frontier, to Cossack garrisons where the girls danced Hungarian horseherd dances for the entertainment of the bored officers. On that freight train Béla was converted, learning to pray in Chinese and, arriving in Buda, he tried hard to gain new followers for Buddha in a country where even the One True God was no longer worshipped sufficiently. The Eastern God had imbued his unhappy little disciple with amazing eloquence. He was perhaps more ragged than ever—but now he knew *why* he was so ragged.

So it was autumn and the clocks struck sadly in the towers of the Tabán. Outside the house there was an ancient sumac tree which may have been planted in the reign of King Sigismund more than four centuries ago. From the window Mr Rezeda kept looking at the tree. He watched day after day how the leaves were reddening; he stared in childish grief after each leaf drifting away. There was a big armchair that had been left in the place. Perhaps aged kings listened to the tale-bearing of their young mistresses sitting in it—for women could tell such wonderful stories! Or perhaps old princesses sat there, smiling at the wit and gossip of young knights and the dowager queen shook her head at the immorality that was rife in the neighbouring court. Now Mr Rezeda sat in the armchair for the rifle wound was healing with difficulty, he was not allowed to move much and Miss Horváth looked reproachfully at every puff of smoke—her reproach being directed at Béla Bonifácz who had found himself a marvellous place in a corner. He sat in a cradle which the former tenants had forgotten here. Perhaps the baby had died and they did not want to take the sad souvenir with them. Little Béla Bonifácz spent weeks dangling his short legs from the cradle and he spoke no more than ten words a day. In the evenings he gathered himself and went some place... He slept somewhere in deserted gardens like the birds of the Lord, for he never accepted the invitation to spend the night...

One day he said, sitting in the cradle:

'Do you two never kiss at all? I'm going for a walk—so you can make love.'

Clara let her head hang sadly and caressed Mr Rezeda's face.

'As soon as my kind lord and master is healed, when he's well again, my lips will always cling to his lips. Now I am only the serving maid of my king.'

Béla Bonifácz hated arguments. He went on swinging his legs and smoking the shag which he mixed, for economy, with dried acacia leaves. Miss Horváth walked softly in the room like a medieval nun who had been canonized; she cooked and cleaned, she gossiped with the woman next door in the corridor for she knew that Mr Rezeda was happy about this, thinking that his beloved was entertained... And she read the serial in the illustrated paper, waiting every day full of curiosity for the next instalment.

'My God, what happened to Count Beerborough?' she said sometimes for Mr Rezeda was pleased about this, too. He did not want his darling to be occupied with nothing but sad thoughts. She always wore low-heeled shoes and gowns rather like dressing gowns, her hair in a fringe and a small cross around her neck; she gave the cooking pots and pans individual names and she played a whole afternoon with Mitzi, the six-year-old girl next door... Mr Rezeda smiled quietly under his eyelashes. His sweetheart wasn't bored, he thought... They turned the pages of a French grammar; Mr Bonifácz sometimes intervened to point out the correct pronunciation and one day Clara brought a gay little bird from the Tabán market. The little bird lived in a romantic, turreted, fretwork hut, and when the rays of the autumn sun emerged from the foliage of the sumac tree, the whistling of the titmouse rose from the fairy-tale cage. Clara placed her finger on her lip and looked at the little bird with almost unearthly happiness... Mr Rezeda closed his eyes. My God, he thought, there *was* something in the world that gave his darling pleasure...

Thus they lived in Buda, in the Tabán, in the ancient house where King Sigismund used to hide his mistresses. The leaves of the sumac tree became redder and redder, the striking clocks louder and louder over the autumnal silence of the quarter. Béla Bonifácz climbed out of the cradle.

'I'm going off to found a religion, after all,' he said and next day he did not return at his usual time...

The day the yellow leaves had become completely red on King Sigismund's sumac tree, Miss Horváth bought two kittens on the Tabán market, a striped tom and a female with yellow spots. She put the tom on Mr Rezeda's lap.

'This is yours, my dear!' she said with a melancholy smile like that of a good mother bending over her ailing child.

She tied a red ribbon around the spotted cat's neck.

'Missy!' she said and laughed with tears in her eyes.

Mr Rezeda closed his eyes again while he stroked the striped tom and thought that soon he would have to send for a priest. How difficult it will be to part with the darling lady! The leaves drifted almost in the rhythm of a minuet from the sumac tree of the long-dead king and the sky had a fairy-tale depth above the roofs of Serb Town. The chimneys smoked as seriously as in the tales of Andersen and the dragon-headed, rusty rainpipes blinked almost slyly with their tinkered eyes at the autumn sunshine, wondering when the cloak-shaped clouds would arrive from the mountains so they, too, could carry out their duties. All the white dogs of the quarter rushed around hurriedly in the street as if they had business that would not brook postponement. Only the ravens sat down now and then upon the eaves and brooded, deep in care, at their high stations. It was late autumn though the little sun promenaded with such holy affection above the twisting little

Tabán streets as bemedalled, red-faced old gentlemen visit their former loves and talk away the afternoon about the beautiful past.

One afternoon Madame Louise's comfortable carriage stopped outside the house of the former royal mistresses. She wore a grey travelling costume and a small, feathered hat; Béla Bonifácz jumped from the box. He looked rather sad and thoughtful as she entered the apartment of his old friends:

'Unfortunately I cannot sit next to Madame,' he murmured as if following an interrupted chain of thought. 'She is far too distinguished and rich for me to take up a place beside her in such shabby clothes. Pedestrians might think that these fat-backed horses had accidentally run over me at the Chain Bridge and that the kind-hearted lady is now taking me to hospital in her carriage. But you can enter the carriage without any fear; we're going to Christina Town, to the Red Frog where there's going to be a great party in honour of Mister Sylvester.'

'Has the good old man died?' asked Mr Rezeda.

'Not yet, but he is close to it... He takes his naps between the wild rose-bushes on Little Gellért Hill, putting his head on a big stone and when he sometimes gets up from the fading greensward, he is highly dissatisfied. He dreams every night about his daughter who committed suicide and in the evening he stares at the sun so persistently as if he did not expect to see it again next day. Let us go and amuse the old gentleman.'

Kindly Madame Louise took care that the convalescent Mr Rezeda should have a warm shawl around his shoulders and on his knees. Miss Horváth put on a shabby and strange little hat that looked as if she had borrowed it from some Buda matron of the previous century. She had darned her gloves in the proper places and now she pulled her somewhat down-at-heel shoes anxiously under her skirts. Madame

Louise measured her with a single look from under her long lashes, then she sighed slightly and gave Clara a red rose.

'Roses suit blondes so well!' she said and her voice sounded apologetic.

Little Béla Bonifácz took his seat on the box and the grey-moustached coachman in his winged cloak (he was as grim as if he were driving a hearse) flicked his whip to urge on the broadbacked greys. In her youth Madame Louise loved the fastest American horses for her carriage and used to make some tenors in check trousers mount the box; but in time, as her blood cooled, she regularly bought her horses from the Chapter of Veszprém—horses which not even an old canon would employ.

So they drove along the twisting Buda streets, uphill and downhill; the greys trotted as diligently as reliable old civil servants performing their duties. Madame Louise sat unmoving and serious under her tiny hat with the thick blue veil; Mr Rezeda inspected the fine autumn landscape which now and then emerged from behind fallen-down fences and wrecked houses; in the Castle one roof shone with a brilliant redness as if it had been tiled recently; the towers and steeples rose with almost sensational sharpness from the thin air; above the distant hills birds flew looking like parentheses. Miss Horváth looked with melancholy confidence into her lover's face. She gazed at his eyes, his face and his neck—the latter being particularly thin and pale. She stared at the young man with devotion, with total life-sacrifice and holy love, remembering how recently it was that he tried to put a bullet in his heart because of her. Her lips closed tightly like the cups of flowers in bad weather; but her eyes, her forehead, her darned gloves and the tip of her down-at-heel shoes all said the same thing: 'My God!'

The comfortable carriage rolled through Christina Town, the wheels turned slowly for it was no longer worth-while to

covered with oilcloth, in his hand. His mistress addressed him in Slovakian:

'Fetch me in half an hour, cousin.'

(It became evident that all the staff on Madame Louise's country estate were more or less her kith and kin. She established her impoverished relations in the farmhands' cottages and consoled herself with the thought that at least it wasn't strangers who pilfered the hams hung up in the chimneys to be smoked. The old coachman being the father of six children spent the summertime in the village, and worked in Madame's vineyard; it was only with the coming of the cold weather that he put on his livery.)

The inn was already resounding with gaiety—if you could call it gaiety that Mr Sylvester had cocked his mushroom-sized hat and was leaning on the broad shoulder of a fat blind man, as if he had drunk more than the needful.

'My friend, Bocskai—alas, not one of the famous Bocskais, but he's still a very decent fellow,' said Mr Sylvester, introducing his companion.

A second later he added with a lavish gesture:

'Bocskai is the most wonderful man in Buda. In his youth he played in a theatre orchestra—but because he peeped too much at the stage, under the skirts of the actresses, he was blinded. So he became a pianist in a night-club and he had never a sad day in his life. He had an excellent job in Embroiderer Street, he played for the most distinguished magnates, the young aristocrats used to frequent the place to the dancing lessons—until fate intervened. My friend Bocskai fell in love with one of the ladies attached to the establishment whereupon he had to leave. Poor man, he was jealous... Now he's only working in Hoer Street...'

The blind man accompanied the biographical account with a satisfied nod. He wore a thick copper chain across his waistcoat and his black tie was fastened with a turban-shaped pin. His collar and his handkerchief were clean. Who

203

supplied a blind man with all these things?... He kept his hand constantly around his thick, stemmed glass. Now and then Mr Sylvester with a student-like enthusiasm filled the pianist's goblet.

'Tonight I'll go to Hoer Street,' he promised, his eyes shining. 'Since my poor wife died, I never slept with a woman.'

Madame Louise laughed out loudly.

'Oh, you all say this, you old scoundrels! That's how you try to seduce women. For how long? Ten years? Fifteen years?... Certainly, it is intriguing if a man has led a saintly life for ten years...'

She was sitting at the head of the table and presently she sent away Béla Bonifácz from her side because of his evil-smelling small cigar.

'Mr Rezeda... you aren't smoking... Sit beside me.'

The innkeeper served salami, onions, small hot peppers. He brought red wine in pint bottles and smoked bacon for which Mr Sylvester immediately offered his own pocket-knife. He touched his glass to the blind man's.

'That's how we used to live in the old days with poor Sándor Balázs. The actresses in the People's Theatre were still of the sort who gladly crossed over to Buda, to the small inns. Here Lujza Blaha sang once and the fairy-like Aranka Hegyi, while Lányi, the composer, thrummed the *cimbalom*. Long-dead authors had a merry time here, my young friend. They held feasts in the manner of Lisznyai, the sentimental poet— and no poet had to grieve because of unrequited love. At night, lying on the sofa of the drawing-room, the young girls of the houses of convenience read the poems of Reviczky to their visitors; but the maidens of the bourgeoisie did not hesitate either to stretch out their white hands in the evening dusk between the flowerpots of the open window. Poets were considered to be saints. Writers and actors often did not have to pay for their lodgings the old landladies in the houses of the Inner Town and the maiden with the auburn hair kept a book of poetry under her pillow. Love, too, was different in those days...'

The blind pianist lifted the wineglass with a self-assured gesture to his lips. He spoke in a melancholy, distant voice:

'On weekdays books are much-sought-after in our establishment, too. Simonia—once she was a governess in respectable houses—sits under the big chandelier in the *salon* and reads aloud to the girls. The other day the whole place was crying over one of the books. *Unwritten Letter* that was the title. Written by Hugó Csergő. "White Nuptials", the poet sang about and we all cried quietly...'

Mr Sylvester gestured violently.

'I don't know the book, but in my opinion there were really fine girls at that establishment in the days when they all knew Reviczky's Perdita poems by heart. And the young writers slept and lived for years on end in Embroidery Street, in that fairy-tale pleasure dome. In my young days I was a great dancer myself... And I taught the famous Gipsy Vilma all the songs of Pest County...'

Madame Louise cast a searching look at Mr Rezeda.

'Tell me, young man, what are your plans with this unfortunate girl?'

Mr Rezeda grew serious.

'As soon as I'm well, I shall marry her; she deserves it, she's a good girl.'

Madame Louise smiled sadly.

'How old are you, my young friend?'

'Twenty-six. I intend to work.'

'At what?' Madame Louise asked, amazed. 'Writing poetry?'

He lowered his eyes.

'I have an old friend, he promised to get me a job at the new daily, the *Journal,* as proof-reader. Ödön Gajári takes care of his employees as if they were his own brothers...'

'A proof-reader has to work nights, you look to me as if you had a weak chest, Mr Rezeda. You'd leave a young widow and unpaid bills at the grocer.'

Mr Rezeda passed his hand over his forehead.

'I always thought, Madame,' he said in a lowered voice, 'that you were of poetic nature. Lo and behold, you are far more prosaic than I believed. I'm not afraid of death. It makes absolutely no difference when one has to die—when we all die sooner or later. But I'd like to be happy before that... Madame, I've never really made love to a woman in my life...'

'Not to Miss Horváth?'

'My God... I love her much too much for that... First we'll get married in some old little church, asking the blessing of an old, saintly priest for our love; a sacristan with a palsied head will be the witness and the lame bellringer will wish us luck at the church gate. If we have enough money, we'll hire a professional to play the Wedding March from *Lohengrin* on the organ. The eyes of the lovely lady, looking a little myopically at me with a brown, moist look, her restless feet and white hands where passion dwells... She is all mystery and I long to learn all about the charms her body and limbs hold in secret... Saints, brown-visaged and framed in black, gaze from the walls and Our Lady smiles a blessing with her lily-crowned head from the altar. Since I had attempted suicide, I have become religious, my lady. I have learned to trust God.'

Madame Louise frowned.

'I, too, am godfearing; and equally since I tried suicide. Before that... in my foolish, extravagant and Bohemian youth I never felt a prayer in my heart. I prayed loudly, fast and as a duty. These days I pause now and then in the midst of my daily chores, I ponder, my heart is filled with warm, happy piety. I'm fifty already. Day after day I am getting ready to go visiting Our Lord. I had a chapel built in my village and took

206

the gold and silver coins which counts and kings gave me as souvenirs in my young days and had them melted down into the little bell that calls the toiling peasants to evening prayers near my country estate. Louise Pommery no longer bottles her blond nectar at Rheims for my palate—the champagne I used to pour into my bath-tub to please an ambassador named Battenberg—and in music Haydn is my only favourite...'

While she talked, she was peeling an orange and offered a slice to Mr Rezeda.

'My young friend, a godfearing person cannot ruin the life of a fellow human being. Let the lady go. Because she is kind, she became your nurse after your suicide attempt—but life does not consist only of nursing an invalid. Once the time might come when she won't create a scandal at Madame Stein's—whom, by the way, I know ever since her youth when she was at the old Somossy Music Hall...'

'You know of it, Madame?' asked Rezeda, turning white.

Madame Louise sprinkled some sugar on the orange.

'I know more or less everything that happens in town. Once my profession was to be beautiful, to be stupid and to let men suffer for months because of me before I yielded to them. Now I am a lady, educated and deeply-read like a principal lady-in-waiting and perhaps I have learned to know people, too... My old gentlemen who visit me and provide for my comfortable life would be bored in my place if I only quoted Sarcey or a Hungarian critic whenever I must offer an opinion about the star of yesterday's theatrical performance... The old gentlemen, reclining on my sofa, their physiological functions restricted to their daily supper at the Casino, now and then like to hear something about the distant life outside the walls. I have to know that Frida Gombaszögi is the loveliest woman in Pest and that Emma Márkus wears a tigerskin fur-coat; what the elegant Count Csekonics is doing and thinking and where Szemere happens to be at the moment. I give regular aid to old crones who bring me the news of the town, while my former girl-friends who have not yet retired from the struggle for life, hasten to me for advice. And thus I knew that your miss who wished to meet the magnificent Alvinczi at Madame Stein's (née Frimette Schwarz) apartment, departed suddenly, disturbed by an unpleasant incident... But my carriage has arrived and I wish you, gentlemen, a very pleasant time...'

After the ceremonial departure of Madame Louise there was soon another little event that survived as a souvenir of Mr Sylvester's anniversary party.

At the very end of the table Béla Bonifácz collapsed suddenly and vomited blood. A doctor appeared from the neighbouring house; later the ambulance service arrived.

'It's undernourishment—and his old tuberculosis,' said the ambulance doctor to Miss Horváth who was greatly frightened by the incident.

Then the ambulance drove off to the St John Hospital and took Béla Bonifácz away. He lay as beautifully on the stretcher as if he were already a kindly and well-behaved corpse. A week later the goodhearted sisters clasped his hands over his chest.

A six year old, tiny girl came for the pianist. She took the blind man's hand, and, as she did every day, she led him to the establishment in Hoer Street where the ivories were already waiting for his touch.

'Bye, bye,' Mr Sylvester called after him. 'If I live long enough, I'll visit you one day.'

The gaslamps were lit and Mr Sylvester supported his forehead in his palm. For minutes he remained in this position, only his chest heaved violently.

Then he took away his hand and his eyes were full of tears.

'Kiss each other,' he said suddenly.

Mr Rezeda and Miss Horváth obeyed the command. They kissed gently, quietly, like children.

Mr Sylvester lifted his forefinger.

'Old people are kind people,' he said, his voice a little embarrassed. 'They seldom get fond of anybody but if they do, they often think of them, secretly. We old 'uns like to interfere with the business of our young friends. Mr Rezeda, my boy and colleague, your sweetheart is leaving you tonight.'

Miss Horváth lowered her eyes in front of Mr Rezeda's startled look.

'This gathering was your farewell party. You must part because Béla Bonifácz, Madame Louise, all of us old people consider this proper and seemly. The young lady's luggage is already at the Southern Station and the train is leaving in an hour—taking her back to the provincial stage company. The engine is already being coaled up for the departure of the princess,' said Mr Sylvester in a solemn tone.

Mr Rezeda behaved heroically—only for a while he was unable to speak.

'You're really going away?' he asked suddenly.

The actress sat with lowered eyes on the shabby cane-chair of the old inn. She looked pale, sad, sick. Her lips even trembled a little. She grasped Mr Rezeda's hand.

'I didn't dare to tell you because you were still ill then... I'd like very much to act again...'

'You're going away?'

'I'm going away because I cannot do otherwise.'

Mr Rezeda pressed her hand.

'God bless you!'

The three of them cried for a long while on that evening. It was mostly Mr Sylvester whose tears started to flow, Mr Rezeda continued and Clara buried her face in her hands when she sobbed. One of her eyes seemed to become smaller than the other while she cried. She looked a bit cross-eyed. Women are the loveliest when they are cross-eyed.

Then they kissed each other once more.

The actress glued her lips fervently to Mr Rezeda's. She pressed her hot face, wet with tears, to his face.

'If I ever give myself to anybody in my life, it will be only you,' she said softly. 'I swear by my dead mother.'

'Good-bye,' said Mr Rezeda grimly.

That night there was an immense number of stars in the sky above the Tabán. It wasn't cool, either, the summer had returned in the darkness. Mr Rezeda stood in the window of the old house until midnight, staring at the stars and repeating to himself countless times:

'Good-bye! I'll call a priest in the morning.'

In the dark heights of the sky wild geese called. Somewhere, far away, in a Serbian inn of the Tabán there was soft cither music. The unhappy young man rummaged for an old ring among his belongings; according to tradition an Angevin queen had delighted in inspecting it on her delicate finger. There was a turquoise stone in the ring, the stone of faithfulness. He decided that he would send it to the actress.

NOTES

45   The actors and actresses mentioned in this page and the previous one are, alas, long-faded shadows and it would be unkind to revive the details of their careers. Lajos Báttaszéki became a legendary figure who spent the last forty years of his life panhandling, a craft he developed into an art of high achievement. It was he who cabled (collect, of course) to Sir Alexander Korda when *The Shape of Things to Come* was first shown in Hungary, saying: 'You already know the shape of things to come, I don't even know where my next meal's coming from.' Korda, not for the first time, sent a generous donation.

     Miss Klári Küry was a lady of ample though shapely charms who preferred roles in which she could shine in tights.

46   Béla Ágai was a much-loved editor and writer.

     Sándor Bródy (1863–1924), a great Hungarian realist playwright, novelist and essayist, was a merciless critic of Hungarian society.

     Temesvár (since the First World War in Rumania) was a flourishing intellectual centre in south-east Hungary.

47   László Beöthy was the Sir Oswald Stoll of Hungary, running a whole string of theatres in the 1920s.

     Andor Miklós became the owner of three daily newspapers, a large publishing house and many other enterprises in the first three decades of the twentieth century.

     József Konti was the early Richard Rodgers of Hungary.

49   Ede Ujházi, the Hungarian Lucien Guitry, was both a great actor and a great character. There is a chicken soup named after him, and the oldest actors in Hungary still remember (and occasionally imitate) his style. His usual salutation to anybody was '*marha*' which can be translated both as 'cattle' and 'ox' though it is more affectionate and less insulting than either.

     Gyula Gál was another fine dramatic actor.

     Mari Jászai (1855–1926) was the greatest tragic actress of Hungary, a very masculine yet passionately amorous lady.

     These three were the leading professors at the National Academy of Drama.

50   Debrecen is a large, sprawling Calvinist city on the edge of the Great Hungarian Plain.

51   Banat—a fertile south-eastern district, formerly of Hungary, now divided between Rumania and Yugoslavia.

57   Nyírség—a country district in north-eastern Hungary, named after its birch forests.

59 Várad (or more properly Nagyvárad) is a large town, now in Rumania; once a flourishing cultural centre where many distinguished Hungarian poets and writers spent youthful apprentice years.

75 János (John) Hill is one of the Buda hills carrying a look-out tower.

82 Prince Ferenc II Rákóczi (1676–1735) was the leader of the Hungarian revolt against the Habsburgs in the early eighteenth century. He died in exile.

84 Madame Déry (1793–1872), the Mrs Siddons of Hungary, spent much of her life with travelling troupes of actors. She wrote and translated plays herself.

The Kisfaludy brothers, Károly (Charles) (1788–1830) and Sándor (Alexander) (1772–1844), were notable romantic poets and playwrights of the early nineteenth century.

Gábor Bethlen (1580–1629), a prince of Transylvania, was the leader of Protestant opposition against the Catholic Habsburgs; his *hajdús* or heyducks were formidable freebooters and guerilla fighters.

92 King Milan of Serbia was a noted playboy of the late Victorian age.

95 Máriabesnyo, a village not far from Budapest, was noted as a place of pilgrimage for the pious.

97 Lajos Kossuth (1802–1894) was the leader of Hungary's 1848–1849 War of Independence, who lived to a ripe old age and died in Turin, Italy.

99 General Hentzi was commander of the Austrian forces during the same war; he was especially hated because he had his guns shell Pest from the heights of Buda. Afterwards, during the period of absolutist rule, the Austrians added insult to injury by erecting a statue of him in Budapest. Patriotic Hungarians made several attempts to blow it up and succeeded in the end.

Károly Eötvös (1842–1916) was a liberal lawyer and popular writer (mostly of non-fiction) in the second half of the nineteenth century.

101 Istóczy and Verhovay were radical politicians who moved from nationalism to anti-Semitism; they began as student leaders and were at various periods members of Parliament. Verhovay died in the United States.

104 The Esterházys were the richest and most powerful aristocratic family of Hungary with immense estates. One of them was Haydn's patron and employer.

122 The Catholic abbot Ignác Martinovics (1755–1795) was the leader of an anti-Habsburg conspiracy in the eighteenth century. He and his fellow-conspirators were executed on the large field named Meadow of Blood.

Count Elemér Batthyány was a famous dandy and race-horse owner.

124 Gyula Reviczky (1855–1889) was a pessimistic poet of more promise than achievement.

Mihály Tompa (1817–1868), a prolific and often moving poet, was one of the literary galaxy during Hungary's Golden Age of the second half of the nineteenth century.

125 Endre Ady (1877–1919) combined the symbolism of Baudelaire and Verlaine with a particularly Magyar passion. He was the greatest Hungarian poet of the late nineteenth and early twentieth century and his heritage still endures.

127 Arthur Görgey (1818–1916) was the general who surrendered the Hungarian armies to the Habsburgs in 1849 and was regarded as a traitor for the rest of his very long life. His son was a psychopath. The Lipótmező (Leopold's Field) was the Budapest lunatic asylum.

128 Béla Révész, short-story writer and essayist, wrote half a dozen books about his friend Endre Ady (See note to page 125.)

Victor Cholnoky and Károly Lovik were highly talented and original novelists and short-story writers whose work remained largely unappreciated during their life-time.

133 Cecilia Carola, of uncertain origins, was the toast of Budapest–a combination of Marie Lloyd and the Gibson Girl.

134 Sári Fedák reigned for many years as musical comedy and straight actress, just as famous for her love affairs and extremist political views as for her performances on the stage.

135 Miklós Szemere (see Introduction) was the great eccentric Hungarian commoner who may have served as Edward Alvinczi's model.

Jenő Szekula was a Hungarian journalist and writer known for his mordant wit.

158 Késmárk—an old, romantic city in northern Hungary, since the end of the First World War in Czechoslovakia.

161 Jenő Heltai (1871–1957), playwright, poet, novelist, editor, was one of Hungary's most polished wits. His play *The Silent Knight* was translated and produced in many languages.

165 The Tabán was an old, romantic quarter of Buda, now, alas, torn down.

Page

173   Mihály Táncsics (1799–1884) was a self-educated pamphleteer and
      writer, an early radical socialist who spent many years in prison—as
      passionate and as ill-starred as Daniel Defoe. The revolution of
      1848 freed him and honoured him as a forerunner of its ideas.
      Visegrád, north-west of Budapest, on a bend of the Danube, was
      once a royal castle where several of the Hungarian kings resided.

174   Mohács, south of Budapest, is a sprawling village; nearby the
      Turks defeated the Hungarian armies in 1526.
      Komárom, now a frontier town between Hungary and Czechoslo-
      vakia, is a historical community north-west of Budapest.

175   Emilia Márkus was a beautiful blonde actress who also taught at
      the Academy of Drama. Later she became Nijinsky's mother-
      in-law.

179   Alag is a modest version of Epsom, near Budapest.

186   Lujza Blaha (1850–1926) was Hungary's most popular musical
      comedy actress who later excelled in straight plays and lived to a
      serene old age. Her autobiography was a classic.

189   Mór (Maurus) Jókai (1825–1904), the Hungarian Walter Scott,
      was the greatest Hungarian novelist of the nineteenth century; not
      much of a stylist yet possessing an inexhaustible fund of invention.
      His books are still widely read.

191   Rákos is an easterly suburb of Budapest; once a pleasant sylvan
      district where, in a large meadow, assemblies of nobles were held.

195   Matthias Corvinus, the great Renaissance king, used the raven as
      his heraldic animal.

200   Veszprém, in western Hungary, has been the seat of an ancient
      bishopric.

205   Hugó Csergő was a Hungarian poet, short-story writer and editor of
      the early twentieth century.
      Ödön Gajári was a notable liberal editor; his *Ujság* (Journal) had
      a long and distinguished career.

207   Frida Gombaszögi was a leading dramatic actress who married
      Andor Miklós (See note to page 47) and died in the 1960s.

47. Ft.